ANOTHER TRY

ANOTHER TRY

GENE KOON

Another Try is a work of fiction. Names, characters, places, and incidences are the product of the author's imagination. Any resemblance to persons living or dead, actual events, companies, or settings is purely coincidental.

Copyright © 2024 Gene Koon.

All rights reserved. No part of this novel may be reproduced, distributed, or transmitted in any form or by any means, electronic or mechanical, including photocopying, without written permission from the author except for the use of brief passages to be used for book reviews.

Rusty Typewriter Publishing LLC
1600 SW Walker Rd. #335
Beaverton, Oregon
97006

Library of Congress Cataloging-in-Publication Data
Names: Koon, Gene, author.
Title: Another Try / Gene Koon.
Description: First Edition | Rusty Typewriter Publishing LLC, [2024]
Identifiers: LCCN 2024904733 | ISBN 979-8-9901595-0-1 (hardcover) | ISBN 979-8-9901595-1-8 (paperback) | ISBN 979-8-9901595-2-5 (Kindle ebook) | ISBN 979-8-9901595-3-2 (ebook)

10 9 8 7 6 5 4 3 2 1

FIRST EDITION

Book Cover Design by Jerry Todd

Interior Book Design by VMC Art & Design LLC

Edited by Ann Aubrey Hanson

Printed in the United States of America.

To Merritt

Both of you

Dad and Grandson

CHAPTER 1

FRANK BEEMER FOUGHT TO KEEP HIS BALANCE AT THE BACK of the metro transit train. He had a tight grip on a grab handle with his right hand and tolerated the steady knocks and bumps from strangers he usually would have considered invading his personal space.

Beemer would have preferred to fly into the smaller Hillsboro airport and take a private town car to his campaign rally in Portland. He had that option. But Lawrence, his son, who Beemer insisted on having as his campaign manager, devised the train idea, and they agreed it wouldn't hurt the incumbent Oregon Senator to rub a few elbows this last time around. It was only a half-hour ride on the MAX Red Line from the Portland International Airport to the Pioneer Courthouse Square, where Lawrence expected a creditable crowd of supporters.

At first, it was no big deal, with plenty of space on the train. Most passengers looked like business travelers or tired vacationers eager to get home. But with each metro stop away from the airport and closer to town, more riders hopped on, and fewer were getting off.

Free from the need to make idle conversation with Lawrence, Beemer watched as the assembly grew. He noticed that the growing crowd now included a couple of rugged guys standing shoulder-to-shoulder in the aisle. Along with rugged jeans and boots, they wore yellow safety vests and budget sunglasses and carried hard hats. Likely a construction crew.

Two big-belly guys were taking up more than their fair share of space on the seats. In their early twenties, dressed in T-shirts featuring epic space movies and black easy-fit jeans. Beemer listened for a minute while they discussed a video game.

Across from the gamers sat a young mother who had her hands full with two active and vocal toddlers, both girls.

Adjusting his stance to allow more passengers to embark, Lawrence turned until he stood toe to toe with his father.

The man to Lawrence's right was a regular guy. Late-thirties, with generic brown glasses and medium-brown hair, dressed in a brown sweater, Wrangler blue jeans, and a pair of brown loafers. Nothing unique about Mr. Brown, Beemer decided, turning to seek other opportunities, thinking it might be time to initiate some short conversations.

A woman to his right stood with one foot atop the other. Almost as tall as Beemer, she also looked to be in her thirties, though her free-flowing blonde hair covered most of her face. She wore black large-frame glasses and a short-sleeve floral-print dress, loose-fitting and fluttering with the breeze anytime the doors opened. Beemer appreciated how she worked to avoid bumping into him when the train jerked to a stop.

He smiled, and she smiled back. He thought she might recognize him, though Beemer knew US senators were not rock stars. Even during a campaign year, unless they were harping on CNN or Fox News, a senator had to stand in line like everyone else. Beemer was okay with that. He did not need adulation. He grinned to himself, thinking that those with the greatest power stayed hidden.

When the train left the Hollywood Transit Center, the lion's share of passengers grew annoyed. First, they had to jockey to make room for two bicyclists with their wheels. Then a chubby man in his late fifties, plastered in puddled ink, long greasy hair, and sporting a bright Hawaiian shirt, parked his enormous yellow, four-wheeled mobility cart in the handicap zone, nudging three other passengers to look elsewhere for seats.

By this point, several of Portland's growing population of the less-fortunate had taken over the last car. Rough skin and bones. Homeless. Talking to themselves in their own world, hitching a ride to nowhere.

Filling in the gaps were a few typical Portland hipsters dressed in the standard hipster uniform: beards, tattoos, piercings, plaid flannel shirts, and clunky boots.

The MAX rolled out of the Hollywood station, the car jammed.

With no ventilation in the stuffy car, the amplified body heat was overwhelming. Beemer could see that Lawrence sensed his discomfort. He nodded and smiled slightly. Part of the job. With three terms in office under his belt, he had learned to go with the flow.

Lawrence's strategy to take the MAX and pick up a few votes on board the public transportation had fallen flat. No big deal. Like his father, he had an instinct when to cut bait and focus on the big picture.

The big picture was to create a throwback image reminiscent of the old-fashioned whistle-stop. First, the MAX would brake at the oldest federal building in the northwest, the Portland Pioneer Courthouse. Then, with son Lawrence by his side, Senator Beemer would step out, and the local news stations, with their cameras rolling, would trail them across the street to the Square, where he would deliver a rousing speech.

Beemer had to admit, it was a nifty publicity stunt and not just because of the exposure for his campaign. It was a foregone conclusion that he had already won the election. Oregon loved and trusted Senator Frank Beemer.

The key to this event was Lawrence.

It was paramount that cameras capture the Beemers, plural. Father and son, standing tall, standing strong, and standing united. A homemade apple pie photo-op.

For years, Beemer had envisioned Lawrence making a political run in his footsteps, a notion Lawrence had only recently dialed into, but ambitiously embraced. It made sense he should be the one to fill his father's shoes.

Before Lawrence graduated from high school, Beemer had mapped out his son's potential future in public service. He would not press him into a life of politics; it would have to be his choice. But Beemer had subtly guided him down a path to make the option palatable. Lawrence attended public schools, played team sports, and devoted extensive time to volunteer work. He had spent a short time in the Marines, followed by law school, and now put his degree to work at a nonprofit. From Beemer's perspective, Lawrence's political resume was already stellar.

Beemer knew his son was one in a million, a born leader. Now with his own long political career running out the clock, Beemer believed that within the next three or four years, Lawrence would be ripe to take over and build on the legacy his father had created. With Beemer's longtime pal, United States President Paul Cahill, on board with the plan, it was time to make the introductory move. To plant the first public seed in passing the torch. And what better place to do that than Pioneer Courthouse Square, the center of Portland and the state of Oregon?

MAX stopped at the Rose Quarter station. The doors pumped open. Eleven passengers, including the Hawaiian shirt guy, squeezed or rolled their way off, creating a little shoulder room. Twenty-five seconds later, the doors closed, and MAX glided on its way.

Catching Beemer's eye, Lawrence fished his cell out of his jeans and checked the time. "Only another fifteen minutes, maybe," he whispered. Beemer nodded.

He saw Lawrence give him a last once-over before he met the public. A trim six-foot-even, Beemer often joked if he had not gone into politics, he would have been a professional tennis player. He kept his snow-white hair on the longish side for a seventy-one-year-old man and had dressed casually, knowing that a suit would not be expected today. Instead, Lawrence had chosen for him a tailored blue open-collar dress shirt, ironed denim blue jeans, black-leather Chelsea boots, and Tom Ford tortoise-shell glasses. To onlookers, he looked like a man who had known success.

The doors closed, and the MAX sped up, rumbling onto the Steel Bridge and crossing the Willamette River.

Through the train's smeared windows, Beemer caught sight of a smattering of sailboats. He smiled. Once upon a time, the Beemer family had owned a thirty-six-foot cutter, the *Robin-Bell*, named after their two high-spirited Boston Terriers. When he had long periods off the Senate floor, he, with his wife, Janet, and their two children, Lawrence and Elizabeth, would retreat to the *Robin-Bell* and do what tight-knit families do. Then Janet passed away, and Elizabeth drifted in a different direction.

The MAX dropped into the southwest blocks, traveling the rails between Front and First Street, the part of Portland not pictured on a postcard.

Beemer imagined he could have been on a different planet. This was not his world. Junkies, dealers, ex-cons, schizophrenics, paranoids, runaways, and homeless outcasts owned the neighborhood. They had inundated the streets with empty liquor bottles and cans, discarded clothes, chewed-up shoes, and the usual garbage. Most of the buildings had been boarded up and tagged with graffiti. Tents, cardboard homes, sleeping bags, and plastic tarps were planted in rows on sidewalks and back alleys. Grocery carts packed and stacked high with the treasures of an entire life.

Lawrence looked at Beemer, his expression indicating his father should not be here. Beemer glanced again at his watch. At least another seven minutes. Three stops to go. He nodded at Lawrence, indicating all would be fine. Then he turned his attention to the young mother, watching her disembark with her girls in Chinatown. They weaved around a cluster of dusty men and disappeared into the shadow of the overpass. Beemer wondered where they were going.

Twenty-five seconds later, the doors closed, and MAX moved on. Passengers shifted, freeing up a couple of empty seats. Lawrence gestured to the blonde woman in the floral dress, but neither she nor Mr. Brown moved toward it. Instead, the woman leaned into Lawrence's shoulder, boxing him in as she made way for others to spread out.

Beemer caught a whiff of garbage and piss. He looked over Lawrence's shoulder. Behind the bicyclist, sitting next to the door, he saw a mess of a guy crouched over, his face buried in his lap. The back of his head looked like a crusty fishing net, with long, stringy, matted hair. He wore a bulky Army field coat covered with stains. The coat draped over his soiled cargo pants made it impossible to size up the guy. He could have been a big man or a small fry. Impossible to tell.

The other passengers avoided looking at the man. But Beemer kept his gaze on him, convinced he was an ex-soldier, now homeless. Beemer wished he could do something for him. He was an elected official, after all. Three terms, one to go. But he was also a realist, and politics is politics. Nothing he did would make a difference. Still, Beemer made a mental note to drop the guy twenty bucks before stepping off the train.

The doors opened at the Skidmore station, admitting three more passengers. Two sat down in the empty seats. The other, a lanky rocker wearing a Van Halen T-shirt and palming a cheap hashish pipe, wormed his way down the aisle to the left of the door. Ignoring the seats, he remained standing.

The second the doors closed, the homeless guy in the Army coat sprang to his feet. He had masked his face with a thick layer of mud. With a gun in his right hand, he popped the rocker in the heart, then pointed the gun down and tapped a hole into the left thigh of the closest big-belly gamer and another into the plaid shirt of a redheaded hipster. He turned to his right, toward Beemer.

Struggling to align his body in front of Beemer's, Lawrence tried to shield his father, but was unable to move. The blonde woman and Mr. Brown had him cornered.

The shooter fired. Three shots. Pop. Pop. Pop. Mr. Brown's head exploded. His body dropped.

The shooter aimed and fired again, but the train jolted crossing an intersection and threw off his balance. Lawrence took a bullet to the right side of his neck and collapsed onto Mr. Brown's body. Beemer shot a quick look at the shooter, head to toe. Something about him did not add up. Something in the man's appearance. His shoes, maybe? Beemer had no time to think.

The blonde woman lurched to her feet, clutching her bleeding left arm, Beemer behind her, untouched.

As he shifted his position, Beemer saw the bicyclist readying to ram the shooter but was stopped by a guy who nudged him with his hard hat. Beemer thought the quick thinking might have saved the bicyclist's life—but allowed the shooter another chance at his intended target. Him.

Twenty-one seconds.

The shooter locked eyes with the blonde for a fraction of a second, then pivoted out the door.

Twenty-five seconds. The MAX doors did not close. Twenty-six, twenty-seven, twenty-eight seconds.

A FEARLESS MAX DRIVER for sixteen years, Gina Hernandez often said she would put her hand on the Bible and swear there was nothing she had not seen or dealt with. Except for a mass shooting on her train. She caught the action on the security monitor. In a split second, the mixture of adrenaline and experience kicked Hernandez into action. Though she had taken several active-shooter courses, in the heat of the moment she could only recall fragments. She went with her gut. First, she kept the doors open, allowing the terrified passengers to storm out of the car. A gnarly eighteen seconds. As the passengers fled, Hernandez called emergency dispatch on her radio, calculating time until arrival.

Before she began her route, she had been briefed that Senator Beemer and his son would be on board, and there would be a political rally at the Pioneer Courthouse Square. Crowds. Traffic. Hernandez was aware the Square was a rented public space. With large crowds, police and medical units were mandatory. The wounded on her train needed immediate help, and waiting for an ambulance was not an option. She calculated that at top speed with no stops it would take fifty-five seconds to travel the eight blocks to Pioneer Square. She laid on the horn and hauled MAX ass.

With the train's horn blasting, Hernandez hit the brakes at the corner of Sixth and Morrison, stopping across the street from the Square. Fifty-nine seconds.

The crowd had gathered to greet their candidate, wave banners, take photos, and eat hot dogs. The usual campaign rigmarole. Instead, they were thunderstruck by the arrival of a deserted MAX with blood splatter and shattered windows.

AFTER THE TRAIN SQUEALED to a stop, Sergeant Carl Baranski ordered Phillips, the junior officer, to keep the Nosy Parkers back from the line. Then, ignoring the cry for help from the train's tail-end car, Baranski and Officer Allen shoved through the mob to the front. He motioned to Hernandez to open all the doors. She did. No one exited.

Aware of the danger that the gunman could be in the crowd, across the street, or atop a building looking down on the Square, Baranski drew his weapon, signaling Officer Allen to do the same. In formation, they scuttled to the last car, toward the cursing and moaning.

Two emergency medical technicians rushed over. Taking a deep breath, Baranski ordered Officer Allen to stay behind, raised his pistol, and poked his nose inside the car.

First looking left toward the blubbering, Baranski saw a big-bellied man sprawled across five seats, his eyes wide and teary, staring at the ceiling. He pressed his pudgy hands against his bleeding thigh, seemingly clueless about the lifeless body in a Van Halen shirt lying dead in a claret stream of muck beneath him.

Baranski swung right and saw a blonde woman crouched over a guy lumped over something resembling a human being, her gloved hands wrapped around the guy's neck, attempting to plug a hemic geyser.

His attention shifted to the broad-shouldered guy standing with his back to Baranski. The guy had a persuasive hold on an older man's arms, like he was about to drag him out of the car against his will.

The shooter? Baranski maneuvered up the step and to the left in the aisle, getting a better look. Senator Frank Beemer, the older gentleman spattered in blood, showed signs of shock. Dull, almost catatonic, eyes fixed downward on the guy with the massive neck problem.

"Police. You move, you die!" Baranski shouted.

The guy with broad shoulders cocked his head just enough for them to identify him.

"Oh, shit!" Baranski said. "You're that guy!"

NOT THE ATTENTION HE had ever wanted. For the past week, Garris Kelley had been That Guy. That guy in the news who had his face broadcast to the world as the covert operative whose identity President Paul Cahill, in one of his famous tizzies, had "unintentionally" revealed on social media. The story Cahill had spun said that Garris Kelley had single-handedly liquidated Hector Trevano, an international drug lord, and more than a dozen of his notorious associates.

Fancying himself to be a maverick cowboy type, President Cahill had invited Garris to the White House for a celebratory dinner. Garris, who had neither confirmed nor denied the matter concerning Trevano, declined the president's invitation, insisting he had plans to take in a Hillsboro Hops minor league baseball game, claiming this was not a presidential snub but a choice. He preferred baseball to politics.

"I need your help," Garris told Baranski.

Garris could see that the officer was a smart cop as he took a moment to decide which direction to take. Baranski as the officer in charge of the scene exuded confidence, but was obviously not driven by ego. Garris saw him gauge their mutual strengths.

Baranski holstered his Smith & Wesson. "What do you need?"

"What's your name, Sergeant?"

"Baranski, Carl Baranski. Six years on the force."

"Baranski, it's too dangerous for the senator to stay here another second. I've got to get him to cover. He'll have staff members in the Square. Tell them I'm taking him across the street to the hotel, to suite 1217. Don't send them there. Just let them know that's where he'll be for now." Garris glanced down at the man with the neck problem. "That's the senator's son, Lawrence Beemer."

The blonde woman squeezing Lawrence's neck glanced up at Garris. Focused on the senator's safety, he paid her little attention.

"There's nothing I can do for him," Garris said to Baranski. "Get the medics. Have them to take him and the other wounded to the hospital on NW 22nd."

Baranski nodded, knelt next to the blonde woman, and took over.

Garris leaned down to Baranski. He lowered his voice and said, "Once the medic takes over, I want you to run to my suite as fast as you can. I'll need to leave the senator and want you to keep him alive. Got it?"

Baranski nodded.

"Good. After this is over, I'll buy you a beer."

NEW TO THE JOB, twenty-six-year-old Dante Green had been a doorman at the hotel for three weeks, two days, and four hours. He had no prior experience but possessed a pleasant, upbeat manner. From the get-go, the hotel's manager had thought that Dante's easy smile and guilelessness would be ideal for welcoming guests.

Dante enjoyed everything about the job, including meeting people from all over the world. He was banking a steady paycheck for more money than he had ever had, putting most of it toward helping his grandfather, who shared his home with Dante. Dante liked getting dressed in a uniform and feeling like he mattered. His day was bright until he saw who had catapulted out of the MAX and stormed toward him—the dude he had seen on TV for annihilating a small army or something. Under his shoulder, the guy protected an older man with faraway eyes whose clothes were covered with blood and speckles of matter.

Scared shitless, Dante raised his hands in the air.

Paying him no attention, Garris Kelley eased Beemer down on the top step closest to the hotel's entry. Then he took off his sports jacket and draped it over Beemer.

Dante grabbed his cell phone to call his supervisor.

"What's your name?" Garris asked.

"Dante Green."

"Get rid of the phone, Dante."

"Yes, sir." It vanished.

Garris pulled out a key card and thrust it into Dante's hand. "Listen to me. I'm a guest at the hotel." He reached behind his back and pulled out his Beretta 92. He checked the magazine.

Gauging the size of Dante's pupils, Garris thought it might have been the first gun Dante had ever seen outside a movie or TV show. He popped the mag back in. "Dante, I need you to take him to my room, 1217. Lock the door and stay with him. A police officer named Sergeant Baranski will join you soon. Don't answer the door unless it's Baranski. Understand?"

Dante nodded.

Beemer was coming around. Recognizing the voice, he gazed up. "Garris?"

"Yeah, Frank. It's me."

"Lawrence. He's been shot."

"He took a slug in the neck."

"Is he dead?" Frank asked, dabbing blood off his cheeks with Garris's jacket sleeve.

"Not yet. He's on the way to the hospital."

"Take me there. Now. I need to be with Lawrence. I need to be with my boy."

"No dice, Frank. The shooter could be in the area, and you're his target." Garris knelt beside the senator and waved the doorman over. "This is Dante. He's taking you to my room. I want you to stay there."

"It wasn't me, Garris," Beemer said. "I know you think I was the one who told the president you killed Trevano. But I didn't. It wasn't me, I swear."

"Now's not the time, Frank. We'll have that conversation later. But right now, I need you to tell me everything you can remember about the train."

Still disoriented, Beemer gave Garris an excellent description of the gunman. He confirmed what Garris had learned from the other few eyewitnesses, and Beemer added two significant details that Garris suspected might be a game-changer.

One. Beemer figured the shooter was a homeless veteran with an ax to grind. The man had painted his face with mud, camouflaged like he was on a jungle mission, and wore a military field coat. But what struck Beemer as odd was that the man wore expensive athletic shoes. Beemer owned the same pair of sneakers and knew they cost north of two hundred bucks. The shooter was prepared to run.

Two. The soldier also wore transparent vinyl gloves. A tiny detail, but it sang in Garris's ears. If a down-on-his-luck army veteran with little to lose chose to carry out a random shooting, then why worry about fingerprints? There was little doubt in Garris's mind. The attack was not random, but a hit. The target—Senator Beemer. His son was collateral damage. Knocked around in the pendulous car at the wrong time, Lawrence got in the way.

Garris leaped down the hotel steps, crossed the street, and charged through the congested sidewalk to the coffee shop at the Square's highest corner.

CHERRY MACKEY HAD PIVOTED out the door and stuck around just long enough to watch the passengers stampede off the train and scurry for cover. Then, he disappeared into the urban scenery.

Nobody takes a second look at the destitute. Cherry was invisible to walk free as a bird to an alley near the river he had scouted three days earlier.

Keeping the disposable latex gloves on, he removed his clay mask and the crappy wig and stuffed them into his coat. He stripped off the cargo pants like a banana peel and now sported black running sweats. He would drop the pile of clothes in the alley, where he was sure they would be snapped up within seconds.

Last off came the crystalline, full-faced diving hood. There would be no hair or skin DNA to be retrieved at the crime scene.

He covered his bald head with a Hillsboro Hops baseball cap, popped in some earbuds, and slipped on sunglasses. Looking every bit a tourist out for a run, he headed southwest. If the MAX driver had any sense, he would not hesitate. He would head to the Pioneer Courthouse Square as fast as possible. Help would be on-site and immediate.

Cutting over to Ankeny Blvd., he followed it down to Fourth, then took a right on Morrison. Downtown appeared as expected. In a state of confusion. Two blocks up, the MAX sat dead on its tracks, pocketed in a mitt of onlookers and those fleeing the Square.

Jogging to the Expedition Hotel located catty-corner from the Square, he quickly passed by the young doorman, unnoticed, the doorman more interested in the terrifying activity across the street than in the comings and goings of the hotel's guests.

Catching the elevator farthest from the entrance, Cherry pressed the button to the eleventh floor. He checked his watch. Five minutes since the shooting.

The doors opened.

It was a given they would record his image on the hotel security system. At first, he had the urge to double-time it. But he slowed his horses like any ordinary guest and walked down the hall to the last room, 1117. If they discovered he had been in the hotel, a low percentage, he might as well give them something to look at. No problem. Not in a hundred years would they uncover his true identity. Well trained, he was a master of vanishing into thin air.

The hotel had twelve floors. Suite 1117 was a corner west suite facing the Square. Two men stood at the window. They were the same blue-collar guys with the yellow hard hats on the MAX. Cherry's backup. They had also ditched their construction crew attire and now wore sweats, in navy-blue and charcoal-gray, now looking less brawny and more athletic.

After shaking hands for a job well done, the guy in the navy backed away from the window, allowing Cherry to assess the scene across the street.

One lone police officer had his hands full, moving the crowd out of the Square. Two other cops stood at the train's nose, advising or being briefed by the driver.

Something caught Cherry's eye at the tail of the train. A man with broad shoulders, tall and lean—a powerful guy. The guy had his head down as he plowed his way through the crowd. Without missing a beat, he rushed inside the bullet-riddled train. Cherry could not see his face, only a dark-blue suit jacket over a green polo shirt, with jeans. A civilian, not a cop. The cops swarmed the Square moments later. The two cops hustled from the front car back down the line of cars, guns at the ready.

This was going exactly as Cherry had hoped. In a minute, they would allow the medics to board and rush Lawrence Beemer to the hospital in the Pearl District. A minute or two later, a mob of police would be on-site to transport the senator to safety.

But plans changed.

A minute went by. The medics had yet to enter the car. Two minutes later, the big guy came out and tactically moved around MAX's tail-end, Senator Beemer cradled under his protective shoulder like a bird's wing, as they headed full-tilt boogie straight for the hotel.

Something about the guy rattled Cherry's noggin. Something familiar, but Cherry could not quite dial it in. A moment later, the guy removed his jacket, draped it over the senator, and left him with the doorman, then sprang down the hotel steps, heading toward the northeast corner of the Square to a coffee shop. The highest ground. He studied the shop's exterior and surrounding area. He scaled to the top of a modern art installation and leaped over to the coffee shop, grabbing hold of a beam. Cherry watched as he monkeyed his way up to the roof for a better view. Nothing. Not wasting a second, the guy vaulted off and canvassed the grid, searching for the active shooter.

Impressed, Cherry figured he could not have done a better job himself. Whoever this guy was, he was making all the right moves. He had to be military or ex-military, or even better, CIA.

There was a knock at the door. Cherry waved, and the guy in navy got off the sofa to answer it. The blonde woman from the MAX joined the party.

Diane Finley was still blonde, but her hair was lighter colored, like wheat in late summer, and in a ponytail. The glasses were gone, as was the baggy dress. Like the others in the room, she now wore athletic wear. Periwinkle-blue tights with a matching sleeveless top accenting her well-toned arms. No visible sign of a gunshot. The injury had been an illusion. A blood squib, like they use in the movies. It never happened.

She tapped the door closed with her heel.

Bob Hawkins, the guy in navy, handed her a black gym bag and returned to the velvet Recamier sofa.

Diane took out her SIG Sauer P226 Emperor Scorpion and tossed the empty bag aside with the three others.

"Overall, it went well," Cherry said.

Diane hovered over an unopened bottle of expensive champagne long enough to read the gift card.

Mr. and Mrs. Stephen and Hannah Gilbert

There was no name attached announcing the bubbly's sender.

They were in the bridal suite. Posh in a rich palette of beige and plum, nine-foot ceilings, a dining room, crystal pendant lights, and ivory satin draperies hung from floor-to-ceiling windows.

Diane didn't give a damn about the Gilberts or how Bob Hawkins and Gordon Parks had hijacked their suite. She sidled up to Cherry at the window. "We have a problem. The senator didn't go to the hospital like we'd planned." She gazed out at the frantic scene, still in full bloom. "A hero showed up."

"Yeah, I know," Cherry said. "He handed the senator over to the hotel doorman." He tapped his knuckle on the window. "He's in the Square now, searching for me."

Gordon Parks drifted in from the dining room and plopped onto the dainty sofa beside Hawkins. Diane thought they looked like a pair of turtledoves.

"You're not concerned?" Diane asked Cherry.

"Should I be?"

"It's Garris Kelley."

"Garris?" Cherry said. "Shit, of course, it's Garris. I should've guessed, the way he's scoping the scene."

"No surprise," Parks said. "I'd think he'd want to be the first in line to wring Beemer's neck after Beemer told Cahill, and—"

"—and like us," Hawkins cut in, "Beemer's rally in the Square was the best chance he had to get close to him."

While Hawkins was speaking, Cherry spotted the big man racing back to the hotel, landing at the top of the steps to scan the Square. He turned ninety degrees, then looked up, giving Cherry his first good look at the man's face. It was indeed Garris Kelley. And he had just realized the shooter was inside the hotel. Cherry had to give credit where credit was due. If his old rival from the Agency figured out it was not an ex-soldier, random-shooting scenario in a matter of minutes, then he would determine it was a hit. Because they had worked together closely in the past and had learned the same playbook, Cherry knew what Kelley would do next. Because it's what he would do. First, he would check to see if the senator was safe. Then he would search the rooms on the top floor facing the Square, knowing the shooter would want a good view of the mayhem he had caused.

"Pack it up," Cherry said.

There was no delay. No discussion. They were professionals, and this was not their first rodeo. They had prepared for a speedy and thorough exit. Hawkins and Parks collected and bagged all gear and miscellaneous items, then double-checked their weapons. Diane cleared all evidence of anyone but Mr. and Mrs. Gilbert ever having been in the room, then double-checked her SIG Sauer.

Finished, Hawkins and Parks returned to the sofa, and Diane made herself at home in an armchair by the fireplace. There was no guessing how long they would be waiting, but they were ready when Cherry gave the word. He had something to think about. The surprise appearance of Garris Kelley had created an opportunity that could change their master plan.

Diane waved her SIG. "If he's a problem, why don't I introduce myself?"

"I know you'd like that," Cherry said. "But I've got something else in mind for Kelley."

DANTE GREEN HUNKERED WITH Beemer in the bedroom with the door shut. If it had a lock, he would have locked it. If he had a little more muscle, he would have moved the wardrobe to block the door. But there was no lock, and could not move the wardrobe, so he propped a chair under the doorknob like he had seen in the movies and prayed it would work.

Baranski stood guard in the suite's living area, standing within arms-length of the door with his service weapon drawn, when he heard a knock on the door. He had it in his head; if anyone but Garris Kelley crossed the threshold, he would put his life on the line to protect the senator and the kid.

"Sergeant Baranski. It's Kelley. I'm coming in. Holster your weapon."

Baranski held fast. Not until Garris was inside and the door was locked did he holster his weapon.

"Bedroom or bathroom?" Garris asked.

"Bedroom," Baranski answered. "For what it's worth, I think the kid has a chair to the door."

"Good," Garris said. "We're going to keep them in there. I think the shooter is in the hotel."

Baranski reached for his radio.

"Tell your team to secure all exits and check floors ten and below. I'll cover this floor and the eleventh," Garris said, then he knocked on the bedroom door. "Dante. This is Garris Kelley. How you doing? Everything okay?"

"I think so, Mr. Kelley."

"We're partners, Dante. Call me Garris."

"Okay."

"How's the senator?"

"He's lying on the bed. He smells terrible. He's got all sorts of mess on him. On your coat, too."

"Are his eyes open or closed?"

"Open. He's on his phone. He was talking to his daughter. But now I think he's talking to the president! He's been talking nonstop ever since we got here."

"They're politicians, Dante. They do that."

"But it's the *President* of the United States. I shouldn't be here. I'm just a doorman. Can I come out now? I wanna to go home."

"No, Dante, I want you to stay in there. And I want you to stay away from the windows. Stay low. Just like what the senator is doing. Lie down on the bed or the floor."

"I'm not getting on the bed with him."

"The floor is fine. I'll be back in a minute. You're safe, Dante. Officer Baranski is right here. If you need anything, or if you get hungry or thirsty, tell Sergeant Baranski. He'll call room service. My treat."

"Really?"

"Really."

"How would they bring it if the hotel's locked down?"

A good point. Garris looked at the mini-bar. At the bowl of fruit on the table. Back at the mini-bar. "How hungry are you?"

"Not much."

"There're bananas and apples on the table. And there's a mini-bar. Help yourself. My treat."

"Okay. Hurry back."

Garris waved Baranski over to stand guard, then went to the suite's kitchen and opened the cabinet door above the sink. He grabbed an extra ammunition magazine he had stashed earlier and tucked it behind his back. Then he gave Baranski a 'you-got-this' nod.

Baranski gave him a reassuring, "Oh hell, yes!"

THE EXPEDITION HOTEL HAD been around for a hundred years. It had been other things before becoming a hotel, including a department store, so it made sense it would have a nostalgic yet modern theme. There were thirteen suites, with eight facing Pioneer Courthouse Square on the eleventh and twelfth floors. They reserved these for the affluent: dignitaries, rich business types, celebrities, professional sports teams, and newlyweds wanting to start in style. If you were somebody or wanted to impress, this was the place.

Garris had sprung for the top-corner suite. It had the best view. With his Beretta, he walked down the hall to the suite he thought would have the second-best vantage point—suite 1216.

He could have called the hotel's front desk to check if the space was occupied. But that would have eaten valuable time. There was only one way to proceed. Knock. If no one answered, he'd put his shoulder into it. Either way worked for him.

He knocked.

The door opened, revealing a heavy-set man with thinning gray hair and a pencil-thin mustache to match. He wore a purple dress shirt under a dark-blue blazer. He held a glass bowl, chowing down his room service, a fusion dish. The television blared; he had been following the live local news coverage from across the street. The man looked at Garris, then like a child meeting his favorite sports hero, eagerly invited him inside.

"Come on in. Come in. You're on TV!" the man gushed, setting his food down and pointing to the flat screen. "Look!"

While Garris executed a rapid inspection for the shooter, weapons, or anything else suspicious, the man gave his name. Marty Moore. Marty claimed he was a celebrity chef from San Francisco.

After his scan, Garris stopped to watch the video of himself dragging Beemer out of the MAX on the gigantic flat-screen mounted on the wall. It was not a pretty picture, nor did it make him feel better to see his name keyed over his image.

"This isn't doing you any favors," Marty said. "Now that President Cahill spilled the beans, you're the guy who wasted Hector Trevano;

the cartel has to know exactly where you are." Marty stared at Garris's pistol. "You did it, right? With that very Beretta?"

Ignoring the question, Garris crossed the room to the window and sized up the scene below. He had just narrowed the odds in his favor. Though Marty's suite was next door to his, it lacked the view of the Square that Garris had assumed. While his own suite on the corner had the optimum view, Marty's room only caught a sliver of the Square, and the long MAX train obstructed a clear shot. No need to search the rest of the suites on this floor. The shooter would want prime real estate, and that was on the floor below. In the suite directly under his own. Suite 1117.

While Garris mulled things over, Marty continued his small talk. He worked into the conversation the name of his restaurant, 'Maison de Prawn,' and its address. Marty had a cable-access television show and had self-published a recipe book. He liked to fish and really loved guns. He boasted about being a grandfather of four, all but one graduated from private colleges.

Now that he had determined the odds of danger were low on the twelfth floor, Garris prepared to move on. Sensing this, Marty chugged over and opened the mini-bar. Garris gazed into it like he had never seen what they looked like inside.

"Here, take this." Marty handed him a bottle of water, then pulled out his cell. "Say, Garris. Would you mind if I got a selfie with you? You're a celebrity."

Garris grimaced. Thanks to President Cahill, it had come to this. From being someone whose career depended on total anonymity to someone caught in the spotlight.

Holding his phone at arms-length, Marty draped his free arm over Garris's shoulder and smiled like they had been long-time army buddies.

Garris had an inkling that Marty was attempting to delay his search. He also thought it was odd that the entire time he had been with Marty, the chef never voiced concern that an assassin might be on the hotel premises.

Garris left the bottled water and moved on

PASSING THE TWO OTHER suites on the twelfth floor, Garris took the stairs down to the eleventh, then guardedly doubled back to the corner suite below his own.

It had been twenty minutes since the MAX had stopped. Garris took the chance that enough time had passed that the suite would be empty. Assassins don't book weekend getaways. They would be there to gauge the damage they had inflicted, and get out. Five minutes would do the trick. Fifteen tops. Being cautious, he stepped back to the wall across the hall and waited to see if a shadow crossed beneath the door. He listened for movement. Nothing. Garris knocked, then stepped aside in case he was mistaken. If the shooter was inside, he would have nothing to lose and might fire a round.

No response.

His experience was that some doors and locks, including luxury hotels, look secure but are made of cheap materials. Pinpointing the spot to minimize the damage to the door and his shoulder, Garris backed up a step to get traction.

He was all set to go when another option presented itself. The elevator pinged, and the hotel housekeeper pushed her cart into the hall.

Not a hundred percent positive that it would work, but figuring it was worth a shot, he thought he would try the lamest trick in the book, pleading with her to let him enter on the pretense he had forgotten his key card in the room. To his surprise, she pulled out a master key before he could ask. She said she had seen him in the hotel and knew he was a guest. And she had seen the news.

As she reached forward with her key card, Garris stopped her. He would cash in on his new "take-no-prisoners" public persona, painted and framed by President Cahill. He motioned the housekeeper to step back, then plowed through the not-so-cheap door.

The room was identical. Same layout. Same decor.

He swept every room, all closets, behind the drapes, under the bed. The bed was untouched. The bathroom was unused. Towels fresh. Not a drop of water in any sink or the tub. The only sign someone had occupied the room was an unopened champagne bottle, complete with a gift card addressed to the newlyweds. Stephen and Hannah Gilbert.

Poking her nose into the living area, the housekeeper took a second look at the splintered door. Recognizing her dilemma, whether or not to call security on a guest who caused serious damage, Garris suggested she should call her supervisor and report him. But there was no need to worry, he assured her. The busted door would be paid for, in full, by the man who was now upstairs in his suite, 1217. Senator Frank Beemer.

Seeing things smoothed over, Garris asked her whether the suite was booked. She checked her cleaning schedule. It was not. The room should be unoccupied. There was no record of Mr. and Mrs. Gilbert due in the room.

That ticked more boxes for Garris. The MAX shooter was exceptional. He had conceived and executed a highly detailed plan, choreographing an assassination to look like a random mass shooting. He had created collateral damage to draw attention away from his primary target and selected the most suitable suite to observe the aftermath.

Shortly, the police would bring their forensics team to the hotel. Garris was confident they would find no fingerprints or DNA. The room was clean ... sort of.

Garris fished the bottle of expensive champagne from the ice bucket and gave it to the housekeeper. "Take it. It's okay. Nobody's going to miss it, and you've earned it."

She hesitated, but only for a second, then tucked the bottle under the apron of her cleaning cart and smiled.

He gave the gift card another look and discovered something he'd missed.

The Gilbert's congratulations were handwritten in some type of calligraphy, using black ink, and printed on a patterned card. Jotted below the sentiments, scribbled in red ink, was the name of a town, Traughber City. Garris thought it might be the newlyweds' home town.

He asked the housekeeper if she knew Traughber City. She had never been but knew it was a small town in eastern Oregon.

He stared closely at the tiny doodle in the lower-right corner of the card. At first glance, it could have been mistaken for nothing but random scratches or a peace sign. Three vertical lines with circles at the bottom of each staff. Garris thought he had seen it before. Crudely drawn, it could have been a bunch of cherries, like those on slot machines in casinos.

Garris slipped the card into his pocket and headed back upstairs.

THE SCENE HAD CHANGED in the short time since he had left his suite.

Beemer sat at the end of the blue sofa in the living area, working his cell. He had trashed his blood-splattered clothes in a wastepaper basket and now sported a hotel robe and slippers. His face was pale and tight. He looked both ritzy and awful at the same time.

Baranski, with his firearm drawn, sat at the opposite end of the sofa, close enough to protect Beemer but far enough to give him space.

There was no sign of Dante.

"The kid got a call from his supervisor. He had to go," Baranski explained.

"I made it clear I wanted him to stay," Garris said.

"It was an order. He didn't have a choice."

"When?"

"Right after you left."

Garris peered through the corner window. There was movement inside the MAX. The forensics team had arrived.

"They've locked down the Square. It's under control," Garris said to Baranski. "You can holster your weapon."

Beemer hung up. "Lawrence is in surgery." He turned to Baranski. "I need to go to the hospital."

"I'll make a call and get an escort," Baranski said, then went into the bedroom and closed the door.

"Thanks for your help," Beemer said to Garris. Garris nodded. "We need to talk about Paul Cahill."

Three days earlier, Beemer had called Garris and asked if they could meet privately after the rally to clear the air concerning President Cahill. It was Beemer's idea to book the hotel room and Garris's idea to book the best suite in the entire building.

"I didn't tell him about your involvement with Hector Trevano, Garris. I promise you, it didn't come from me."

"Zip it, Frank. I've told you, now's not the time. Lawrence is your priority."

"You're right." Beemer shrugged. "My head's not clear."

Garris nodded and picked up his duffel bag. He pulled out a pair of jeans and a gray T-shirt and tossed them to Beemer. "Here. You can't wear a hotel robe to the hospital. They'll think you're a patient. Besides, I'd get charged for it."

Baranski returned. He tuned in on the vibe between Garris and the senator. "A police escort will be here in ten minutes. I've been told both wounded are being attended to."

"Both?" Garris said. "There were three injured. Who are the two?"

"Lawrence Beemer and the guy who took one in the leg. The others died at the scene."

"What about the woman?" Garris asked. "The woman helping Lawrence. She was wounded in her left arm."

"That's right. I forgot her," Baranski said, then got back on his phone. Minutes later, he confirmed that no woman had been treated in connection to the MAX shooting. Whoever she was, she had flown under the radar. Baranski said he needed to make another call and left the room. Needing to change, Beemer was right behind him.

Garris dug into the duffel and pulled out a green polo identical to the one he wore.

Baranski and Beemer came back at the same time. Garris's clothes didn't quite fit Beemer. Big in some areas, tight in others.

Garris handed Beemer his key. "Check-out is tomorrow at eleven." He picked up his bag and headed out the door.

CHAPTER 2

ALONE BY THE POOL, EDGAR TREVANO STOOD BARBECUING A tenderloin when his cell phone chirped. It was his man Ozzie, from San Antonio.

"Have you seen the news? I don't think so. You would have called me."

"Then why ask?" Trevano said. "Get to the point."

"There was a mass shooting."

"There's one every day. Why would I care?"

"Watch the video. Right now. You won't believe it."

"Send me the link."

"Yeah, of course. Just sent it."

Seconds later, his phone chirped. Edgar opened the text and clicked a link to a headline news website. He flipped the steak and clicked another link to a three-minute video. The MAX, Portland's transit light-rail train, had been on its way to Senator Frank Beemer's campaign rally, with the senator and his son, Lawrence, on board. An army veteran with a handgun had opened fire inside the senator's car. Lawrence had been shot. The hospital had not yet released an official statement, but it was rumored he was in critical condition. They played a video from a witness's cell phone recorded moments after the shooting. Dramatic.

Terrified passengers pushing and shoving to escape the train to save their lives. The camera focused on the senator. He looked pale, in shock, as another man dragged him off the train. The man could have been an actor. Not the star, but the guy behind the star. An extra. The type who is easy on the eyes but not handsome enough that he would steal the spotlight from the leading man. The guy who blends into the scene. He is there, but not.

Trevano called Ozzie back.

"Did you watch it?" Ozzie asked immediately.

"I did."

"It's Garris Kelley. He's in Portland." Ozzie paused, allowing Edgar time to think, then said, "I'm going to Portland. Right?"

"Yes, Ozzie. You are going to Portland."

Hanging up, Trevano turned his attention back to the barbecue. He had let the tenderloin go too long. Driving a fork into the steak, he tossed it to his dog.

CHAPTER 3

BEEMER SAID GARRIS WOULD BE HARD TO TRACK DOWN, BUT the senator's daughter, Liz Beemer, had to try. The last time they had been together, he had made a slip, lending a hint to his Oregon hideout. That was two years ago. It was a long shot but all she had.

Listening as the GPS navigated her through the tight, winding curves down Bald Peak Road, she dropped into the valley's forested hills and acres of sun kissed wildflowers and berries. She drove along a stretch where llamas and goats in front yards were as common as dogs on porches. And rusted automobiles served as statues.

The GPS announced her arrival, and a rusty metal sign buried in a shroud of blackberry bushes verified it. She turned her pearl-white Lexus sedan onto a gravel road, reducing her speed to a snail crawl to avoid rock chips.

About a quarter-mile in, the gravel spun to short brown grass and opened to a sprawling field with black asphalt running through the middle. A private airstrip. Nothing special. A mile and a half long. Blacktop and weeds, but it did the job. A Cessna 150 was on deck, gunning its engine, and Liz waited to watch it take off.

The field had about twenty airplanes tied from wings to the ground.

Two- and four-seaters. Cessna, Pipers, three antique biplanes, and a couple of home-builts. Five rows of T-hangers built out of wood and corrugated sheet metal hunkered just beyond the planes.

The airport office sat at the east end of the strip. A simple building, just a roof and four walls. Big enough to house a radio, bathroom, card table, and a soda machine.

A few pilots hung about, drinking coffee and tinkering with their airplanes. None of them was Garris.

Cutting the sedan onto a rocky washboard artery so rugged that it could have been part of the Oregon Trail, she followed it to the first row of hangars. No sign of anyone. She rounded the corner, to a hanger with its doors half-opened. Music from a radio blasted from inside. It was a country western song. One of her father's favorites. She could not recall the title or singer.

She got out of the car and met an older pilot, who had been there for years, gauging by the heap of odds and ends inside his hangar. She introduced herself and asked if he knew Garris Kelley. Nope. She gave him Garris's description, thinking Garris might not have used his real name. Nope. But the flicker in his eyes suggested he might not be telling the truth.

She returned to her car, which wore almost a month's worth of dust, and drove to the next row. She passed an old Volkswagen Beetle mounted high on concrete cinder blocks: no windows, no tires, and no sign of its owner.

Halfway down the next row, she headed for a red-and-white ice chest and two webbed aluminum lawn chairs, folding chairs invented by a WWII P-38 pilot. Garris sat in one, scrutinizing a small piece of paper. Once he saw her coming, he slipped the paper into his chest pocket.

She put the Lexus in park and checked herself in the rearview mirror.

Garris flipped the cooler's lid, swirled his hand inside the ice water, fished out a green beer bottle from Holland, and popped its top.

"You're not surprised to see me," she said, approaching the chairs.

"Cold beer?"

"Wine. White in the summer. Red in the winter."

"Beer's all I've got. But it's got your name on it. Take it or leave it."

He handed her the bottle, and she took a peek. He'd written her name on the side of the label.

"This is your home, Garris? An airport?"

"Don't knock it until you try it. I've got hot running water. My neighbors keep to themselves, and I never have to mow the lawn. How's Lawrence?"

"Alive. He's had surgery, but the doctor says it'll be touch-and-go for a while."

"It was a neck wound. I've seen worse survive. He's fortunate, Liz. He's a senator's son. They'll do everything they can for him."

"Dad asked me to find you."

"I know why you're here."

"And?"

"The answer's no."

"Don't be so quick. He only wants you to find the guy. He doesn't want you to .... you know."

"Think again, Liz. If that's all Frank wants, he can count on the FBI. Tell your father he needs to calm down, not take it to the next level. Besides, haven't you heard? My cover's blown."

"You'd want me to believe that's a problem for you? FYI, Garris, we know who you are. We know what you're capable of."

"Thanks to Frank, the whole world thinks they know."

"Dad swears he kept his mouth shut. Besides, so what, if he did? Cahill is the Commander in Chief. He was going to hear you orchestrated the Trevano hit sooner or later. It was your fault you had to go to a baseball game instead of the White House, knowing it would piss off Cahill. You took your chances, and he took a swing. But look at the bright side. Now you have loads of free time on your hands. So why not help us? It wouldn't be your first time sticking your neck out for Lawrence."

During Lawrence Beemer's short stint in the military, Sergeant Garris Kelley had been assigned to keep the senator's son alive during his tour in Afghanistan. During a transport mission, there had been an ambush. Lawrence panicked and ran, putting himself in a vulnerable position. Garris chased after him. He saved Lawrence's life but took two rounds doing it, and had been in the Beemer family's favor ever since. After he left the military, he had crossed paths with the Beemers on occasion. Garris got to know Senator Beemer a little and thought he was different from most politicians he had encountered, that is until the previous week, when he put two and two together and figured out that the senator part of Frank Beemer had spoken to his good pal and golfing buddy President Cahill about Hector Trevano, leading Cahill to divulge Garris's identity.

"I need to get back to the hospital," Liz said, downing her beer. "Garris, I'm just the messenger. But please think it over."

"Message received. Always nice to see you."

Liz opened her car door and slipped behind the wheel. "If you don't do it for us, how about for the kid? He deserves justice, too." She closed her door and rolled down the window.

"What kid is that?"

"The kid you asked to babysit Dad at the hotel. The doorman."

"Dante Green?"

"What? You didn't know? Yeah, he's in the hospital. The officer said Dante got a call from his supervisor. They think he must have tangled with the attacker once he left your room."

Garris had dropped the ball. He should have checked Dante before leaving the hotel. "What's his condition?"

"What do you think? He took a helluva beating."

She could see it in his eyes. He might not budge for her family, but he had a soft spot for the underdog. "Dante wouldn't be there if you hadn't got him involved. That makes you responsible. Garris. Find the son of a—"

The window rolled up before she completed the sentence. He got the gist.

Garris had been expecting her visit. He knew Beemer would not ask him to find the shooter unless he had to. Seasoned incumbents like Beemer, high on the political ladder, knew better than to put themselves in a position to be held accountable if they found themselves in a courtroom. They made their requests and demands through the back door. So, Beemer sent his daughter to do his bidding.

Liz didn't know that when she pulled her car around the corner to Garris's hangar, he had already been thinking about the card that accompanied with Gilbert's champagne. He had seen something similar to the cherry doodle scribbled on the card before and wondered whether the shooter had deliberately left HIM a clue. It was a crazy notion, but why not?

He also weighed the ramifications of his recent media explosion. Now that his face had been on the evening news, Garris was sure Hector Trevano's little brother, Edgar, would send a crew to Portland. Maybe they were already here.

Once Liz's sedan disappeared around the corner, Garris opened the hangar doors.

Finding it funny that Garris called the hangar home, Liz would have thought it more eccentric that he owned hangars in all four corners of the country, all of them based on small, out-of-the-way airstrips. They were all inconspicuous and minimalist. A refrigerator, coffee machine, AM/FM radio, and a single mattress.

In each hangar, he had five duffel bags containing any clothing he needed, depending on the job. In each hangar, he had five aluminum cases containing the right type and number of weapons he needed, depending on the job.

After studying a map of Oregon, Garris chose his smallest bag, suitable for four days.

He popped another green bottle as he chose his weapons. It was like choosing a wine for a party and not knowing the host. He had a wild guess whose party he would be crashing, but not why. When in doubt, take a friend. He pulled out his oldest aluminum case, with its share of dents and scratches. Just for kicks, he threw in his Colt single-action Army revolver, since he was heading to cowboy country.

Garris had four hangars but only one airplane, a 1958 Piper PA-23, painted yellow-and-white with black trim. Gorgeous and reliable.

He wheeled it out into the sunlight. A perfect day for flying.

CHAPTER 4

THE 1958 PIPER HAD TWO ENGINES, A PUDGY COCKPIT, AND an instrument panel that looked like a dozen chocolate donuts glued to a coral-blue surfboard. The pilot's seat was slightly higher than the other three. The upholstery had a diamond pattern, a design popular in the fifties in bowling alleys and malt shops. It was stitched with the same coral-blue and ivory-colored leather to match the instrument panel. The plane was a creation from a time when post-WWII overlapped with the dawn of the Space Age, a magnificent time for those who embraced the offbeat, square-in-the-round-hole misfit.

Once he was up and had reached a comfortable cruising altitude, Garris headed east along the Columbia River.

He put on his headset and called Olive Peña, his number one, at the Agency. He reached out to her anytime he needed something as big and round as the moon or as small as a Lincoln penny.

Never having met his communication analyst face to face, Garris knew squat about her. Not her age. Not her hair color. Not whether she was single, married, divorced, or had kids. And though she had been his support going on six years and a dozen missions, she knew diddly about him, personally. But he relied on her. And she knew him better than anyone through his work. From her desk, she had a front-row seat to his world. It was not pretty, and some things he had done were out-and-out terrifying. Nevertheless, she would help him any way she could, as he risked his life, time and time again, relishing the thought that they were a team of two.

"I thought you'd want to lie low. Disappear until the Trevano disaster died down," Olive said.

"That's the plan."

"You fooled me. By the way, Conrad banged on my door first thing this morning. A fishing expedition; he wanted to know if you're still on the payroll. Are you?"

"Am I?"

A couple of beats passed before they shared a laugh.

"Conrad's speculating," she said. "I think he bought into the hype that you're holding a grudge. He's been watching a particular news channel who's been saying they wouldn't put it past you if you were in Portland to take care of Beemer like you did Trevano, but the active shooter beat you to the punch."

"After all these years of practice, I've finally become an overnight sensation."

"You're national news, Garris. Fair game."

"Agreed. Let's move on. I'm in my plane, flying east. Can you find a place to land in Traughber City?"

"Traughber City, Oregon? You really do want to disappear. It's a little late, but understandable, seeing how Edgar Trevano undoubtedly has his guys in Portland as we speak. Hightailing it to a place where there're more cows than people makes all kinds of sense."

Garris heard her fingers flying across a keyboard. "Did you get a Beemer prelim packet?" he asked.

"Yes. First thing this morning. It's been less than twenty-four hours, so you know it's light as a feather. It includes the coroner's report, the medical reports, and the latest status of the injured, including Lawrence

Beemer. It also contains links to videos produced by the media and eight amateur videos from witnesses using their cell phones, recording you extracting Beemer from the scene. I've watched them five times now. You look good."

"Keep going, Olive."

"Sure thing. The FBI is involved. But I don't know to what extent. The Portland police are primarily handling this as a random shooting by a disgruntled homeless Army veteran. No specific target. Lawrence was just in the wrong place at the wrong time. They've been canvassing the city. No leads except for what you've dropped in Sergeant Baranski's lap."

"I think they've got it wrong. I think the shooter is a pro. And if I'm right, he's now in Traughber City."

"That's why you're going? Not because of Edgar Trevano?"

"No, I haven't given Hector's baby brother much thought. I will, but right now I'm concentrating on the MAX shooter. My gut tells me he left me his calling card."

"And you think he wants you to follow him?"

"To Traughber City."

"Why?"

"If I knew, I'd tell you. Maybe, like Conrad, he believes the hype. Thanks to Cahill, I'm supposed to be this year's new super-assassin. Some pros need to have their ego stroked. He might see me as a challenge. When I find him, I'll ask him."

"Do we want to alert the local Traughber authorities the guy might be in their area?"

"We could. But I've got no proof. I'm acting on a hunch. Let's wait until I get there and see if I'm on the right track."

"Hang on. I'm almost done." Olive paused for a moment. "Okay. I've found six private airstrips. But you're going to love just one."

"Tell me."

"McCoy's."

"As in, General McCoy?"

"Retired, thirty-six years in. Air Force. General Eddie McCoy. Three stars."

"He made some noise when he left the Pentagon. I watched his hearing on C-SPAN," Garris said.

"You might have found your soulmate. Like you, they tossed him out for snubbing the president. I'm sending his location info now."

"Olive, did I snub the president?"

"You did. For a baseball game."

"The Hops were on a winning streak."

"Did they win?"

"Nope."

Garris heard his phone ping and pulled up the location coordinates.

"I have his cell number," Olive said. "Would you like me to call him and ask him not to shoot you down?"

"You think of everything."

RETIRED GENERAL EDDIE MCCOY'S airstrip was 2,800 feet long and 100 feet wide. Additional notes Olive provided included: don't land midday in hot weather, and circle before landing to ensure no obstacles in the field, such as farm equipment or a cow. Also, General McCoy strategically designed the runway. There is a wide river at the north end and a wall of pine trees in the south. It was not ideal for a twin-engine plane like the Piper. But it could be done.

Garris had flown the eighty-mile gorge, a route made famous by Lewis and Clark, enough times to pick out a few landmarks, but he had never dropped further southeast than Pendleton. The highway split away from the Columbia River at Boardman. Banking the Piper to the right, Garris headed straight into cowboy country.

A gossamer batch of cumulus clouds stayed behind with the river, displaying an azure-blue sky and a western landscape worthy of a

Frederic Remington painting. He cruised above a network of rivers and streams, valleys, hills rich in ponderosa pine, and patchworks of ranches, farms, and orchards for more than an hour.

Surrounded by towering evergreens on three sides and a river on the fourth, McCoy's runway was a bare-bone grassy field with a buzz-cut down the center. Viewed from above, there was no sign of a home, though there could have been, hidden within the pines.

Taking Olive's suggestion, he circled the runway twice. A handful of cows huddled at the south end but were far enough away not to be at risk. Landing would be no problem. After another pass, he dropped the landing gear, then side-slipped the Piper over the river. Like skipping a stone across a lake, he skimmed down the field, stopping just short of the trees.

Spinning the tail around, he taxied to the hangar tucked under a canopy of trees. The hangar was built with timber cut from the surrounding area and capped with a green double-skin roof.

It was a hot day in Traughber City. A heavy dry heat. No wind. The hangar doors were wide open, allowing the slight breeze to drift in. General McCoy waited inside. Once Garris had switched off the power to the engines, McCoy made his way to the back of the hangar to pull a couple of beers from a vintage Coke machine and popped the tops.

"Not a bad landing. I designed the runway to give pilots something to think about. I call it crick or tree," McCoy said with a sly grin as Garris stepped off the left wing. "Come inside. It's cooler."

McCoy had set a couple of folding lawn chairs near the propeller of a blue-and-silver biplane. A 1935 Waco. It was a beauty, as was the classic sky-blue 1977 Corvette parked beside it. McCoy had some toys.

Taking for granted that Garris would be curious, McCoy waved him to take the seat with the best view of the hangar's interior.

Garris looked around. It was spacious, and the battleship-gray cement floor was spotless. Above, hanging down from the rafters, were more toys. Five large-scale model airplanes, including a yellow Piper Cub trainer and an F100 jet. Garris figured they might be sentimental reminders of planes gone by. There was a basic white porcelain sink, a two-burner stove, and a fridge. In the back, on the workbench, sat a small tube television tuned to a baseball game with the sound muted. Next to the television, a portable radio played a country music ballad. To the right, in the back corner, was a door. Garris figured it led to the toilet. Over on the opposite side of the hangar sat a single bed, made tight to military standards. You could bounce a quarter off it.

Like Garris's, the hangar had all the bare essentials needed to live. However, what Garris did not spot but knew were there somewhere were the general's firearms.

General Eddie McCoy was in his late seventies and outfitted in working-man blue jeans and a vintage red Tragically Hip T-shirt. He was six-foot-two and in tip-top shape, like he had never eaten a hollow calorie in his life. Out of the blue, Garris recalled an offhand remark by Olive that McCoy might represent the older version of himself.

"You look different on television," McCoy said.

"So do you, General."

"Good. Now that we've established we're both movie stars, what's the story?"

"I'm looking for the guy who hit the MAX yesterday, and I'm playing a long shot that he's in Traughber City, lying low."

"I got that from Ms. Peña. She gave me the long brushstrokes. Said you think he's professional. But what I want to know is, are you still working for the Agency or are you on your own?"

"Does it matter?"

"It's a simple yes or no question. From what I surmise, what happened yesterday was a local police and FBI problem. It was tragic, but I don't see it as an act of terrorism. Therefore, not an Agency matter. Therefore, not in your wheelhouse. I'm going to be direct, Mr. Kelley. Did Senator Frank Beemer ask you to find and knock off this active shooter? Word is you're part of Beemer's extended family. His inner circle or some bullshit like that. That leaves me scratching my head. Frank Beemer has the president's ear. It's no secret Cahill is no friend of mine. Considering recent events, I can't imagine he'd be one of yours. So, what gives?"

"With all due respect, General, I'm not going to discuss my relationship with Senator Beemer. But for the record, I don't do revenge requests. Not for anyone. And trust me, I've been asked. Who Beemer is friends with is no concern of mine. The media assumes you and I have a bone to pick with Cahill. It doesn't matter to me if they're right or wrong. I'm choosing not to play in their sandbox."

"Good. So, what you're saying by not saying is, this is Agency business and not a personal favor?"

"I'm saying, I'm not saying."

"Smart guy, you are. You get it. You understand President Cahill did you a big favor by blowing your cover. Now you're a celebrity. You've bought yourself a golden ticket. From now on, it won't matter if you're working on behalf of the Agency or not. The public will always assume you are, even if you say otherwise. That's a golden ticket. Carte blanche. I like that. A lot." McCoy chuckled. "Your assistant, Ms. Peña, thinks you and I are kindred spirits."

"She told me soulmates."

"She'd better be wrong, for your sake. I wouldn't wish my sorry-ass soul on anyone," McCoy said with a wry smile.

"Olive sees the best in people. Even in guys like us."

McCoy nodded. "How can I help you, Garris?"

"I need a place to keep my plane for a day or two. I have a bedroll. I can sleep under the wing. I won't be any trouble."

"I have a cot for the occasional visitor. You can sleep inside the hangar if you don't change the radio station."

Garris tilted an ear to the radio. "Buck Owens, 'Pick Me Up on Your Way Down,' written by Harlan Howard, who also wrote 'I've Got a Tiger by the Tail.'"

"I think we'll get along just fine." McCoy heard something that caught his attention. "Let's go outside. I think you'll want to see this."

To the east, Garris spotted a plane flying low, circling to land. He couldn't identify it, but guessed it had to be a private corporate airplane.

"It's a Beechcraft King Air," McCoy said. "It belongs to the new neighbor. It's been flying in and out of Traughber City for almost a month now."

"Nice plane. Who's the neighbor?"

"Not verified, but there's a rumor that it's the Oregon billionaire Rudyard Coleman."

"The winemaker?"

"I believe he calls himself a vintner. It rolls off the tongue easier when peeling off a hundred bucks for an average bottle. But, from what I'm told, no one's seen him. So it could be country gossip."

"Flying in, I didn't see any vineyards. What would he be doing here?"

"The same thing as me, I suppose. Traughber City is the kind of place where you're left alone. Nobody cares who you are, what you're doing, or what you've done. Here, you have time and the space to think. Meditate, practice yoga, and stay healthy. There was a mining company that went bust in the seventies. The Travis Mining Company. They abandoned it years ago. Lots of land, and it has an airstrip. Besides the main house, there are some bunkhouses on the property. It's very secluded and ideal for someone who values privacy for themselves and their high society friends. Speculation is Rudyard Coleman bought it and has been using the runway to fly in a skilled construction crew to convert the property into another of his playgrounds. If it turns out to be a health spa, count me in."

"If no one's seen him, why's his name being passed around?"

"There's been a handful of unfamiliar faces in town—a tough lot. One of them was at the hardware store, buying supplies. He was running his mouth and let it slip."

Jiggling his bottle, McCoy signaled he was moving off-topic. "Let's go back inside and grab another beer."

Garris did not budge.

McCoy traced Garris's line of sight. He was sizing up the canary-yellow truck parked in the shade left of the hangar.

"It's a 72 Jeep Commando. All original, except for the tires. It doesn't look like much. A little rust here and there. But it runs well enough to get you where you want to go."

"In the morning, I'll go to town for coffee."

"You'll want to go to Rosie's Cafe." McCoy had easily read what Garris had in mind. "The coffee is better at the Painted Wagon, but Rosie's is where you'll have a better chance of being seen."

"Is that what you'd do?"

"Thirty-six years and three gold stars on the lapels. Me, I'd have more boots on the ground. But you're flying solo, so you'll have to be thrifty. If the guy you're looking for thinks you'll take the bait and come after him, which you did, all you have to do is to be visible. Let him know you've arrived. Get a coffee to go, then walk around town. Go antiquing. Buy a postcard for the lovely Ms. Peña. Let him come to you. If your long shot pays off, he could make contact before lunch. But then what? What do you think he wants?"

"It could be anything. But if I had to guess, if I'm as popular as they say I am, maybe he'd like to put a bullet between my eyes. In our world, killing is business. His asking price would go up."

"That's true," McCoy said. "What do you think a guy like you would be worth?"

"Why? You thinking 'bout cashing in?"

"I need a lawnmower."

"Help me out and I'll buy you one."

"New or used?"

"Used. And it will be a push-mower."

"Forget it. I'm getting my shotgun." McCoy laughed. "But if you're right about this guy, you'll be going after his employer, too?"

"I'll have to. This isn't one of those 'don't kill the messenger' scenarios."

"Then, what?"

"One day at a time, General. First, I find him."

CHAPTER 5

DRIVING A VEHICLE FOR HIRE HAS ITS ADVANTAGES. FLEXIBLE working hours. Getting paid instantly, occasionally meeting interesting customers, and the opportunity to earn cash for delivering food and packages.

It was a good fit for a young guy like Jimmy Jimenez. He was not a morning person. He liked to get behind the wheel of his red Ford Escape in the evening around eight and have his app turned off by two. Once he got home, he would eat cereal and play video games for the rest of the night. He thought he might play better if he lit up. He wanted to, but he never did. Never. Not that he worried about the company he drove for. He could not care less what they thought. But if Cousin Renn ever got wind, it was lights out, game over.

Cousin Renn was not his natural blood cousin. But he was family. The Trevano family.

Working for Cousin Renn had its advantages. Flexible working hours. Getting paid well and instantly. The occasional interesting customer and the ease of delivering small packages. It was a good fit. But not perfect. It filled Jimmy with anxiety and sleepless nights. When Jimmy had found himself between jobs and vulnerable, Cousin Renn had recruited him into the Trevano outfit. It was a mistake but there was little he could do about it now, and that was that. So Jimmy toed the line. He followed the rules to the letter and followed Cousin Renn's every order with a nod and a smile.

He was told to arrive at the Portland airport terminal at nine o'clock. Keep the car doors locked and be on time. Of course, he would never, ever be late. Whoever he was to pick up would be important and possibly harmful to his health. So, he cleaned up extra special. He showered. He clipped his fingernails and palmed the perfect amount of product into his hair. Then he put on a fresh shirt, polished his black dress shoes, and was out the door.

He pulled the Ford to the curb seventeen minutes early and waited. Three minutes later, he panicked. Assuming Homeland Security had wired the place with a million security cameras, he thought it might raise suspicion if he spent too much time parked in the terminal. Maybe driving the loop around the airport parking lot would be best. But traffic might be a problem, and he might not return in time. Too risky. In the end, Jimmy did what he always did. He waited. It was the right decision. Ten to nine. The door locks clicked open. The passenger had his own key fob for the Ford: a reminder the car was not his car but a loaner from Cousin Renn.

Chin up and eyes forward, Jimmy avoided looking into the rear-view mirror. He sometimes had customers who were squirrelly, alone in a car with a stranger while carrying things they might not should have. Privacy. That was Jimmy's rule number one.

His passenger settled in the backseat and fastened his seat belt. No luggage. Not even a tote.

"Hey, Jimmy. Turn around. Let me get a look at you."

Jimmy detected a slight accent but could not place it. Before he turned, he closed his eyes tight, signaling he would not see the man's face.

"Yeah, that's you. Lucky for you, you don't look like your cousin Renn."

Jimmy kept his mouth shut. He was not about to correct the guy. Instead, let him think he was Renn's kin. Judging by the tone in the guy's voice, being Renn's relative could be a perk.

"Let's get out of here, Jimmy."

Direction unknown. Jimmy did not get far. Not even to the airport's toll booth before his passenger ordered him to turn around and return to the terminal.

He pulled into the same space he had left less than five minutes earlier.

A squat guy with bug-like eyes who resembled the end product of a steroid experiment stood curbside. He sported a polo shirt similar to the one Jimmy wore. Same color. Same collar. Jimmy thought the guy's looked more expensive because the fit around his enormous biceps was much tighter. The guy got into the front beside Jimmy. He reeked of alcohol. The cheap kind that came in tiny bottles served on short flights. He had no luggage. No tote. Nice Rolex.

"Look at us. We're twins," he said to Jimmy, then turned to the guy in the backseat. "How was your flight?"

"I cracked open a new book," came the reply.

"Any good?"

"Why do you ask? Do you read?"

"I watch a lot of movies."

"Jimmy, drive to the Flying Dutchman," the passenger said, assuming Jimmy would know the place. He did.

Getting to the Dutchman, a dive bar in northeast Portland, would take twenty-five minutes. If he put on the gas, he could be there in twenty without traffic. Then, he could cut them loose. But he would not dare speed. It took little imagination for Jimmy to visualize what would happen if a cop pulled him over with these two in the car. Then again, they had no bags, which meant they had no guns. An idiotic assumption on his part. He told himself to get a grip and drive. Everything would be okay.

Driving for the Trevano family was infrequent. This was Portland.

Not Vegas, not Chicago, or New York. Until now, Jimmy had only driven one passenger at a time. And those passengers were in town for drug deals or money laundering. This was a different scenario. This was a crew. There was a violent vibe radiating from these fellas. Just looking at them made Jimmy's hand twitch. That had never happened before. He inhaled a few deep breaths through his nose and prayed they would not refer to each other by their names or mention where they were from. He wanted to know nothing about them. Bad things happen if you know too much.

With company in the passenger seat, Jimmy thought it was safe to glance in the rearview mirror to steal a quick look-see. The guy calling the shots was in his late thirties. He looked like he took care of himself. A clean-cut, healthy guy. He, too, was wearing a polo shirt. Black as his hair.

"Did you hear about the shooting, Jimmy?" he asked, making Jimmy jump.

Jimmy gathered he was the boss, the crew chief, and swept his eyes back to the road. "Yes, sir."

"Sir," Bug-Eye said. "Listen to that. We've got us a driver with manners."

"Tell me about it, Jimmy," the crew chief said. "I heard he was one of the zombie blokes wandering 'bout your town?"

"I don't know much. I was sleeping when it happened, and I only saw a little on the news while I was eating a bowl of cereal. But I guess he wanted to kill a senator."

"A senator?"

"Yeah. I think they said his name was Senator Blumer?"

"Do you know who your senators are, Jimmy?"

"No. I guess I should. But now I think I know one."

"You should take an interest in politics. It will help you in life."

"Okay."

"But you were close, Jimmy," the crew chief said. "It was Senator Frank Beemer. And they shot his son. Did you hear that on the TV while eating your bowl of cereal, Jimmy?"

Oh, geez! Jimmy felt a panic attack coming on. He was way over his head, with no chance of jumping out of the car and leaving them in it. "No, sir, I didn't."

The crew chief continued. "Then you might not know Garris Kelley rescued the senator."

"Oh yeah, Garris Kelley. I saw him on TV. They said he was the badass who took out a narco leader or somebody like that. That was cool!"

"No, Jimmy. It wasn't cool. Kelley's the guy who killed Hector. Your boss."

Silence. Nothing more was said until they reached the Flying Dutchman. "Pull around to the back," the crew chief said.

The Flying Dutchman had its heyday in the late forties and early fifties when the post-WWII neighborhood flourished. Built with old cedar and stained in Netherlands bright-orange, the bar made a statement, with its paintings and cheap posters of ghost ships and seafarers garnishing the walls. Green Heineken beer decals plastered every window. Eight cars, all beaters, filled the front lot.

In the back, the tight eight-car parking lot was dark and empty.

Following instructions, Jimmy nosed the Ford as close as possible to the steps leading up to the kitchen on the second floor. He killed the headlights. Jimmy immediately spotted the 'Beware of Dog' sign at the bottom.

The crew chief made a call, and the Dutchman's kitchen door opened.

An orange vaporous glow from a single bulb illuminated the entry. Then it switched off.

"What are you waiting for?" Bug-Eye asked Jimmy. "Go help."

As Jimmy got out, the silhouette of a man appeared on the kitchen porch. There was a loud thump, like a pair of barbells. Jimmy froze.

"Go!" Bug-Eye yelled.

As Jimmy pussyfooted up the twelve steps, he tried not to think about what kind of dog waited at the top. The closer he got, the easier it was. The rancid mixture of pickled fish, hamburger grease, onions, dirty dishwater, stale beer, and more unidentifiable foulness lingered in the air, making it hard to think about anything but getting out of there.

Two duffel bags sat outside the kitchen door. No dog.

"Toss them in the car, then come back. There's more," a man's voice shouted from inside.

The bags had the right amount of heft and give, and Jimmy figured they contained clothes. Placing them in the trunk, he hurried back up the steps to find another two bags waiting for him. One was about the same weight as the two he had just stowed. The other was much heavier and clanged as he bumped down the steps. Guns. Had to be.

Bug-Eye had his window down. He called out to Jimmy as he headed up for a third trip. "I'm hungry. See if they have any fresh fries. And ketchup. Don't forget ketchup."

"Leave him alone," the crew chief said.

"Hey, I'm hungry."

"Look at this place. Do you think there's anything here that won't kill you before we leave the parking lot? We'll eat later."

Two more bags sat outside the door. Maybe a combination of weapons and clothing? It was hard to tell. A nervous wreck, Jimmy was no longer sure of anything. He needed to get these guys where they wanted to go as fast as he could and never see them again.

An intimidating guy pulled the kitchen the door and tugged at it, ensuring it had locked. "That's the lot. We can go."

We? Great! Another passenger.

In better light, Jimmy checked the guy out. He was tall and had a full head of wavy black hair. Unlike the other two men, he dressed sharp, in an expensive fitted jacket, blue open-collar dress shirt, and jeans.

Jimmy assumed he was the gunsmith. The other two guys had flown in, so could carry no weapons. This guy had to be their arms guy.

While Jimmy loaded the trunk, the gunsmith crammed into the backseat beside the crew chief.

When he finished arranging their stuff, Jimmy reached into the car and switched on the headlights, then walked around the Ford to make sure he would not be pulled over for something as lame as a broken bulb. He got back in and buckled up. Though he had filled the gas tank before leaving for the airport, he checked the gauge.

"Jimmy. What's the hotel right across from Pioneer Square? The nice one," the crew chief asked.

"You mean the Expedition Hotel?"

"Yeah. That's where we're going."

"Yes, sir."

"See what I was saying, Dom?" Bug-Eye cracked to the crew chief. "We got us a genuine gentleman for a driver. He shows respect."

Shit!

In his rearview mirror, Jimmy caught the crew chief's eyes lasering into his. They both understood what had just happened. Bug-Eye had said a name. Dom.

Shit!

Jimmy started praying a mental rosary. Praying he would not be told to take a detour down a lonely road or stop at the river.

The fastest way to the Expedition Hotel was not the scenic route. It was a risk on his part. But it was dark, so Jimmy thought he could get away with it. He drove parallel with the MAX line, dropping into the southwest blocks.

"Jimmy. You know where you're going, right?" Dom, the crew chief, asked.

"Yes, sir. I thought you'd want to get there faster, so I took a shortcut. We're almost there. Just another minute or two."

"It smells, Jimmy," said Bug-Eye. "Like a sardine and old shoe sandwich."

"Welcome to downtown Portland," said the gunsmith, sounding like a local.

Fortunately, the light was green, allowing Jimmy to make the last turn without pause. "That's it right there," Jimmy said, pointing to the hotel two blocks up.

Prayers answered. No detours. Jimmy pulled into the valet space in front of the hotel.

They all exited the Ford and eyeballed the damaged MAX anchored across the street. The police had it lassoed in yellow crime-scene tape.

The doorman informed them there had been a bit of excitement the day before. All was good now and there was nothing to be concerned with, and he hoped they would enjoy their stay.

The gunsmith told Jimmy to pop the back. The guy grabbed three of the six duffle bags. Then he closed the trunk.

Confused, Jimmy wondered why the guy had left the rest of the bags: the heavier loads—the bags with the guns.

Dom pulled out his wallet and plucked out a twenty, handing it to Jimmy. "See you tomorrow morning. Eight-thirty sharp. Don't be late."

CHAPTER 6

WHILE GARRIS CONTACTED OLIVE IN THE PRIVACY OF HIS plane, McCoy was slinging eggs with hash browns.

Olive had nothing significant to report. The Portland police had worked throughout the night gathering close-circuit video. The FBI promised to add more agents. There were no new leads. The homeless veteran had vanished.

When asked about the hotel doorman, Olive said, like Lawrence Beemer, Dante was not out of the woods. In a joint press release, Senator Beemer and Lawrence's wife, Meredith, announced they were at his bedside and would stay until further notice. They also thanked President Cahill, who continued to tweet his support for their family. Dante Green had his grandfather. No tweets regarding him from Cahill or anyone else.

Olive had prepared a file on Dante and his grandfather. She apologized for its brevity. It was all she could dig up. She sent it to Garris's phone. It took less than a minute to read. When he finished, he asked her to send five thousand dollars from his personal account to Dante's grandfather, who would probably be at the hospital.

Sunlight folded over the eastern partition of pine, casting a knobby shadow on the runway. Garris thanked Olive, then signed off.

ANOTHER TRY

It was going to be another hot day in Traughber City. McCoy had the hangar doors open and had breakfast waiting on the workbench. Waylon Jennings sang "Good Hearted Woman" on the radio.

Garris brought his Beretta from the plane, set it down next to a power drill, and planted himself on a stool at the workbench.

"I can make some toast if you promise not to shoot me," McCoy said, gazing at the pistol.

"Butter or margarine?"

"Raspberry jam."

"Right answer. You'll live another day."

Past the workbench in an overhead cabinet, McCoy grabbed a loaf of bread that might have been the healthiest Garris had ever seen: golden brown, at least six kinds of seeds, nuts, and some oats.

"May I?" Garris asked.

McCoy handed it over. It had the weight of a cannonball. Garris switched on the table saw, then ran it through, cutting off four slices. Perfect in every dimension. He dropped two pieces into an archaic chrome toaster next to a jar of flathead screws and box nails, and returned to his eggs and stared into space.

McCoy set his fork down and waited. Garris had something to say.

"There's a young man, Dante Green, who works at the hotel where I secured Beemer," Garris said. "A few minutes ago, I read his file, which wasn't a file. It was one page. Double-spaced. He had a tough start in life. He lost both parents to the street and lives with his only relative, his grandfather. Two months ago, he caught a break. The hotel hired him. He's not paid much, but most goes to help his grandfather. Yesterday, I asked him to watch Beemer while I searched for the shooter. After I left, he got a call from his supervisor, ordering him to leave Beemer and report to the office. What happened next, I don't know, but Dante got his skull cracked. In the wrong place at the wrong time, and it was my doing. I somehow put him in the path of the shooter." Garris glanced at his Beretta. "Now he's in the hospital fighting for his life."

Seeing no good reason to speak, McCoy went for the toast. He got what Garris was saying. He was going after the shooter, not for the influential senator, but for Dante.

IT WAS APPROACHING THE hour when business at Rosie's Cafe would be humming. McCoy insisted Garris take the Corvette instead of the Jeep Commando. It would attract more attention. Garris agreed.

Garris felt pretty good with the T-top off and stowed, zipping down a winding country road. Within a mile or two, Garris discovered the breathtaking panoramic scenery he had seen from the plane. The land was flat and brown as a pancake. A deserted field, an apple orchard, a crop, a ranch, a farmhouse here and there. Wooden fences. Wire fences. Cattle, pigs, and goats. This was cowboy country.

Not another car or truck on the road. Nary a soul in sight. When in Rome. Garris laid his boot on the gas and confirmed that a 77 Corvette could indeed go from zero to sixty in 6.8 seconds.

IT WAS NOT A good idea, but Gordon Parks did not argue the point with Cherry. Still, clearly, this was counterproductive. Not to mention it was boring as hell. A well-oiled crew usually has a big man. A guy who stands out in a crowd. The muscle. An intimidator. The guy who is tucked away until absolutely needed.

To bring the new guy, Bruce Gillman, a.k.a. the Beluga, to the coffee shop instead of Bob Hawkins ... well, he might as well light a box of firecrackers. But Cherry was the boss. It was his call. Besides, this was not the first time the Beluga had been off the ranch. The crew had been in Traughber City almost a month, so the town was getting used to seeing him lumbering about. But this was different. This was surveillance. The idea was to keep a low profile while they waited to see if Garris Kelley showed up.

In the end, Parks made the best of it. The Beluga was not a bad guy. Parks would have just preferred having his morning coffee with Hawkins.

Parks and the Beluga had been at Rosie's since seven, having taken the booth in the back corner nearest the single-occupant restroom. Parks believed that customers avoided sitting near the toilets.

For a month, they had been dressing like locals, but not entirely pulling it together. Parks wore a red trucker's cap, mirrored shades, faded denim jeans, work boots, and red-plaid flannel shirt with a Blackberry Smoke T-shirt underneath. The Beluga dressed almost the same, minus the trucker hat and T-shirt. There was no way he could squish his fat head into a baseball cap. He had gone another direction by going with a black Stetson. The Beluga stood six-foot-six. Easily two hundred and eighty pounds, with black hair so thick he could not run his meat hooks through it. And droopy hound-dog eyes with matching cheeks. The cowboy hat worked in his favor.

Most of Rosie's Cafe customers were hardcore regulars. The place looked like it had never been updated since it was built in the early thirties, with its ceramic horses and ceramic steers in the front window and black-and-white rodeo photographs hung on all four walls. Cowboy salt and pepper shakers, dishes, and rodeo cowboy coffee mugs completed the look on all the tables and the countertop. Gene Autry and Roy Rogers album covers were strategically placed to draw the eye to the jukebox. The menus were the size of barn doors and laminated in tired, peeling plastic.

Killing time, Parks and the Beluga ordered more food than they could eat. Or than Parks could eat. Pancakes with blueberries, country sausage, bacon, and toast with orange marmalade. Bob Hawkins did not realize what he was missing.

At eight o'clock on the button, Parks scooped up his last runny egg. The Beluga had cleaned and waxed his plate.

Garris Kelley stepped inside Rosie's and bellied up to the counter.

IT COULD BE BECAUSE he had been on Fox News as recently as one day ago, or because he was the guy who took Hector Trevano off the game board. Whatever the reason, in this cowboy town, Garris believed his fame resulted from being the target of the president's malicious social media campaign. The locals were on Team Cahill. He was not. Whatever it was, it was his advantage. Within ten seconds of his entering the cafe, the clamorous tonality of clanking plates, cups, saucers, and Western silverware hushed to a whisper. Cooks, servers, and customers were all spellbound as if a movie star had just walked in, allowing Garris time to register and evaluate them all at once.

While standing at the host desk waiting for his large black coffee, Garris listened to the jukebox as Kris Kristofferson sang "Sunday Morning Coming Down."

Coffee in hand, he left Rosie's. There was no need to stick around. The MAX shooter would get the message. Garris Kelley was in town.

In addition to the coffee, he had left Rosie's with a discovery. At first, Garris thought the shooter might stake out the area from a distance, a parked car, across the street, around a corner, or behind a tree. Not from inside the coffee shop. He made the two guys at Rosie's, the two in the back booth across the aisle from the toilet. It was easy to pick them out. Could not have been easier. Garris could go along with the new plaid shirts, spotless blue jeans, and even the unsoiled work boots. The black Stetson on the whale of a guy was a nice touch. He wore it well. But in the end, it was the guy wearing the red trucker's cap who betrayed them. There is a specific terminal spark in a killer's eyes, which Garris had seen many times before. This guy had it in spades.

Right away, Garris realized he had underestimated the situation. The attack on Beemer and the others on MAX might not have been by one shooter. Likely there was a crew. But if that was the case, he was still not concerned. The game would change, that was all. He excelled at adapting.

Rosie's was located north of Main Street. Garris headed south. The street was clean and wide. Most buildings were no higher than three stories, giving the illusion that Traughber City was more prominent than it was. A handful of funky breweries seemed to be the new thing. But the plethora of spruced-up antique, resell, and thrift shops, hardware, and general stores preserved the overall sentiment of Eisenhower's fifties, while giving the nod to the historic Oregon Trail and the booming days of the Gold Rush.

About halfway down Main, one building stood above the others. The historic Grand Meeker Hotel had been built in the Italianate Victorian-style architecture of the late 1800s. The clock tower and a two-hundred-foot cupola atop the northwest corner suite made it Traughber City's tallest structure, built to capture everyone's attention, including Garris's. He had to peek inside.

Keeping a safe distance, the two guys from Rosie's followed him three blocks behind on the east side of Main. Parks adjusted his red trucker cap, fished out his cell from his new 501s, and called Cherry to let him know he had hit it on the head. Garris was in Traughber City, staying at the Grand Meeker. Which Cherry had also predicted. No wonder he was the boss.

Cherry told Parks to give it a few minutes, then go inside and suss things out. Leave the Beluga outside. No reason to send in a billboard. Send him to get himself an ice cream.

The Grand Meeker prided itself on preserving the luxury found in the grand hotels of the late nineteenth century. The spacious lobby boasted ten chandeliers imported from Venice, a high stained-glass ceiling, marble flooring, Honduran mahogany balcony railings, Honduran mahogany paneling, a Honduran mahogany front desk, oversized Western paintings in hand-carved wooden frames, photographs of politicians and celebrities visiting the hotel, an emerald-green European sofa, and a baby grand piano. This was the place to stay in Traughber City. Perhaps in the entire state.

Garris figured he would see the two guys tailing him in about ten minutes. Ten minutes was the usual time before patience ran out and the brain thought it safe to continue the chase. He puttered around the hotel's lobby, helping himself to a glass of water from a pitcher full of lemons and limes. The glass pitcher was antique crystal, which he believed added to the piquant flavor. He browsed a few paintings. Then he sat on the sofa to check if it had any spring. He tinkled the baby grand's ivories. He drifted to the connecting dining room north of the front desk, more of a saloon than a formal restaurant. More cowboy- and pioneer-themed artwork, cozy mahogany booths and tables. Lots of expensive alcohol twinkled behind the Honduran mahogany bar, and a glass wine cabinet featured Rudyard Coleman wines.

The dining room/saloon was mostly empty. But even if it had been standing-room-only, one woman would have stood out. She was alone, sitting in a booth, working on her laptop with a glass of red wine to the side. Straight black hair, blunt cut at the shoulders, trim, athletic, and smart looking. She wore a fitted black suit, a white open-collar blouse, and a gold snake-chain necklace.

Garris knew her. Not personally. But he had seen the modest bulge under her jacket only a holstered weapon could make. FBI.

What was she doing in Traughber City? Had the Feds caught a lead Olive was not aware of? If so, how did the agent get here so fast? Did she know he was there? He would find out later. The way she used the dining table as a workstation, he could tell she had been there awhile.

He walked to the front desk and took out his wallet. He asked for four rooms in four corners, on four different floors. One room had to be the Clock Tower Suite, advertised as the hotel's most elegant.

The receptionist recognized Garris and opted to be difficult. He dragged his feet. He put on a show. He shook his head and flayed his arms about, acting like the request was a joke. Nobody books four

ANOTHER TRY   65

rooms just for themselves. He said he just couldn't do it. Without a doubt, the receptionist was on Team Cahill.

Narrowing his eyes, Garris gave the guy a hard stare, the kind only a reported lethal CIA agent with a history of liquidating cartel kingpins could make. He told the receptionist he was one hundred percent confident he could manage it, and at a discounted group rate.

The hotel's manager saw them from the dining room. She rushed to the desk and took over.

About that time, Garris spotted the guy in the red trucker cap pretending to appreciate a bronze statue of a wagon wheel. Eight minutes. He was impatient.

The manager picked up the desk phone and called someone above her pay grade. She tapped on her computer keyboard. Two intense minutes later, she gave one last flourish as if she had hit the final note of a concerto, then smiled. They could accommodate Garris's request. In fact, one of the four rooms would indeed be the elegant Clock Tower Suite—compliments of the hotel's owner.

Things were looking up. Maybe she was on Team Kelley? Garris thanked her and the receptionist. He said to skip the group discount. But if he were ever to come back in thirty years, they had better count on giving him the senior rate. He headed to the elevator, leaving Trucker Cap to spy on what floor he would poke. Once Garris was inside the elevator and the doors closed, he did what any school kid would do. He hit the buttons to every floor.

THE BLONDE WOMAN, DIANE Finley, spotted Cherry and Hawkins messing around with something near the mock-up communication tower on the hill.

They had seen her coming from a half-mile away. Literally.

Hawkins was showing Cherry the latest addition to their arsenal:

the McMillan TAC-50, manually operated rotary bolt-action rifle. A beautiful weapon. Hawkins bet he could name the nail polish shade on Diane's pinky finger simply by peering through the rifle's high-powered Leupold scope.

He had sold Cherry on the weapon based on its reputation for holding the longest confirmed sniper kill at 3,871 meters, over two miles. Perfect for what they had in mind.

Hawkins thought firing one round near Diane's feet would be a laugh. It was a shot he could have made blindfolded. But the thing about Diane was she had zero sense of humor. None. So Hawkins resisted.

Running up the steep dirt road, Diane conquered the hill with ease in her tracksuit and mirrored aviator shades. She wore her hair in a ponytail.

"Kelley's here," Cherry said, handing her a bottle of water.

"You called it," Diane said. "Staying at the Meeker, no doubt."

Lying flat on his stomach, Hawkins peered through the scope. There was a barn more than a half-mile away. It had a small target like archers would use with their bows and arrows, a bullseye in the middle. He fired. Direct hit. He glanced up at his boss and flashed a satisfied grin.

"He booked four rooms," Cherry said.

"So there might be others coming you didn't count on?"

"Parks said Garris had his eyes on a woman in the bar, giving him the impression they could be working together. But he might have booked the additional rooms to keep me on my toes. Just showing up tells me he suspects I'm the one who led him here. But he's not sure. He'll want to make the first contact in a room to give him the upper hand."

"I was thinking," Diane said, "he could recognize me from the MAX. It's doubtful, but possible."

"What's your point?"

"I should go back to Portland. Avoid Kelley for the next couple of days, just in case. By then, you'd have your hooks in him. I'll go to the hospital and take care of the senator's kid."

"Good idea. Get the ball rolling again."

He wrapped his arms around her waist, and she leaned into him. She glanced down at Hawkins, who was futzing with the new rifle. "Just promise me when this is over, you'll put a bullet between that one's eyes," she whispered to Cherry.

Hawkins stopped what he was doing, curious whether Diane was joking.

GARRIS POPPED OUT OF the elevator on the second floor and took the stairs down to the street level. He had avoided elevators since he had been trapped inside one when he was eight. Besides, he had never intended to go to his room … or rooms. Instead, he wanted to give the guy in the red trucker cap something to report to his boss. Shake the tree. He assumed the guy was good at something. Everyone has one thing to make their momma proud. But leading a crew was not in this guy's universe. Too sloppy with surveillance skills to be the boss. He was a doer, not a thinker—a foot soldier.

By now, Trucker Cap had time to grease the palms of the receptionist, who would gladly sell him out. Then Trucker Cap would know which room … rooms, Garris had booked. Twenty bucks should do it. The receptionist might give him up for free to show his supervisor he was attempting to be more helpful in the future like she had suggested he be. Trucker Cap would call his boss, the MAX shooter, and give his opinion on why Garris would want more than one room. The shooter might think Garris had backup on the way.

Garris walked back onto Main Street. Having started south but stopped, spun around, and headed back to Rosie's. If there was more than one shooter involved, there might be someone staking out the General's corvette. There were three in the crew for sure, not including the person footing the bill: the shooter, Trucker Cap, and the jumbo guy in the black cowboy hat Garris had spotted in a dessert shop. Jumbo sat in the front window at a table with an ice cream cone, the cream dripping down his chin. Garris gave him a friendly nod, as one would do in a small town. Jumbo nodded back.

Five stores down, Garris stepped inside the Hello Deer, a boutique hunting store for those wishing to shoot in style. In addition to top-shelf guns, rifles, and hunting bows, they had an excellent selection of men's clothing.

Like the two guys from Rosie's who were tailing him, when Garris worked, he would find a run-of-the-mill store and select a wardrobe to blend into the local setting. He was already wearing jeans and a T-shirt, so a plaid flannel shirt was the only item lacking. Maybe a baseball cap to give Trucker Cap something to think about.

The kid behind the counter gawked at him like he was a circus pony, reminding Garris of his cover blown. He chose the first plaid shirt on the clearance rack. Dark-green. Nothing fancy about it. He paid twenty dollars cash, ripped the tags off, and put it on. As he was leaving, the kid behind the counter pulled out his cell and asked if he could get a selfie.

"Sure, why not?"

Two country bumpkins were waiting in a white Chevy pickup truck parked three spaces down on the 'Vette's passenger side. The driver had rusty-red hair. The passenger's hair was also red, but five shades lighter, like bubblegum. Both were in their twenties and wore matching Harleyville, Howdy Doody-style Western shirts, a brand Garris had seen at the Hello Deer. Every few seconds, one of them would take a quick peek out of the corner of his eye, waiting. For him. It was possible Howdy and Doody might work in cahoots with Trucker Cap and Jumbo. But Garris was not a hundred percent sold. The redheads looked more homegrown, whereas the other two were not; still, they were worth considering.

Seeing they were not bothering the 'Vette, Garris left them to wait and headed back to the hotel. If Howdy and Doody were part of the big picture, it would be best to have them far from the hotel if he had to deal with the other two guys.

He was halfway up the steps leading into the Grand Meeker when Trucker Cap spun the hotel's revolving door on his way out. They passed each other, giving each other a friendly nod, as one does in a small town.

Poking his nose into the saloon, Garris checked for the woman FBI agent.

She was having another glass of red wine. Perhaps she was waiting for him to show up. That is what a saloon was good for—meeting people.

He had a room. Four of them. Might as well put one to use. Garris hoofed it to the Clock Tower suite, electing the stairs over the elevator.

The enormous suite under the hotel's exterior clock tower had a 180-degree view of the countryside, an octagonal dining room, antique gilt mirrors, fourteen-foot ceilings, and chandeliers. And, of course, a plush king bed with French linens. Nice. But Garris was only interested in a shower.

The shower was separate from the tub and was spacious enough to accommodate his broad frame. The carefully positioned intense water jets hit the spot. The easy-to-use golden fixtures were a plus. He would like to have stayed longer but wanted to get downstairs. So, a military shower, in and out. He re-donned his clothes, and used the hotel-provided comb. It would do. He was an extra, not the star.

Peering through the suite's living area window, Garris checked to see if they had stationed anyone outside. Clear.

He searched for the hotel's complimentary stationery and pen inside the antique desk, finding them underneath a stack of restaurant ads that featured free delivery. Tearing off three pieces, he wrote the same message on all three.

Take a seat and stay here until I get back.
Hands off the mini-bar.

He stuffed the notes into his front pocket, then hung the Do Not Disturb sign on the door, just because. Then he hurried to the other three rooms, on three different floors, in three different corners. He placed the notes on the beds, easy to spot.

But he left no note in the Clock Tower suite, where he was sure the shooter would be waiting. It was basic psychology. Tell a bad boy to wait and he will not. But show him a lavish room with no strings attached, and he will take that bet every time. Garris thought if he were on the right track, and the shooter wanted to meet, then the shooter would wait. Whether he would stay out of the mini-bar was debatable.

Notes in place, it was time to meet the FBI agent.

Entering the saloon, Garris found the woman absorbed with her laptop. But she sensed his presence as he neared. He appreciated the seamless finesse with which she maneuvered her hand to her concealed firearm without drawing attention.

"No need to draw your weapon. I'd just like to talk a bit," he said.

"Why?" she asked guardedly.

"Because you're with the FBI."

"Interesting. In less than fifteen seconds, you've made two impressive assumptions. Consider me intrigued. What else have you got?"

"I'd just like to sit down and ask a question or two. Then I'll be on my way."

"No, I insist. When I was a young girl, I'd go to the carnival. I loved the fortune tellers," she said. "You've got my attention. Tell me more if you want to keep it. Then maybe I'll ask you to sit down."

"I don't read tarot cards, but here goes," Garris said. "You graduated from the academy at twenty-four. You spent four years in D.C., and you've been in the field for two. If my high school education paid off, that puts you at a solid thirty. The right age for an agent to prove their mettle. And you're prepared to do just that. You've tucked an FBI-issued SIG Sauer P226 on your right hip, under your suit jacket." Glancing down at the mess of papers covering the table, he continued,

"Right now, you're reviewing the Fed and Portland police reports. Am I close?"

Keeping her eyes on Garris, she shoveled the papers into a pile, then determining he was not a threat, relaxed and reached for her glass.

"My age is none of your business. I've been in the field for three years, and it's a Glock 22, not a SIG. Now I'm curious. Who are you?"

"I can't tell if you're serious. Are you aware of the recent event in Portland a couple of days ago?"

"No. I've been off the grid, working on a personal matter that has nothing to do with Portland—and you haven't answered my question."

"I'm Garris Kelley."

"Gayle Wilson," she said, motioning him to take a seat. "Tell me about Portland."

"Okay, short version. A couple of days ago, Senator Frank Beemer and his son were in Portland to attend a campaign rally held at the Pioneer Courthouse Square. For a publicity stunt, they took the MAX. The MAX is Portland's transit train."

"I've been to Portland. I know the MAX."

"Okay. A guy disguised as a homeless army vet shot and killed two passengers and wounded others."

Gayle leaned in.

"The shooter missed his mark—the senator, but a stray bullet clipped his son in the neck. I was there to talk with Beemer after the rally. I think the shooter spotted me and intentionally left me breadcrumbs on a path leading to Traughber City. I'm here to find him. As an FBI agent, I thought you were working the case and might have information you'd share."

"I'm not and I don't. But why you? What makes you so special that both the senator and a murderer would want anything to do with you?"

"If you hadn't been off-grid, you would already know, but I find it refreshing that you don't." He motioned to a chair, seeking permission. She nodded. "Beemer passed some information concerning me to President Cahill that should have remained confidential. It's not a secret that Cahill gets bored easily, and when he does, he has a habit of stirring up trouble. Especially on social media. I got caught in his crosshairs, and he put it out there that I had something to do with the way Trevano came to meet his maker."

"Hector Trevano?"

"That's the one," Garris said. "I'm betting the guy I'm looking for is a contract killer. These guys are businessmen, first. Assassins, second. I think he sees an opportunity to raise his rates by having a showdown in a Western town, far from the big city."

"Now I think on it, I do recall hearing about you," Gayle said. "You're the covert op who chose baseball over a visit to the White House. Not the sharpest move. You look nothing like the photo I saw on the internet."

"Is that a good thing?"

"Take a wild guess," Gayle said, allowing a beat before taking a sip of wine. Then she continued. "Did you? Take out Trevano?"

"Do you believe your commander-in-chief?"

Conceding she was not going to get a straight answer, she let it go. She would try again later.

"Okay, your turn," Garris said. "Why are you here?"

"The FBI has rules about discussing cases."

"You said you're working on your own time."

"That's true. I'm on vacation."

"Perfect. The Agency doesn't need to know how you're spending it. You can spill the beans."

"I suppose I could," she said, thinking it over. "Why not? It appears we're in the same business. Brothers from a different mother, sort of thing."

"Works for me."

"Short version. An agent friend at the bureau, Ron Boyle, thinks he's stumbled on to something in Traughber City. Something big. But he doesn't have the evidence to bring it to the office, so he's moonlighting until he finds something solid."

"Using his vacation time?"

"Totally off the books."

"You guys must enjoy working for free."

"Sometimes you have to. President Cahill and budget cuts go together like alcohol and depression."

Garris nodded.

"Last week, I got an urgent voicemail from Ron. I could hear something odd in his voice. He said he'd been working undercover and had infiltrated a suspicious group. Said he'd made progress but suspected they were on to him. I tried texting and calling him for days but never connected. It's not like Ron not to answer my calls. So, I took a few days off and came here to find him. I've been racking my brain. What kind of group in Traughber City would get his attention? At first, I thought it only logical it could be cowboys or farmers. But Ron used the word 'infiltrate.' Nobody infiltrates a dairy farm or a cornfield. The two words, infiltrate and group, gave me the idea he got himself involved with some sort of militia. Maybe some white supremacists or religious extremists?"

"Militia groups? Wide-open spaces. Plus, the spirit of the Wild West. Not to mention pleasant weather and great steaks. Yeah, I can see a bunch of knuckleheads would set up shop here," Garris said.

"I've been looking at maps and old land management documents all day. That's until you showed up and offered to buy me a glass of wine," Gayle said, leaning back, a playfulness in her eyes.

"Right I did."

"I was about to clear my desk," she said, "and go for a drive to check out the cultural center outside of town. Besides having information on the Oregon Trail, pioneers, and gold miners, it's supposed to have some older topographical and geographical maps of the region. I want to see them. Want to come along for the ride?"

"I would. In fact, I'll drive. I have just the horse and wagon."

CHAPTER 7

JIMMY JIMENEZ COUNTED HIS LUCKY STARS. HE HAD FOUND A parking space, on a weekday morning. Finding a parking space downtown was like fishing for a Goliath Tigerfish. Never expect to land one. Be thrilled if you do.

Arriving at ten after seven, Jimmy was downtown an hour and a half early, allowing himself ample time to circle the city blocks. He had started with the cubic strategy, first following Morrison Street, then taking a left on Broadway, another left on Yamhill, another left on Sixth, and so on. Not a bite. Eight times around the horn, then he got lucky, finding a spot right in front of the hotel. Not knowing how long he would be waiting for Dom and his party, Jimmy played it safe and plugged the meter for the maximum time allowed.

Ordered to be at the hotel at eight-thirty sharp, Jimmy had not been told where he drive, when they would leave, or how long they would need him. Nothing. There was no agenda. He could be there for five minutes or all day. He was now officially on-call. Be ready for anything. At eight-thirty sharp, Dom walked through the lobby.

Dom was a morning guy. He greeted Jimmy with a smile and a firm handshake. Jimmy appreciated the friendly gesture. They were off to an excellent start. He suggested that he give Dom his cellphone number. That way, they could reach him when needed, and he would not have to wait around. Dom did him one better. He plucked Jimmy's phone out of his hands and put it in his pocket. Then Dom headed back to the elevator, leaving Jimmy stranded in the lobby.

Restless, with no phone to occupy his time playing video games or checking email, Jimmy leafed through some magazines and local newspapers. He eavesdropped on a few hotel staff conversations. A door attendant had been severely wounded during the incident the day before. He was in critical condition at the hospital.

By mid-afternoon, nature called. It was more like a primal scream than a call, and Jimmy broke down. He had no choice. All he could do was cross his fingers that Dom would not choose that moment to come looking for him. Making a mad dash to the men's room, Jimmy did what he needed to be done in record time. Relief. Now, his attention turned to his stomach. His breakfast had been a single frozen waffle. He was starving.

He asked the front desk if he could see the hotel's restaurant menu. A ham-and-Swiss sandwich with a pickle cost twenty dollars. It was a lot of money, but he ordered it and paid up front.

Three minutes later, Dom and his pals stepped out of the elevator.

THE TWO REDHEADS WEARING the Howdy Doody shirts parked their white Chevy truck two spaces closer to the Corvette. It was a better vantage point. They rolled down the windows and tried to blend in. Doody, in the passenger seat, fiddled with the radio. Way too obvious. Howdy had his arm hanging out the driver's window, looking in every direction in the universe except Garris's.

Walking to the 'Vette, Garris gave Gayle an abbreviated primer. The two guys in the Chevy might be part of his problem. As they neared the truck, Garris committed the license plate to memory. Then he went around the 'Vette and opened the passenger door. As he did, Gayle glanced through Rosie's window. A handful of customers were craning their necks to get a peek at Garris. Acting like she had not noticed, she slipped into the blue-leather bucket seat.

Garris decided the car had been built just for her. She looked good.

He got them out of town, and she navigated them southbound.

It was a typical Traughber City sultry afternoon. The 'Vette's T-top was stowed, the whole wind-blowing-through-the-hair thing happening. No one else on the road but the white Chevy pickup, following a quarter-mile behind. Gayle spent a little time twisting the radio knob, finding a classic country western station on the dial, a Merle Haggard song. Garris pushed the gas pedal. It was a good day for a drive.

Gayle slipped on her sunglasses. Italian. The real deal. The style Garris had seen in shop windows while walking the Via del Corso in Rome. For a split-second, he took his eyes off the road. Long enough to see that the sunglasses complimented her high cheekbones and dark hair. She would definitely be the star if he were casting an FBI movie.

She glanced at her phone. Four miles to go.

With Gayle busy on her phone, Garris took in the scenery. A hodgepodge of uniform potato-sack shades of nothingness, with parcels of spectacular amber hills staked with majestic evergreen trees. He recognized a few orchards and cattle ranches he had seen from above as he landed his Piper. Bottom line: a lot of land and sky.

Garris spotted the Beechcraft King Air. Rudyard Coleman's airplane. It was flying east low, circling to land. Garris looked around, then checked his rearview mirror to see if he had passed any vineyards.

Gayle's voice cut through his thoughts. "You don't exactly scream CIA."

"I don't what?"

"You don't look like CIA."

Sitting straight, Garris studied himself in the rearview mirror, then looked at her. "You look exactly like the FBI."

"Thank you."

They drove on a little further, the wind flapping over their heads filling the void.

"So what's a CIA guy supposed to look like?" Garris asked, curiosity getting the better of him.

Gayle shrugged. "Not sure. Just not like you."

"Isn't that the point? The agency frowns on us wearing name tags and badges, shouting, 'Hey, look. I'm CIA.'"

"And yet, everyone in the world knows you're a covert op, specialist, or assassin. Whatever you guys call yourselves."

Thinking it would be in his best interest, Garris shut his mouth and kept driving.

"You still active? With the CIA?"

"I know a retired general. He says it's to my advantage not to say."

"Excellent advice."

"It came from a general."

They drove another long, silent mile.

"Okay, I've got to know," Gayle said. "Did you liquidate Trevano, as Cahill said? All by yourself?"

"You've already asked."

"And you didn't answer."

"Do I look like I could do something like that?"

"I don't know. Maybe. With each mile, you're looking more capable."

Taking another peek in the mirror, Garris seemed pleased.

"I'll let you off the hook for now. But I'll get it out of you later. I was at the top of my interrogation class at the academy," she said, slipping her cell phone into her pocket. "The cultural center is up a quarter-mile. Driver's side."

Garris turned left into the parking lot of the Historic Oregon Trail Interpretive Center and noted a hand-painted wood sign designed to look old and rustic. "Be on the lookout for original Oregon Trail wagon train ruts."

It was a special day at the museum. Immersion Day. A troop of twenty local actors had dressed up as pioneers. Men, women, and children were reenacting what a regular day in the life was like for the Oregon settlers. Four full-sized covered wagon replicas were visible in the adjacent field above the parking lot. A woman with gray hair dressed in a blue prairie dress was casting wax candles. An older man with no hair who wore wireframe glasses was waving a tin pan as he shared his story of being a gold miner. Three children under twelve, dressed in less-elaborate costumes, sat around a campfire. Their mother was serving baked beans and potatoes while a muscular man with greasy black hair and a matching fake crowbar mustache played the part of a blacksmith.

The museum was holding up its advertised interpretive portion of its advertised billboard.

Gayle led the way inside the center, and Garris forked over the sixteen-buck admission fee for both of them.

Following the natural flow of interested tourists, they came upon a full-size wax figure of pioneer Ezra Meeker. No doubt the grand hotel's namesake. Ezra stood beside an ox-drawn wagon, scowling.

"He doesn't look happy to be here," Gayle said.

"I think that's his resting face."

They walked on, experiencing other life-size displays and reading details of the explorers, settlers, and Native Americans who had occupied the Oregon frontier.

Stopping to watch a short film about the railroad that had once run through the area, Gayle left Garris to run down the maps she had come to see.

The film ended, and he moved along, semi-interested, keeping a lookout for the two guys in the white Chevy. No sign yet. They might be waiting in the parking lot, too cheap to spring for the sixteen bucks apiece.

Picking up the pace, he skimmed a few displays until he came upon another wax creation and stopped in his tracks.

The exhibit featured a young couple and their child, a baby girl. It was hard to say whether wax figures captured a good likeness. Not important. The models were sitting on the buckboard of a covered wagon. Garris took for granted they were heading west. Unfortunately, the wagon's wheel was stuck in a turbulent river. The woman grasped her husband's buckskin shirt with her left hand and clutched her baby girl, like a football, with her right. The husband held the reins tight in both hands. Their eyes were wild, full of fright. The display's lighting was effectively dark and moody. The hidden sound speaker played an audio loop of crashing, thunder, and lightning. Overall, it was a theatric and moving experience, one that did the museum proud.

Though Garris also enjoyed the presentation, a testament to the unwavering determination, courage, and heroic deeds it took to make this land, their land—it was the young family's name that caught his attention, displayed on a plaque next to the exhibition:

STEPHEN AND HANNAH GILBERT WITH DAUGHTER ISABELLA

Stephen and Hannah Gilbert, the newlywed couple from the Expedition Hotel, whose names were included on the card with the champagne. The card had three scratches, like little cherries scribbled in the lower right corner. Maybe the lines represented the three Gilberts? Or maybe it was the shooter's John Hancock? This was the trail Garris was following.

Stumbling upon Gilbert's exhibit was like discovering a gold mine and had saved Garris hours running around the county, asking questions if anyone knew or had heard of the family. It also gave weight to his suspicions. But why was he being lured to Traugher City? A bullet between his eyes was still on the table, but now Garris had another theory, something else in play. Something more murderous than the attack on the MAX. President Cahill had painted a picture in the press of him being a rogue agent, an assassin with mad skills. Did the killers want to recruit him?

Gayle found Garris in the museum's gift shop. He hoped to find a book telling Gilbert's story. Something in their history might explain why their names had been used in the suite at the Expedition Hotel.

The gift shop was a bust, featuring only the standard T-shirts, coffee mugs, posters, and postcards. Gayle bought a map that was supposed to represent the area, as they had plotted it at the turn of the century when Traughber City experienced its golden years. There were several books on the shelves and tables. Garris leafed through them; none mentioned anything about Stephen or Hannah Gilbert or their daughter, Isabella.

Exiting the museum, they followed the path to the front, bypassing the pioneers' performances.

Garris gave the parking lot a once-over. The white Chevy pickup truck was nowhere in sight. Fine with him. They had been on his heels all day; they would surface again.

He slipped behind the 'Vette's steering wheel. Gayle buckled up and donned her sunglasses.

Garris took the right turn out of the lot and followed the same route, backtracking to town, the T-Top off in the heat of the afternoon. The radio played one classic country song after another. They enjoyed the drive, but it was also a time to scout. He hung a left the first chance he had.

"What are you doing?" Gayle asked.

"Taking a road less traveled."

"Do you know where you're going?"

"Nope."

"Okay."

"Keep your eyes open for a place rednecks might want to party and fire off a few rounds. Someplace that fits in with the scenery. A place the sheriff wouldn't take a second look."

"The local law? That would be everywhere in fifty square miles."

Gayle took the map from the gift shop and unfolded it just enough to look at, but not let it fly out of the car.

Roaming two of the four corners of the county, they passed one tumbledown barn after another. Feeling uneasy, concerned she might miss something hiding in plain sight, she took photos on her phone, a picture TripTik.

They arrived at the hotel just as the sun called it a day. The drive was excellent, but there were no signs of vineyards or good old' boy keggers. No militia.

Garris half-expected to catch Trucker Cap and Jumbo lurking about the hotel. But they were nowhere in sight. He half-expected to see Howdy and Doody. No sign. He fully expected to find the MAX shooter waiting for him inside the Clock Tower suite.

"Thanks for the lift," Gayle said as they approached the elevator.

"My pleasure."

"Can I buy you a drink? For your time and gas?"

"I should be going."

"Going? I thought you had a room in the hotel?"

"Yep. Four of them," he said. "How about breakfast tomorrow?"

"I'm not much of a breakfast person," Gayle said.

"But you drink coffee?"

"Who doesn't?"

"Great. Rosie's at seven?"

"The Painted Wagon at seven-thirty," she countered. "When we walked to your car parked outside Rosie's, I saw how the customers were eagle-eying you like you were on the menu. Face it. You're a celebrity. We wouldn't have any privacy. Besides, I heard the coffee's better at the Painted Wagon."

The elevator door opened, and they stepped inside.

"I thought you weren't staying?" Gayle said.

"I'm not. I'm expecting company."

"You have a guest?"

"Hardly a guest."

The elevator stopped on the third floor, and they entered the corridor.

"Are you following me?" Gayle joked.

"I enjoy taking the stairs. But I want to make sure your floor is clear," Garris said, then waved goodnight.

Garris pulled his pistol as he ascended the narrow, inky staircase to the top floor. He was not expecting to dodge a bullet before hearing a sales pitch, but, as he recently admitted, he was no fortune teller. Better to plan a future with a Beretta in hand.

The hotel was working against him: old hotel, old door, old wrought-iron key. When he inserted the key bit into the lock, part of his body would be vulnerable. He would be an easy target. He imagined whoever was inside waiting for him would sit in the overstuffed chair he had placed to the left near the fireplace. It was the grandest of chairs in the suite. His visitor would want to look impressive for ceremonial sake. To appear powerful and in charge. Sitting in the chair with weapon aimed at the door. He figured they would either invite him to take a seat or blast him at first sight. A toss-up.

Beretta in his left hand, he inserted the long ornate key. He preferred to use his right as his primary shooting hand, but for now, he was a lefty. He tapped the door with his boot, then agilely leapt back and waited for an invitation.

Nothing.

Guardedly, he stepped inside.

The chair was empty.

He searched the suite.

Nobody.

The only sign anyone had been in the room was the turned-down bed and a piece of Belgian chocolate on the pillow.

He repeated the process in the other three rooms he had booked.

No one was waiting to shoot him or make an offer. But it was not a total loss. He got four chocolates.

On his way out of the hotel, Garris poked his head inside the saloon. He had a feeling he would find Gayle. He was right. She was in the same booth, the documents and the maps bought at the museum spread over the table. As before, she had a glass of red wine. She had settled in, and Garris imagined she would be there until closing to work the puzzle, to find her friend and colleague. There was not much to go on. Only a voicemail saying he had infiltrated a group, and they were on to him. Garris put himself in Agent Boyle's shoes. He would be outnumbered. Four-plus days and counting. The odds were not in Boyle's favor. And he had instructed Gayle that no matter what, she was not to get the FBI involved. Garris knew she was going to need help. His help. But not tonight.

Garris waved goodnight to the receptionist at the front desk, then hit the road back to General McCoy's.

CHAPTER 8

PARKING THE 'VETTE AT THE HANGAR DOOR, GARRIS SWITCHED off the ignition.

Having moved the two folding chairs outside, McCoy sipped a bourbon as he evaluated the night's sky. A half-moon and a thousand stars. A solid ten, an atmosphere that could only be experienced far from the city's bright lights.

McCoy nodded toward the bottle and an empty glass. "Make any headway?"

Garris poured himself a drink, then lowered himself into the lawn chair. He took a sip. Not a cheap bottle. "You ever hear about a pioneer family that settled around here? The Gilberts? Stephen and Hannah."

"No. I'm not current with the local folklore. Why? They important?"

"I think so, but I don't know how."

"I can search for them on the computer."

It occurred to Garris he had not seen a computer or any other tech devices in the hangar. McCoy must have a laptop stored somewhere.

"I booked the Clock Tower suite at the Grand Meeker," Garris said.

"Nice room. Nice saloon. How come you're drinking with me?"

"What would I do with a comfortable bed?"

McCoy chuckled, a knowing look in his eyes. "You've set a mousetrap to catch the shooter. Smart move. You thought he'd want to meet at a location, giving him the upper hand. You thought you'd do the same. But here you are. Obviously, he didn't take the bait."

"Not the right cheese."

"Smart mouse."

"Smart mice. I think there's more than the one."

"I could have guessed. Present company excluded, lone assassins are rare. The best work in teams."

"And if I had to guess, I'd say this is a group of five or six." The instant the words left his mouth, it hit him. He and Gayle might be looking for the same bunch. Their individual investigations might be entwined.

"There's a chance to lower that number if you wanted to," McCoy said, glancing down at his left hip. He had his pistol ready. "We have company. They're out there in the field, a few hundred feet out. Ten o'clock."

"By the gas pump?"

McCoy nodded. "They've been lying on their bellies since sunset. Waiting for you, I suppose."

"Any idea who?"

"Nope. I haven't seen them."

"But you know they're there?"

"There's two of 'em, guaranteed."

"What do you have in mind?"

McCoy glanced at the 'Vette. "Nice night for a drive, don't you think?"

Garris caught McCoy's lead. He reached into his pocket, fished out the car keys, and handed them over. "I call shotgun," he said.

"I don't think we'll need to take it to that level. But I could get you one if it makes you feel better."

"No. I'm good."

Nonchalantly, the two stood and play-acted a little. They pointed at the moon and the stars. Then McCoy said, "Hey, let's go for a drive."

He said it out loud for their audience. Then they strolled to the 'Vette, McCoy taking the driver's seat.

Garris pulled his Beretta. He had packed his Wild West Colt revolver in his bag, but it was still in the Piper. He wished he had it—to suit the overall Western vibe he was getting.

The standard 350 cubic-inch engine in a 1977 Corvette has 185 horses at 4000 rpm. Garris had already proved the Corvette could travel a distance of five hundred feet in 8.5 seconds. McCoy's Corvette was in pristine condition. A real gem. He fired it up, turned on the high beams, and shifted into reverse. Garris twisted his torso to face the rear and raised his pistol. McCoy floored it. He covered the five hundred feet in nine seconds, which was still pretty good, considering traveling in reverse.

Nine seconds is not much time to react when seeing a classic sports car's taillights coming at full speed, spraying rocks and dirt. McCoy slammed the brakes at the last second and cranked the wheel, spinning the car in a 180. Executed perfectly. It was as if he had practiced the maneuver in his backyard.

The high beams lit up, and Howdy and Doody, the two guys from the white Chevy pickup truck, got off their tummies and waved their hands above their heads.

McCoy and Garris marched over.

"Damn it, Tommy. Do you want to get yourself shot?" McCoy barked to Howdy.

"Not really," Tommy said.

"How about you, Andrew?"

"No, General. Not me either," Doody answered.

"Garris. Let me introduce you to the Mitchell brothers, Tommy and Andrew. They're on my squad."

"Squad?"

"Occasionally, I hire men to help work the property."

Garris tucked his pistol away.

"Why are you two knuckleheads hiding in my field?" McCoy asked.

Tommy, whom Garris took to be the brains of the family for no other reason than he was the brother driving the truck, began picking pebbles and weeds off his shirt and jeans.

"We wanted to see him," Tommy said. "That's all. We didn't mean to make any trouble." He turned to Garris. "People in town think you got something against the president. They don't like you much. But we think you're awesome. You killed Trevano, just like in the movies. And we asked Tristan, the receptionist at the Meeker, who the woman was. He said she's FBI. That's frick'n awesome. We wanted to see you guys in action. That's all. We kept our distance. We were trying to be respectful."

"Okay, boys. You saw him. It's late," McCoy said. "Now, get on home."

"All right. Sorry, General," Tommy said.

Andrew, who Garris thought came across as shy, stepped forward. "Mr. Kelley, sir?"

"Yes?"

"Since we're here and all, would you mind if I got your autograph?"

"I'd like one too, Mr. Kelley," Tommy said.

Seeing how the brothers had the best intentions and meant no trouble. No harm, no foul. Garris shook their hands and signed his first autograph.

It had come to this.

CHAPTER 9

EDGAR TREVANO LOUNGED IN HIS FAVORITE CHAIR IN THE whole damn mansion. Not a classic chair found in a CEO's office or bright board room. Not a fancy French design or Italian. Just a black leather recliner he had bought from a movie theater. A whole section of recliners for his own home theater.

He was alone, five rows back, center, from the enormous screen, his legs extended and half a bucket of buttered popcorn on his lap. Previewing a new investigative crime show. With so many streaming services popping up, networks were dying for original content. Documentaries were cheaper to produce than scripted dramas or comedies. There were no actors. No elaborate sets. No craft services.

The current episode was about the Trevano crime family. He found it amusing and satisfying. The program hit most of the notes of a typical investigative film. Interviews with unrecognizable eyewitnesses and former cartel members, protected with face and voice distortion. Third-string former law enforcement officers who were cashing in on the fame game. The film tossed in a few exotic and domestic locations. And the program had almost nothing accurate. Perfect.

Edgar believed money could produce average fiction. Enough money could create an illusion. Cartel money would make a documentary film and rewrite their version of history, and the public would believe and form an opinion that supported his fairy tale.

Though Edgar's name did not appear in the credits, he was the film's executive producer. He had put up the money and told the director what would go in the movie and what he would leave out. Because he was taking over his brother Hector's business, they would leave him out of the storyline. Edgar had no need to see his name in lights. It was better to create a fictional character for the role to lead the CIA and the DEA on a wild goose chase. Eventually, they would figure it out, but it would cost them time and money. That would be hilarious.

The entire movie was bullshit, but the public would never know. If they did, they would not care. They only asked to be entertained. So even if the DEA, the FBI, or even President Cahill himself disputed the show's content, the kernel of doubt would be planted.

The film profiled Hector Trevano not as a violent drug lord but as an innovative, successful business entrepreneur, targeted by the government to justify their soaring budget.

The film was nearing its completion before Garris Kelly came into the picture. Now that Hector was dead, Edgar paid a boatload to finish the program quickly to get it on a streaming platform as soon as possible.

The film reached the final climactic scene. The CIA operative had tracked Hector to The Hague, a city in the Netherlands. The operative slaughtered Hector Trevano in cold blood. This part of the film was mostly accurate and not pretty. But, thanks to President Cahill's tweeting frenzy, the movie named names. The star of the show was Garris Kelley.

Edgar's cell chirped. He muted the film's sound. He had seen the ending before and knew what was coming.

"It's me."

"Dominic. How goes it?"

"Slow. You know how these things can be. But we'll find him."

"I know you will."

"We checked into the hotel. We thought he'd come back. Now I'm outside the hospital with Jimmy. Ozzie thinks Garris will pay a visit to the senator's son."

"What is his status?"

"I don't know. One minute, I hear he's going to be fine, then they say he's probably a goner. There are a few well-wishers here doing the candle vigil thing. Cops are in and out. Doctors and nurses come and go. Jimmy and I have our eyes open, waiting for Garris to show up."

"Good. Stay on it." Edgar said. "Who is this Jimmy?"

"Our driver. You know, Renn's cousin."

"Right. Long term, how bad do we need a driver in Portland?"

"Don't worry. We'll take care of any loose ends once we get Kelley."

"I know you will."

DIANE FINLEY FLASHED HER official nurse's ID badge to the two police officers standing guard outside the hospital's main entrance. Even with the Oregon senator and his dying son, the cops' reason they were getting paid overtime, they allowed her inside. No problem.

Like fishing, she had waited for the tide to turn—the time when the late shift drifted in and the day shift drifted out. The foot traffic had finally picked up. It was the optimal time to breach security.

Padding her sleek greyhound figure to achieve a much heavier appearance, Diane dressed in blue scrubs, a short auburn wig, and black glasses. For detail, she drew a tiny red peace sign on her right hand. It looked like a tattoo and would get noticed. She looked like she belonged.

Snaking her way through each wing, she said hello a few times when she had to but never lingered. They had their jobs and she had hers. She had memorized the hospital layout from the map on the hospital's website and knew where she was going.

She would walk the halls to let the hospital staff and the police get comfortable seeing her moving about. She had learned the turnover rate at the hospital was high. There was always a new kid on the block. As long as she wore an ID badge and look like she ran the place and had seen it all, she would be accepted. Her badge was perfect in every way, and deep down, Diane was an actress at heart. She could play any part. She would sit in the cafeteria awhile and make small talk when she had to. She knew enough about the healthcare industry to pull it off. She had sent her fair share to the hospital, and more to the morgue.

Every hour, she would make another round, widening the net, getting closer to Lawrence Beemer's wing, then the corridor, eventually passing by the two or three officers outside Beemer's private room. It was a waiting game. She would be there all night. She would be there when the dayshift filed in. She would be there when the following day's police officers came on duty. They would see her and accept she was part of the staff. She had an ID badge.

It was a few minutes past midnight. She sat at one of the three tables in the break room eating her lunch from a blue insulated food container. Shrimp salad. And though she was hungry, she did not take a single bite. It was a prop.

As she had anticipated, Senator Frank Beemer eventually strayed in. He needed coffee. Diane thought he looked like he had not slept in days. Unshaven. Thin, pale face. He did not recognize her. Why should he? The woman standing next to him on the MAX was blonde. Not a slightly pudgy redhead. He had been up for hours, never leaving Lawrence's bedside for too long. Only to stretch his legs, make a pit stop, and grab a coffee. His mind was not clear.

"I'm so sorry about your son," she said.

"Thank you," Beemer answered, turning toward the nurse. Elizabeth Anderson, according to the nametag pinned to her uniform.

"My daughter's name is Elizabeth. You might have seen her," he said. "She's been here throughout the day."

"Yes, we've met," Diane lied. And she had carefully chosen her alias to match the Beemer Princess.

"Would you mind if I sat down to drink my coffee?" he asked.

"Please do." Diane/Elizabeth, gestured to a chair. "I'll be checking on your son throughout the evening. Until tomorrow afternoon, actually."

"That's a long day," Beemer said.

"I volunteered to work a double. The hospital is short staffed these days, and I want to ensure your son's well taken care of."

"Thank you."

Diane Finley wore an ID badge. She was accepted.

CHAPTER 10

GARRIS WALKED INTO THE PAINTED WAGON AT TEN-TILL. Wearing the same clothes as the day before, minus the green plaid, he looked homegrown. Close enough to local stock.

Gayle sat in the corner booth near the window. The morning sun struck the corner of her left shoulder, casting a shivery shadow on her pile of papers. It was easy to guess she had been at the Painted Wagon before seven-thirty. She had on the same dark-blue suit jacket, today with a different blouse. Black.

Garris sat across from her and set four Belgian chocolates on her coffee saucer. "This doesn't count as breakfast. Think of it as a snack," he said. "Any word from Boyle?"

"No. I had my cell and my computer on all night. No calls. No text. No email. Nada."

Like an accordion, she compressed the museum map to one-quarter size, revealing a flat satellite image on the tabletop. "I called in a favor from a friend at the bureau. They took this at three this morning. I've been over it and over it, searching for a location a militia might think they'd be safe from prying eyes. Do you know how many barns are around here?"

"Is that a trick question?"

He held off telling her he now had doubts about her militia theory and that they might be after the same bunch. Not a militia, but worse. Instead, he asked what else she had.

"I've got nothing," she said.

"Why don't we take another drive? See if we can't stumble onto something at ground level."

"You're reading my mind," she said as two coffees in large to-go cups arrived at the table.

Stepping outside the Painted Wagon, she looked around for the 'Vette.

Garris opened the passenger door to McCoy's canary-yellow 72 Jeep Commando. "Mind if we drive something that won't draw attention?"

"It's a convertible. Why would I mind?"

He headed south, down Main. Past the Grand Meeker, he cut to the east, where he had seen the plane, rumored to be Rudyard Coleman's. It had been circling to land. Garris aimed to find out where.

The drive started out the same as the day before. Long, winding country roads. Intersections, few and far apart. Old farmhouses and barns at the end of long gravel driveways. A mixture of wood posts and barbed-wire fences. Not another car or truck on the road. Garris was appreciating the serene country drive.

Gayle broke the silence. "The satellite image wasn't the only thing I perused last night," she confessed. "I also took a detour through your FBI file."

"I have an FBI file?"

"Who doesn't? I wanted to read the bureau's assessment concerning you and what happened in The Hague."

"Why?"

"I'm the FBI. We want to know everything."

Garris did not disagree.

"Would you like to know what's in the report?" she asked.

"I'm as curious as the next guy."

"On the morning of September nineteenth, Hector Trevano flew to a private airstrip off the southern coast of England. He then slipped into Rotterdam via a cargo ship. Once in Holland, he and his five bodyguards, not the dozen reported by President Cahill, split into two groups of three. They risked traveling to Holland to attend a meeting that would take place at a hotel in Scheveningen. Scheveningen is one of eight districts in The Hague. It's on the North Sea. Which you already know."

"If you say so."

Garris kept driving, mostly listening to be polite. He knew what had gone down in The Hague, and that information would not be found in any FBI report. The file Gayle had was fiction. Manufactured by Conrad's team.

He was also keeping an eye out for something different about the countryside. Something that did not fit. Anti-government and radical groups were hard to pin down. The cluster that Ron Boyle had possibly infiltrated might be local farmers, cowboys, or ranchers with an ax to grind with the government. Or they could have come from somewhere else. Shipped in. They could be ex-military, where more than one rebel got their start. It was possible they had slipped up and set off a red flare. Garris kept his eyes open.

Gayle continued. "The Netherlands has a relaxed opinion concerning drugs. We know that. Cannabis, amphetamines, and psychedelics. Soft drugs. They're big on their personal freedom. It's a live-and-let-live society. But then a game-changer came along. A new super club drug called Belatrox hit the market."

Garris nodded. That part was true. There was a Dutch college student, a chemistry major, who had stumbled upon a formula for the next big thing. He called it Belatrox. What else was in the FBI file? Garris listened up.

"Hector rarely left his compound. But he had no choice if he was going to take the lead in what would surely be the biggest moneymaker on the planet. Perhaps of all times. The broker said whoever would be lucky enough to secure sole distribution and make endless billions would have to come to The Hague to make it happen. Ironically, The Hague is the International City of Justice. Anyway, it was a deal-breaker. Take it or leave it. There was absolutely no way the college kid or his broker would risk traveling to Trevano's home turf. He had grown up watching mob and narco movies. A close confidant convinced Hector he would be fine. If the king of the Netherlands could walk unescorted through The Hague's city center and not one local would blink an eye, then Hector could too. Hector rolled the dice. But what he didn't know was that his confidante was CIA. One of you guys. An agent who'd worked six years undercover."

So far, the story was holding up. But it was nuts and bolts. Nothing that had not been posted as a rumor on the internet or discussed on news programs. The generic CIA undercover fable. Garris predicted the storyline would divert from the script soon.

"This is the part where you come in," Gayle said.

"Wait. Hold that thought," Garris interrupted.

"What?"

He pulled over to the shoulder and turned off the ignition to listen. But not to Gayle.

A high-pitched whine was trailing off to the north. Working for the Agency, Garris knew the sound of a drone when he heard one. Once they hit the market, they had instantly become a helpful tool, and he had used them himself. The one he had just heard was likely being operated by a farmer or a rancher, but Garris did not want to rule out the chance the guys Gayle was looking for might be at the controls. Best take a look.

On the other side of the road, a barbwire fence ran down and out of sight. Eyeballing it, Garris reckoned it was five feet high. High enough to keep cattle in, though there were no hoof prints to say there ever had been any in the area. So what was its purpose?

He got out and crossed the road, dipped down into the bar ditch, then up, and plodded through the scrub brush to the fence. Gayle right behind him. He suggested she keep her eyes out for rattlesnakes and cautioned her about the fence. Not only was it barbwire, but it was also electric. Four parallel lines loaded with juice.

He left her at the fence and trotted back to the Jeep, returning with the spare tire and jack.

"What are you doing?"

"I'm going to see what's over that hill," Garris said, gesturing to the slope.

Garris knew of five good ways to get past an electric fence, but he lacked the right hardware on hand for any of them. It was time to add a sixth. He slid the rubber tire horizontally between the two inner wires, then pulled it upright as far as it would go. Inserting the hydraulic jack inside the inner rubber lining of the tire, he cranked the handle. The tire stretched and bent the electric wire, but not by much. Maybe a three-foot gap.

Gayle glanced at his broad chest. "You're not going to fit."

He took off his belt and tucked his T-shirt into his jeans. "The thing with most electric fences is they have a low current. And they pulsate. If I touch it, I won't feel like tangoing. But it's not going to kill me. Worth the risk."

"I'll save you the last dance," Gayle said.

The lower middle wire was two feet above the ground. Not a problem to step his right foot over. From there on, it was all gymnastics. Bending his torso at a forty-five-degree angle, Garris focused on the lower wire and visualized the upper. It was not the time to think about his head size. But he did. His was not small, but it was not a bowling ball, either. If he kept his nose down to within an inch of the lower wire, he would clear the top by two inches. Two-and-a-quarter, if he was splitting hairs. Shifting the bulk of his weight to the ball of his right foot, he straightened his arm, kept his right hand flat, and sailed underneath. Made it look easy.

Leaving Gayle at the fence, Garris dogtrotted to the hill, trudged up, then disappeared from view.

It was no surprise that the other side of the hill was more of the same. Flat, cracked, and barren. Except that about a quarter-mile to the northeast stood what appeared to be a shooting target, probably built with plywood, maybe twenty-five feet high and ten feet wide. Garris thought it looked a bit like the Empire State Building. He had to go down and check it out.

He was almost to the bottom but stopped. He heard the whirring again. Having a good idea of what would come next, he nestled behind a patch of sagebrush.

Seconds later, a drone the size of a cello case flew up. Carbon-fiber propellers. Modified brushless electric motors. Cameras and microphones. Weaponized. It swooped down and flew less than five feet above the flat surface at twenty miles per hour plus. It lined up dead center to the target, then fired, hitting it with an explosive shell filled with white powder. Then, banking left, it circled back around, heading straight toward Garris. It shot straight up about twenty-five feet and hovered above him.

Because it was there and it seemed like the right thing to do, Garris picked up a rock the size of a hardball and threw it at the drone. He missed. He picked up another. Missed again.

The drone tilted downward. Hearing gears click and tumble, Garris figured it was replacing the white powder ammo in its chamber with a different, more lethal shell. Its barrel rotated and locked into position, aiming right between his eyes.

He had never stared down a weaponized drone before. Time to improvise. But what to do? His gun was in the car and he was not about to hang his hat on his rock-throwing ability. Not when his life was at stake. He slowly raised both hands in the air. Then, putting himself into the drone operator's frame of mind, he came up with two plausible scenarios. First, if he stood still as a statue, showing a non-threatening position, that he was just a guy who had lost his way, they might think he was not worth the bullet and fly away. The second scenario, they would think he was armed, so they would likely wait for him to make the first move, then shoot.

But there was a third scenario he had not anticipated.

Gayle had charged up from behind and took his left side. She had drawn her Glock 22.

"Maybe you should holster your weapon, Gayle."

"I don't want to."

"What?" He was caught off guard.

"You heard me. I think I might want to shoot the shit out of that flying robot just to say I did."

"Sure. That's one way to go. If I had my gun, I might want to do the same. But let's take a moment."

"Garris, open your eyes. You don't have a moment."

"Technically, we're trespassing on their property. I think they just want to scare us off. They were using powder, not live ammo. Whoever's operating that thing might just be some country boy with a new toy. Like shooting tin cans and empty beer bottles. Target practice."

"Do you know what I think? I think you're overthinking. I think it's the militia Ron is involved with. And you've become a slightly better target than a Budweiser bottle."

"It would take a damn good pilot to zip in here the way it did and hit the bullseye dead center," Garris said, mulling it over.

"Ron could do it. He's got a garage full of those things. He competes in tournaments. Drones could have been how he bought his way into their group."

The drone rocked its rotors, left and right, like it was signaling a message, then swiveled its barrel to Gayle. Then it exploded into bits.

Gayle had fired four rounds into it before one piece hit the ground.

"Do you know how much one of those costs?" Garris asked.

"What do I care?" Gayle holstered her pistol. "Let's go find Ron."

IN THE JEEP, GAYLE picked up her story where she had left off.

Down the road, two miles as the crow flies, a newish Audi sedan had blocked both lanes, making it hard, but not impossible, to pass.

Trucker Cap leaned against the car, his arms folded. Alone. No Jumbo to lend a hand.

Garris could have driven around the truck, but he had a hunch and saw an opportunity. Maybe the guy had a role in the MAX attack or knew something about Gayle's partner. Garris pulled over, snatched his Beretta from the back of his jeans, laid it on the seat, and stepped out of the Jeep. Gayle stayed but surreptitiously drew her Glock.

HAD CHERRY GIVEN HIM a choice, Gordon Parks would have stayed with Bob Hawkins and played with the new rifle. Let the new guy, the Beluga, play traffic cop. But orders were orders and Cherry was the boss. If Cherry said to keep Garris far away from the ranch for the afternoon, he would do that. At least Cherry had not specified how to keep him away. So Parks had some fun showing off the drone. At least until the FBI agent showed up and displayed her short fuse. Now he had some explaining to do about the destroyed drone. But that would happen later. For now, he had to follow Cherry's orders and stop Garris from getting closer.

He told himself he wasn't looking for a fight, but if Garris wanted to start something to impress the FBI agent, he would help a brother out. He had heard about all he could stomach regarding Garris's reputation. Hawkins would not stop blathering on about the guy and what he was allegedly capable of. He had had enough, reminding Hawkins that he was not afraid of Garris or any other operative. Not even close. Those guys took every advantage of the hype personified in Hollywood movies and thriller novels. They were smug, promoting their myths to sound more mysterious and lethal than they really were. They had a bloated and undeserved reputation. There was no question in Park's mind that he could easily take Kelley out. Any time, any place—only not now. Cherry had said they needed him alive. And Cherry was the boss.

"Stop right there. This is a private road," Parks told Garris.

Garris kept walking toward Parks.

"What? Can't you hear? I said this is a private road."

Not counting the flyby on the hotel steps, this was Garris's first good look at Trucker Cap. Like himself, the guy was built, over six feet tall and two hundred-plus of solid muscle. A sense of fearlessness emanated from the guy, and his hands were battle-scarred. Garris easily deduced that, also like himself, Trucker Cap came from military stock. Because he was there, and it was the right thing to do, Garris tested the waters to find out which branch.

"Seems to me, out here with nothing better to do than to pull guard duty, you must be the low man on the totem pole," Garris said. "Can't say I'm surprised. I made you yesterday, at Rosie's. You and the little fella."

Parks took off the cap and tossed it on the ground. He balled his hands into fists. "Turn your truck around."

"Why?"

"Because I say so."

"Not going to happen. But I tell you what. Let's start over. But we're going to switch roles."

"What?"

"I'll tell you to turn your tail around. And you're going to do it."

Parks scoffed. "No, I won't."

"I bet you do."

Parks charged Kelley. He was slow, though admittedly it was hard to get any momentum going in six steps. Parks should have known better. He left himself wide open. Garris had more choices than a Rosie's menu to level him. But he resisted. Not now. Maybe later. Garris had a bigger picture in mind. He needed information, and that required him to keep this guy in fairly good working condition and to have the ability to form complete sentences so he could run to his boss and get the ball rolling. For that reason, Garris took it easy. He allowed Parks the time and space to maneuver himself into a combat position. Parks raised his arms to throw a throat punch. Information received. Parks was most likely an Army Ranger. The throat punch was typical with the Rangers.

It can brutally crush the windpipe when properly delivered. It is also very tough to execute. Besides being easily telegraphed, the chin can be a problem with that attack. The chin is not always in the proper position when you need it to be. Seeing that Parks would give it the old college try reminded Garris it was better to give than to receive. Parks planted his left foot, his right fist aiming at Garris dead center. Mistake. Without momentum, there was no wind in his sails. Garris timed a whole step to his left like he was line dancing. Parks missed him by a country mile. Garris flattened his hand into a rock-scissors-cut-paper position and snapped his right arm backward, catching Parks' Adam's apple. Then, because it was there and seemed like the right thing to do, Garris popped him in the nose.

Watching from the Jeep, Gayle was impressed. Garris made it look like there was nothing to it. She made a mental note to try that strike if ever she was in a bind.

Parks bent over, clutching his throat. He would be okay. It was just a tap. He would be quiet at dinner but a Chatty Cathy by breakfast.

Garris sauntered over to the Audi. He would be friendly and open the driver's door for the guy. The scenario took an unexpected turn with the arrival of a metallic-gray Range Rover. It passed by the Jeep and stopped in front of the two men. Dark-tinted windows made it impossible to see the driver as it idled for a moment, then drove off. It rounded the Audi and kept going. It had stayed just long enough to send Parks a message. Not saying another word, Parks slid into the Audi and followed the Rover.

Reclaiming his spot behind the Jeep's steering wheel, Garris stuffed his Beretta back where it belonged. "You hungry?"

"Starving," Gayle said.

"Let's go back to town and get a bite to eat."

"Don't you want to see where they're heading?"

"They'll expect us to tail them and go for a Sunday drive to shake us off. We'll make more progress by getting lunch and giving them time to pow-wow."

"Do you know who they are?"

"The guy with the sore throat and his partner have been tailing me since I arrived. The sidekick is a big guy who wears a five-gallon cowboy hat on top of his ten-gallon head. You might have seen him at the hotel. He's the hard-to-miss, hard-to-forget type."

Gayle nodded.

Garris fired up the Jeep, pulled a U-turn, and headed to town.

After a short negotiation, they were back at Rosie's. While the Painted Wagon had the reputation of having the best coffee, Rosie's conquered the battle of the burger. It was worth the prying eyes. Garris was still on display. And now that they had seen Gayle with President Cahill's bad boy, she was also fair game for small-town gossip. She was unused to being under a microscope, but so was he. There was nothing they could do about it now but breeze through the lunch menu.

In keeping with Traughber City's mining town theme, Garris ordered the Gold Nugget Special, a cheddar cheeseburger served with golden Ore-Ida tater-tots. Gayle ordered a modest chicken Caesar salad and picked a few nuggets from Garris's plate. They were both satisfied.

Afterward, they were back at the Grand Meeker. Gayle wanted to run down a lead on her laptop she had meant to do after her morning coffee—a lead she had not mentioned to Garris.

Retaining four reserved rooms, Garris used one to clean up. The shower at McCoy's hangar would work, but it would be hard to beat the Clock Tower suite's ambiance and the shower's intense water pressure.

Garris stuck in the iron key, twisted the knob, opened the door, and saw a guy sitting in the overstuffed chair near the fireplace.

He was not holding a gun. Instead, he raised a glass, offering red wine.

Garris paid little attention to the glass. It was hard to get past the guy's eyebrows, which were freakishly raised in the middle. Either it was terrible plastic surgery, or he was forging a dominant expression like he owned the place.

CHAPTER 11

"PLEASE, COME IN AND MAKE YOURSELF AT HOME."

"You're in my room," Garris said.

"You're in my hotel."

"Ezra Meeker, I gather." For the time being, Garris dismissed the guy in the chair. He was no threat. Not at this stage. The guy wanted to drink, not shoot. Roaming from room to room, Garris checked whether he would be entertaining additional guests. He thought the shooter might have made an appearance the night before. He had put it on the back burner when that had not happened. Let his guard down. Fortunately, this guy was not the one who scribbled cherries on gift cards. He was not the MAX shooter. But he was somebody. The guy in the chair reeked of money. He was a fit forty-something. His hair was brown with blond highlights, cut to the perfect length to frame his jawline. He was tan, just the right tone of copper. His face and hands were moisturized, and his fingernails were manicured. Wearing an expensive red-plaid flannel shirt over a blue Henley, tan corduroys, and suede desert boots, he was the epitome of outdoorsy type with tons of money.

Garris judged this man was the billionaire winemaker.

"Relax, Mr. Kelley. I'm alone. Come sit down. Join me."

The room was clear. Sitting opposite the guy, Garris glanced at the opened bottle of wine. "If you got that from the mini-bar, I'm not paying."

"The bottle is from my private collection," he said, handing Garris a pinot glass. "I'm Rudyard Coleman. And in addition to my vineyard, I own this hotel."

"Prove it."

"I've comped your rooms. All four of them. You are now my guest."

"You've got my attention," Garris said, playing along. He would let the guy play the rich big shot and see if it led anywhere. But at the end of his stay, he would put the total amount he owed in an envelope and leave it on the pillow for housekeeping.

"I apologize for catching you off guard," Coleman said. "I use this suite when I'm in town. It's only occasionally available for guests."

Garris sampled the wine. It was good, but he agreed with McCoy it was not worth a hundred dollars.

"Is there a problem with the hotel I should know about?" Coleman questioned.

"Why do you ask?"

"Housekeeping said you didn't use the bed. Not one of them."

"I sleepwalk."

"That must be difficult."

"Depends on the shoes."

"Mr. Kelley—"

Garris interrupted. "You're footing the bill. Call me Garris."

"All right ... Garris—"

"What about you?" Again, Garris cut in.

Puzzled, Coleman said. "I'm sorry?"

"Rudyard, or are you a Rudy?"

"I prefer Rudyard. But Rudy is fine."

"Works for me. Okay, Rudy, why are we talking? I'm not cheap if you're considering asking me to shill your wine."

"No, of course not. I'm here to invite you to dinner at my ranch this evening."

"Why would you do that?"

Coleman flashed his pricey Rolex wristwatch so Garris would see it and stood up to leave. "You've been making headlines. You're more famous than I am. For the time being."

"Me? You must be confusing me with someone else."

"Don't downplay your celebrity status, Garris. You'll be getting many invitations from now on."

"Thanks for the warning."

"Garris. Did Senator Beemer ever mention we are old friends?"

"If he did, it didn't register."

"We are. We've done business together for years. That was a helluva thing you did for Frank. I've watched the videos on YouTube a hundred times. Inviting you to my ranch for dinner is the least I could do. My way of thanking you for taking care of my good friend. Not to mention, I've been quite busy at my ranch for the last month. I'd enjoy the company. An evening with you would be welcome."

"Didn't I see you just fly in?"

Coleman chuckled. "Ah, you saw my Beechcraft. It was loaded with supplies. Items I can't find here in this rural area," Coleman said, walking to the door. "Be downstairs at eight." The boss giving an order.

Garris shrugged it off. Guys like Coleman could not help themselves. He could permanently straighten Coleman out later if it came to that. But for now, it was better to find out what the winemaker really had in mind. There might be a little truth behind the Beemer friendship story, but Garris could see through the smoke and mirrors. Guys like Coleman rarely spoke the truth during the first meeting.

"There's not much light on the back roads. It's dark and dangerous if you don't know where to go. I'll have my driver waiting for you in the lobby. And bring a guest. I insist," Coleman said, then nodded goodbye.

TAKING THE STAIRS DOWN to the third floor, Garris knocked on Gayle's door. She wore the same suit, now with a pale-blue blouse. Her hair was straight as an arrow and hit squarely on her shoulders. Her makeup accented her lips, and her eyes lit up. Stunning.

They stepped into the elevator. Gayle had accepted his invitation as his date for the evening. He could hardly ask her to take the stairs.

"FYI," she said. "I don't use the elevator when I stay at a hotel with less than fifteen floors. It keeps the legs in shape."

"FBI agents think of everything."

Garris told Gayle he believed the dinner might be a set-up and they should go together. Word had reached Coleman that not only was he in town, the exposed covert operative, but had been seen roaming the countryside with a female FBI agent. This would raise suspicion in any man's army. Coleman was a billionaire business entrepreneur. It made sense. Coleman would want to know why a duo of bloodhounds were sniffing around. But if that was true, how and when did Coleman learn that Gayle was an agent?

The elevator door opened and they stepped into the lobby. Under the thousand twinkling crystals hanging from the lobby's chandelier, Gayle seemed to shine even more brightly.

A man stood outside the saloon's entry. He looked like he fell in line with the five-star luxury crowd. His eyes were trained on the elevator as he held a cell phone to his ear. When he saw Garris, he bee-lined toward Garris and stuck out his hand.

"Mr. Kelley, I'm Bob Hawkins. I'll be driving you to Mr. Coleman's ranch."

Garris judged Bob to be in his mid-thirties, in the prime of life. In great shape. Probably a perfect BMI score. He wore fitted black jeans, a chest-hugging navy-blue polo, and tan desert boots. An expensive ensemble when you throw in the pistol tucked on his right hip, concealed under his black blazer. Garris knew the type. He might moonlight as a chauffeur, but his day job was Coleman's bodyguard.

"Good to meet you," Garris said, shaking Bob's hand.

Not to be ignored, Gayle introduced herself by her first name, and also shook Bob's hand.

Bob asked them to follow him to the car. A black Toyota 4Runner waited outside the hotel's door, the custom SUV glistening like it had come hot off the lot. Opening the rear passenger door, Bob expected the two guests to pile in.

"I'll ride up front," Gayle said.

Driving south, down Main Street, Bob drove past Rosie's and kept going for about ten miles, then cut east. Another five or six miles down the country road, they drove past the spot where the guy in the red trucker cap picked the wrong place to park his Audi. Garris asked Bob to pull over. He got out of the vehicle and returned a moment later with the red cap the guy had tossed earlier that afternoon. "Okay, Bob. I'm good."

Gayle gave Garris a questioning look.

"What?" Garris shrugged, bending the cap in half to tuck it into his back pocket.

The road went over one hill after another. Garris was pleased. It saved him from making the reconnaissance trip he had planned for later. With each mile traveled, there were fewer farmhouses and more hills and valleys.

With Bob's attention focused on driving, Gayle nodded to Garris, signaling to look out the right-side window. A high-voltage electric security fence ran parallel to the long road. No cattle, no agriculture. Nothing but barren land. Why the fence, and who was the owner?

Five minutes later, Bob turned left into a driveway and stopped in front of a massive timber and stone gate. Bob made a call, and the doors opened inward like a castle.

They followed a winding road. It looked new and smelled like asphalt. And, like the fence, it, too, went on and on.

Bob hooked right, then drove along the private airstrip. Close enough, Garris could glimpse Coleman's Beechcraft King Air. It was not a cargo plane as Coleman implied it might be. Instead, it had a fancy logo and Coleman's name painted on the fuselage. Purely a luxury item. Noting its tail number, Garris would ask Olive to check its flight and ownership history.

The airplane's hangar was in a category all by itself, at least four times the size of his own. A custom barn design, tall and wide, stained a light shade of washed-out red, with white trim to give it an aged feel. Garris admired the oak plank doors in the front and back, making it possible to taxi inside at one end of the hangar and taxi out the other. He coveted them.

Traveling further on, they passed a lake. Bob took a right and followed along its shoreline. While Bob was not exactly a tour guide, he did mention that the ranch spanned more than a thousand acres. At first, Garris was skeptical, thinking Bob might like to exaggerate, but after taking another five minutes to reach the main house, he was a believer.

Using the same building materials as the gate, the main house was a mixture of fine timber and large stones. It was more in line with a Spanish villa or hacienda than a traditional Oregon farmhouse.

Garris waited for Bob to open his car door, thinking it would create an opportunity for Bob to shift into a position where he would expose the pistol he had holstered under his blazer. Bob complied. A Glock 19, a popular weapon for Navy Seal teams and US Secret Service.

Gayle took Garris's arm. He realized this was the first time they had made physical contact, having never so much as shaken hands.

"Thank you both for coming," Coleman said, stepping onto the porch to greet them. "Gayle. May I get you started with a glass of red or white?"

"Excuse me. I don't believe we have met," Gayle said.

"Ah, yes. I'm sorry. I assumed Garris had told you. I'm Rudyard Coleman. Besides the winery, I own the Grand Meeker Hotel. Bob called me when you entered the lobby with Garris. I made an inquiry with the front desk. You are Gayle Wilson, correct? And you were staying in room 311. But now your luggage has been transferred to a suite on the upper floor. My treat."

"White wine. Thank you," Gayle said.

Coleman gestured toward the entry. "Follow me."

The entry opened to showcase a selection of Coleman's wines displayed on a table. The table, Coleman pointed out, was custom-designed and made from an authentic pioneer wagon wheel and an Italian wine barrel.

After Coleman poured a glass for Gayle, Garris picked up the bottle. The white wine was a blend, Jamais Oublier, 2009. *Never Forget*. The label depicted the silhouette of a woman flying a kite, unfortunately caught on a tree branch.

"2009. Expensive?" Garris asked.

"Not tonight," Coleman said. "Would you like a glass?"

"It's delicious," Gayle said. "You should try it."

Holding up his forefinger and thumb, Garris pinched them close together. Coleman poured him a smidge. Then he uncorked a bottle of red. "Let's have a seat while we let this breathe."

Leading the way into an airy salon, Coleman guided them to a mahogany wood with a turquoise-inlay dining table with twelve rustic plank chairs to choose from. They did not look the most comfortable, but they fit in with the pampered, outdoorsy vibe.

Gayle had her eye on the chair midway down the table, and Garris pulled it out for her. Once he settled beside her, he glanced through the window. A woman walked a horse near the lake. Though seen from a distance, she bore an uncanny resemblance to the figure on the wine label.

For now, he was more interested in the room than the woman. He wanted to get a read about what kind of man he was drinking with. He knew no significant details about Coleman. No books, music, or family photographs that identified his personal taste. Nothing. The room was generic Western, as though he had tried to recreate something once seen in a Ranch & Pasture magazine. Cowboy paintings, bronze sculptures, rugs, and pottery, that sort of thing. But one object that caught Garris's immediate attention. An oil painting of the pioneer Ezra Meeker. The hotel's namesake. Ezra had the same scowl as his wax figure at the cultural center. That was Ezra. But nothing in the room gave any insight into who Coleman was, except his selection of wines. The same went for the adjacent room.

Six southwestern upholstered chairs were positioned in a semi-circle by the fireplace. Garris wondered why. And why were there six place settings on the dining table when he thought it would only be the three of them?

"Are we having a backyard barbecue or a business meeting?" Garris asked.

"I've invited a few of my men to join us. I didn't think you would mind."

"I'm good. Just asking."

Entering through the back door, Bob was the first to show. He picked up the bottle of red and poured himself a glass, then sat down across the table, facing Gayle.

Garris would have bet the ranch that Coleman would take the chair at the head of the table as if he were in a boardroom. He did.

"You've met Bob," Coleman said.

Garris gave Bob a friendly nod, as one does in a small town.

Garris caught Gayle surveying the room.

Coleman caught her, too. "Gayle," he said. "What brings you to Traughber City?"

"I'm on vacation," which was technically accurate. "I have a friend in town, and I thought I would join him."

"Would you like to call him and invite him over? I could send Bob to pick him up."

"No. This is fine," she said.

"Are you sure? It wouldn't be any trouble."

Hawkins looked like he would be crushed if he had to leave.

"No, thank you." Game over.

"How about you, Garris?" Coleman said. "It's unexpected you'd turn up in our small town just a day after such a horrible shooting incident."

"I'm on vacation, too."

"Is that so? I didn't realize our chamber of commerce was doing such an outstanding job on tourism." He noticed two men entering. "Ah, here's Gordon."

Gordon, who Garris recognized as Trucker Cap, strode in, sporting a shiny red nose still showing significant swelling.

Trailing behind Parks was the jumbo guy. Up close, Garris thought he looked big enough to be Park's shadow.

Parks had dropped the lame trucker disguise. After losing the cap, it was easy. He wore a tight gray T-shirt and jeans. He took a seat beside Bob.

"And Bruce," Coleman said by way of introduction.

The jumbo plodded to the far end of the table. He tossed his black cowboy hat onto the table, then slogged over to the half-moon of chairs by the fireplace. He eyed the chairs like he was buying a car, eventually choosing an oversized hickory rocker. Besides being more comfortable, it looked like it had the best chance to support his weight. Picking it up effortlessly, he carried it back to the dining table. No problem. Shifting in his uncomfortable plank chair, Garris wished he had thought of that.

"Good. We're all settled," Coleman said. "Garris and Gayle. I'd like you to meet Gordon Parks and Bruce Gillman. Or, as we fondly call him, the Beluga. Along with Bob Hawkins, who you've met, these men are my security team."

Security team. Garris considered this. The night before, Garris had set a plan to entice the shooter to his suite, allowing the MAX shooter to lay his cards on the table. In Portland, the shooter had left the card with the three cherries, dropping Garris an obvious clue to come to

Traughber City. But Coleman showed up in the suite instead. Garris mulled it over. To immediately connect Coleman to the shooter might be jumping the gun.

Coleman could have merely been playing the ego card, letting himself into Garris's room as he, being the owner, easily could. Harmless. However, it raised red flags. But then, Coleman insisted he bring a guest to dinner, assuming he would bring Gayle, the FBI agent. She was the only person in Traughber City they had seen him with. And now, Coleman was showcasing his clout, parading two powerful guys and a whale. And not just to him, but to Gayle. Why? If he had discovered she was the FBI, did he know she was looking for Ron Boyle?

"Garris, I have united the best and most experienced private security team money can buy. I won't go into their backgrounds. I'll leave that to them. But I'm certain even you will be impressed. That said, with my highest respect for these expert professionals, I don't have someone with your—"

"Notoriety," Garris cut in.

"I was going to say elite skill set," Coleman said, "but, yes, your recent notoriety is highly appealing to someone like me. I'll get straight to the point. I do a lot of business domestically. But now, my wine has taken off internationally. And, as the spokesperson for Coleman wines, millions worldwide know who I am, making me a target for kidnappers. Wouldn't you agree?"

"If you say so."

"I do. These professionals have the experience, the skills, and the dedication to protect me."

Garris glanced at Parks, who still showed resentment over the broken nose thing. Parks was on the same page as Coleman. Hawkins, too. But, the whale guy, the Beluga, not so much.

Except for the Beluga, who was in his own category, the men seated at the table had the right physique for a professional security unit. They exuded confidence and were self-assured. Hawkins carried a Glock. No doubt the other men had similar weapons. Garris thought Parks and the Beluga had been a little too amateurish when tailing him. But that was minor.

Garris's assessment: These guys had potential. They would be able to protect Coleman. With monetary incentives, they could have also been the same bunch behind the attack on MAX. But, if that was the case, someone was missing—their leader. No one at the table could have orchestrated such a complex mission.

Garris thought it would not ruin the entire evening if he poked the nest just a little. He reached into his back pocket and pulled out Gordon Park's red trucker cap. "You dropped this," he said, and flung it at Parks. "A thank-you isn't necessary."

If looks could kill.

Parks did not care so much if Kelley made fun of him in front of Coleman, but in front of Hawkins, his partner … unacceptable. Garris would pay. Glancing at Coleman, Parks sought permission to teach Garris Kelley some table manners. But Coleman signaled him to stand down. Not the time. Fine. He would wait, but not forever.

Garris's plan worked. He saw Parks do as he was told. He was a doer, not a thinker, and showed significant signs of restraint—a quality found in the best soldiers. Also, good to know Parks sought Coleman's permission. Not Hawkins's or the Beluga's. Confirming the security team's leader was definitely not present.

Gayle had an idea what Garris was up to. He had measured the unit's temperament with a simple nudge while conveying a message. *Hey, Gayle, look at these guys. They're a GROUP of lethal professionals.* Message received. Ron Boyle might not have been investigating a militia. It could have been another radical faction. Maybe these men?

Coleman resumed where he had left off. "Garris, because the president exposed your cover as a CIA operative (keyword: operative, being another word for government assassin), you're now out of a job."

"I was? I am?"

"I would say so. It's widely accepted on social media that you and Cahill have lost that loving feeling. Some say you'd kill him yourself if you had the chance."

"Your words, not mine."

"Garris, I'd like to make you an offer."

"Endorse your wine? Rudy, we've been over that."

"No. But you're close. I'd like you to be the face of my security team."

Before Garris could respond, the woman he had seen walking the horse now pushed a dining cart into the room. She was close to Coleman's age. Short, sandy-blonde hair. Garris detected a hollow sadness in her eyes. He wondered what her connection to Coleman was. Coleman did not introduce her, and she said nothing, which brought again to Garris's mind that he knew diddly about Coleman's personal life. Only that he was connected to the wine business. The woman could be anyone: Coleman's wife, a hired hand, a neighbor, or a mistress. The way Coleman ignored her, however, Garris thought highly disrespectful.

Gayle also tried to place the woman, thinking she had seen her before. Maybe at Rosie's?

Seeing that the woman was a distraction, Coleman stopped his sales pitch and waited for her to finish and leave the room.

"I'm holding a special event at my Willamette Valley tasting room," Coleman said. "It's an international vintner's conference. Winemakers like myself from France, Italy, Spain, and all over the world will be attending. A number of these elite winemakers will be concerned about their safety. Some travel with bodyguards. Some don't. I want everyone who steps foot on my property to feel safe and secure. Garris, recently a security team member unexpectedly dropped out, and I need to replace him. I would like to hire you for the week. My guests will be thrilled to see they are in the company of the infamous agent who, as you guys say, 'liquidated' Hector Trevano. And the icing on the cake … you could give my team some pointers. Like a Master Class."

Parks rolled his eyes.

"I would, of course, make it worth your time."

Coleman might be okay making wine, but he was a horrible actor. Garris saw right through him. Coleman had another motive, one that might involve either Frank Beemer, the FBI agent, or both. Like a fine wine, Garris would let the offer breathe.

Coleman shifted a little in his uncomfortable rustic chair, turning to Gayle.

"So, Gayle. You're an FBI agent."

CHAPTER 12

"OZZIE GOT IT OUT OF THE HOTEL'S HOUSEKEEPER," DOM reported, touching base with Edgar over the phone.

After setting his pistol down, Edgar took off his goggles. He had been in the middle of a virtual reality video game. It was a shoot-em'-up that Ozzie had given him as a birthday gift. Ozzie gave it a solid review, but was careful not to oversell it. Nothing could ever, ever beat the real thing.

"The housekeeper said Kelley busted into a room and ransacked the place. He was interested in the couple who were staying there. She said he inquired about a place called Traughber City."

"Never heard of it."

"I looked it up. It's a small town on the other side of the state."

"And?" Edgar said.

"And Ozzie and I are going there tomorrow. If it doesn't pan out, we'll come back to Portland. Eventually, Kelley will show up. At some point, he'll want to check on the senator's son in the hospital. I'm leaving Armin behind to cover our asses."

"What about the hotel maid?"

"If Ozzie thinks he needs to stay, I'll leave him to take care of her and take Armin instead. Either way, it's all good."

"I want Kelley dead by the end of the week. It would be good for my movie." Edgar hung up, then slipped on his VR goggles. He started shooting at a DEA agent. It was not a perfect game. Nothing can beat the real thing, but it would have to do for now.

"EXCUSE ME?" GAYLE SAID.

"I simply commented that you're an FBI agent. Was that supposed to be a secret?"

Coleman knew. She had asked one too many questions. At Rosie's or the Painted Wagon? Given Coleman was the Grand Meeker's owner, it was likely an employee, or possibly a nosey housekeeper or a restaurant server who had seen her documents and maps on the table.

Annoyed with Coleman's game, she would have to let the moment pass if she was going to find out what else he knew. "No secret. As I've said, I'm on vacation. I leave work at the office."

"Gayle. Your friend, he's with the FBI, too," Coleman said.

"That's right," Gayle said evenly, wondering what he knew.

"When was the last time you talked to him?"

"I don't see how that's any of your business."

"Gayle. FBI agent Ron Boyle was staying at the Meeker. He checked out four days ago. You're here to work a case with him. Isn't that right?"

"If I were, that would be FBI business."

"You're on vacation, Gayle. Ron Boyle claimed the same thing. That would mean whatever you and he are doing is technically not an FBI matter. And that, Gayle, would leave the door open for discussion. I'm a concerned taxpayer. If there's trouble in my backyard, I want to know. In fact, I'd like to help. So, to move forward, let's agree the cat's out of the bag. I know you're on an unofficial investigation. What I don't understand is why FBI agents love working for free."

Garris nodded an amen to that, and Gayle smacked him under the table.

Coleman continued. "Agent Boyle approached me while I was having breakfast with the Beluga at the hotel. He knew who I was and assumed the Beluga was my bodyguard. Initially, Boyle claimed he was on vacation and asked if I knew someone who could show him around the area. I suggested he use the Beluga. Boyle must have already told you this?"

Disregarding Coleman's assumption, she turned to the other end of the table. "Do you know where Ron is, Bruce?" She would not call him anything other than his Christian name.

The Beluga waited for Coleman to give him the go-ahead to speak. He continued to wait without answering.

"That looks like a solid no," Coleman said.

Garris wondered why Coleman did not let the Beluga speak for himself. The guy had a tongue. Garris had seen him inhaling an ice cream cone.

Coleman continued. "After hearing Boyle was with the FBI, I upgraded his room. Then I dropped in for a chat."

"You like dropping in," Garris said.

"He didn't seem to mind."

"I do."

"Noted." Coleman continued, "After a glass or two, Boyle leveled with me. He said he had come to Traughber City to investigate a hate group headquartered in this area. He believed they were ramping up for something serious that was happening soon. He was tight-lipped but said they were actively recruiting like-minded sympathizers to take back their country. He was vague, but I got the idea. I had the Beluga drive Agent Boyle around and ordered Parks to help him if needed.

Parks looked like he was about to say something, but a look from Coleman stopped him from interrupting. "One thing you might want to know. Agent Boyle asked if I knew of anyone who might be using drones in the area. I didn't, but Parks knew of a couple of brothers, Tommy and Andrew Mitchell. They've been seen flying the things all over the county, at all hours of the day and night. Maybe it's nothing. I heard farmers use them. But I think Agent Boyle met with the brothers and discovered they were involved."

"Did he say in what way?" Gayle asked.

"No. But he asked Parks if he'd check into recent drone sales in town and nearby counties. Then he asked if I had a Portland connection willing to help."

The Mitchell brothers, Tommy and Andrew. The two young men Garris and McCoy had almost run over in a 'Vette. Garris considered this. McCoy said he had a crew of four or five helping him with his property. Could the retired general be playing war games out in the sticks? Had he organized a group into a militia? The same militia Gayle was interested in? General McCoy fit the profile, being a highly decorated officer with a reputation for being a little on the idiosyncratic side. Plus, Garris thought McCoy's reported public disdain for President Cahill was on par with his own.

"I told him I have someone posted at my vineyard in the Willamette Valley who could assist him. He packed up and met with her the same day. Naturally, she's reporting back to me. The last I heard, she said he's in Salem."

"Salem? Do you think it has something to do with the state capitol building?" Gayle asked.

"You're asking me? I don't know. I'm just a vintner. But what else is there in Salem?"

"Does she know where he's staying?"

"No. She said she asked, but he avoided her questions. But they were supposed to have coffee yesterday. He never showed. I called her this evening, before you arrived. If you want to speak with her in person, you're welcome to stay at my tasting room until you and Boyle conclude your 'vacation.' The Beluga can drive with you and fill you in on what he and Agent Boyle discussed in more detail. And, if Garris accepts my offer, you would both be there at the same time. How kismet is that?" Coleman let the offer hang. "Tonight, I've offered opportunities to the both of you. Think them over. But now, dinner is waiting."

CHAPTER 13

GIVEN A CHOICE, NURSE ELIZABETH ANDERSON PREFERRED TO work the night shift. The day shift had been a revolving door, much like a grocery store or the DMV. Mostly patient appointments and scheduled procedures. Too slow. Thankfully, there had been two automobile accidents, one broken arm, and a three-year-old boy who had swallowed half a bottle of baby aspirin. Doctors pumped the boy's stomach. He was fine.

The day shift was nuts and bolts. In contrast, the night shift was a high-voltage three-ring circus. Crazy shit happened at night. Bar fights, shootings, stabbings, and drug overdoses kept the emergency room hopping. It was easy for Diane, or Nurse Elizabeth Anderson as her nametag identified her, to go unnoticed. She had stuck to her plan and kept moving, inching her way ever closer to Lawrence Beemer's room.

She checked her watch. Senator Beemer was due to make another coffee run soon. He followed the caffeine-every-four-hour health plan.

Worming her way through a labyrinth of corridors on her way to the staff break room, she passed by Dante Green's room. His door was open a sliver. She turned back and peeked in. The room was shadowy. Lit by one reading lamp and a starry night of multi-colored buttons and switches glowing from four medical equipment towers surrounding

Dante's bed, he looked like Snow White tucked inside a Christmas tree. As far as she could tell, he was either sleeping or in a coma. What did she know? She was not a nurse.

At the foot of the bed, an elderly man slumped in a chair, a book in his lap and eyes closed. Diane assumed he was family. She studied him for a while. A long time ago, she had had a family. Not anymore.

She wondered, had it been necessary to clean the kid's clock and send him to the hospital? Yes, it was necessary. It was his fault. At the hotel, he had whipped around the hallway corner and smacked into her. Wrong place, wrong time. He had seen her face. Seen her SIG Sauer. And though he was a frightened little bunny, he had tried to stop her. Stupid kid. She could have just grazed him for his foolish act of bravery. But given a chance, there was no doubt he would've identified her. One hundred percent.

Satisfied that she had done the right thing, Diane moved on. She would not give Dante Green another thought—unless Cherry ordered her to.

Narrowly beating Beemer to the break room, Diane bought two coffees out of the machine. Minutes later, he entered. A creature of habit, right on time.

"That wouldn't be for me, would it?"

"It is, Senator," Diane said.

Taking a seat, he ran the palm of his hand across the lunchroom table. Three feet in diameter. One and a quarter-inch thick, high plastic laminate top, stain- and water-resistant.

"If I'd known I was going to spend so much time here, I would've lobbied for better furniture when I had the chance," he said.

She smiled, not even remotely sincerely. Who gives a rip about what he could have bought? Instead, he could take one minute to think about why he was in the hospital and why his family was chosen.

"How's your son?" she asked, as though she cared.

Tearing open two pink packets of sweetener, Beemer dumped them into his coffee. "I don't know. The doctors speak in riddles. I can't get a straight answer out of any of them."

"Senator Beemer, doctors are like politicians. They give their opinion and let you believe you have input. Then, they do whatever they want. In the end, they send you a big bill, and you won't understand what you're paying for, but you still pay. And they line their pockets."

"Sad take on my profession. But true. Thank you for being honest."

"Present company excluded. I didn't mean you, Senator."

Lost in thought, he seemed not to hear. "My son is paying my bill. I never should have got him involved in politics."

She did not say so, but she agreed. They would not be having coffee together if he had only done more with the political power he wielded instead of wasting time trying to build a dynasty. This old man sitting three feet from her across a cheap plastic table was so self-absorbed that he did not even realize she had been at his side when Cherry shot his son.

"Don't be too hard on yourself," she said.

He nodded, then took a sip and let the moment pass. "You have a slight accent," Beemer said, changing the subject. "Russian?"

"Bosnian," she lied. She was in character. Acting. However, she was careful not to stray too far from the truth. Her parents were from Belgrade. Many Americans did not know the difference between the two accents, Bosnian and Serbian.

"My parents immigrated to Portsmouth, Ohio, after the war."

That was a lie, too. It was only Diane and her mother who had moved to Walla Walla, Washington.

"Yes. Bosnia. A beautiful country. I've been to Mostar. Three years ago, I crossed the old bridge."

"It's new."

"Sorry?"

"The bridge. It's new. They destroyed the old bridge during the war."

"Right. Horrible what happened over there."

"I was a child. Too young to remember most of it." Another lie. She remembered almost everything. She remembered her mother's Cevapi, the delicious oblong-shaped kebab made from lamb and raw onions and served on a slice of pita bread. She remembered the traditional polyphonic Ganga droning music, sometimes played with bagpipes and wooden flutes. She remembered her father and three brothers forced outside their home and butchered.

Beemer tilted his paper cup. Not much coffee left. He downed it, then checked his watch. "I thought I'd see you with Lawrence by now."

"I've been working downstairs for most of the night. I was just about to start on his floor."

"Good. Walk with me, will you?"

"Of course."

Nobody noticed her. Instead, they had their eyes locked on the prominent senator from Oregon.

They had posted three police officers outside Lawrence's room. Two officers were reporting to their commander, a stalky, compact man, hair cut tight to the scalp. His uniform was dry-cleaned and pressed, his boots spit-shined. He was the cop she'd seen on the MAX, who had introduced himself to Garris Kelley as Sergeant Carl Baranski.

Baranski greeted the senator with a firm handshake. It was Baranski who had guarded Beemer in Kelley's suite. Baranski who had tried to keep Dante Green safe, but failed.

"Officer Baranski, this is Nurse Anderson," Beemer said.

Baranski gazed into her eyes longer than anyone had so far. There was something familiar about her. Heading off trouble, Diane glanced at her phone like she was getting a call. Acting.

"Excuse me," she said to Baranski, "it's my babysitter." She turned to Beemer. "I'll be right back to check on Lawrence," she said, then strolled down the hallway to the women's restroom to call Cherry.

"How is he?" Cherry asked.

"Maybe better. I think it's a good that I came back when I did."

"Anything else?"

"The cop that was on the MAX. He's here outside Beemer's door. His name is Carl Baranski."

"If he's a problem, deal with it. Try not to leave a mess."

Diane grinned, her eyes sparkling with a touch of mischief. "You know how I get with authority figures."

"I do. But listen, I have something extra special for you."

"What?"

"Not what. Who."

"Okay. Who?"

"Another Fed. Boyle's partner."

"Well, now. You're spoiling me."

"The Beluga is driving her to the villa. The rest of us fly back tomorrow. I'll see you in the afternoon."

"Okay. I better get back now. Love you, Cherry on top."

"Stop that."

"Never."

CHAPTER 14

"WOULD YOU LIKE TO COME IN AND SEE MY NEW SUITE?" Gayle asked, standing outside her door, three rooms down the hall from his, a shiny brass key in her hand.

Just in case Hawkins was listening, as surely he was, they had kept their conversation limited to small talk during the drive back to the Meeker.

"Let's talk here," Garris said. "I'd like to get back before General McCoy bunks down. Coleman tossed the Mitchell brothers under the bus. They're the redheads in the Chevy truck that's been following us. They work for the General. They're probably okay, but the General has made a lot of enemies, President Cahill being one of them. It was Cahill who pushed him out the door."

"Are you listening to yourself?"

"Okay, I admit, McCoy and I have that in common. But he was a military General, a commander for decades, and leaders need to lead. It's in their blood."

"Do you think he's the type to hold a grudge?"

"My impression, maybe. I like McCoy. He snores. But who doesn't? I'd like to hear his take on retirement. Besides the two brothers, McCoy said he also has a couple of other guys who help. A couple more guys equals a group. McCoy could have had the Mitchells tail me."

"You're staying at his place. Why would he do that?"

"To keep informed. As the saying goes, information wins battles."

"True. What about Coleman?"

"What about him?"

"Forgetting he's high maintenance, I don't trust him. He's coming off a little too gung-ho for me. Way too helpful. Sure, he's ultra-successful, but how exciting is it to make wine? He could have grown tired of his airplanes, his horses, and his unnecessary elite security team. Did you notice his art collection? Boring. I have a hunch he's in the market for new toys to give him a thrill. Like an FBI agent. Coleman clearly got a charge out of meeting Ron. Then you show up and he wants to hire you for some bullshit babysitting assignment so he can act out his secret agent fantasy."

"I agree. There's more to his offer than what he's letting on. But I don't know if it's that. Have you decided if you're going to stay at his tasting room, his villa?"

"Sure, I'm taking him up on it," Gayle said, running her fingers through her hair, a gesture that did not go unnoticed. "I need to meet the woman, Diane. I hope she'll talk. Did you notice how Coleman controlled his puppets? He didn't let them say a word."

Garris nodded.

"Bruce Gillman is meeting me at eight," she said.

"He's a big fella."

"It would be nice to have you there, but I get the feeling you might want to stay behind in Traughber City."

"I'm having breakfast with Coleman. He wants to show off his guys in action. Then he'll ask if I'm accepting his offer."

"And?"

"It will depend on how it goes with the MAX shooter. He'll show himself tomorrow. Early."

"You sound sure about that."

"It'll be three days. He's waited long enough. I think he's smart enough to know if he doesn't make his play, then there's no need for me to stick around."

"And if he does?"

"If I'm right, he'll only want to talk. But if things don't go his way, then he might try to shoot me in the head. Then it's anything goes."

"Sounds fair," Gayle said. "So what's your plan?"

"Tonight, I'll talk with McCoy. I think he'll have a reasonable explanation concerning the Mitchell brothers, and I can clear him off the militia game board. If I'm wrong about the shooter and he doesn't show tomorrow, and if Boyle hasn't contacted you, I'll accept Coleman's offer. And, if you like, I'll help you find Boyle. And I'll find out what Coleman is really up to. I agree with you. Something else is going on. For some reason, he wants us both to stay at the villa at his Willamette Valley vineyard. I'm not doing that. I have my own place, not far from there. I could make you dinner."

"You own a home in Oregon wine country?"

"Calling it a home would be a stretch. It's an airplane hangar." Reaching into his pocket, he took his iron key to the Clock Tower suite. "Here. Take this. In case you'd like to upgrade your upgrade. Just make sure you lock the door. And don't touch the mini-bar."

"What if things don't work out with McCoy? You'll need a place to stay tonight."

"I'll knock."

SHE WAS LAWRENCE'S WIFE—NO question about it.

Flipping through pages on a police clipboard, Meredith Beemer fished a Mont Blanc pen from her purse. She signed her signature with the flair of a modern artist, then handed the board back to Sergeant

Baranski. Though she had not slept in days, she was focused and driven. She had declared that Lawrence was going to make it through this. End of story. She reminded herself not everyone who gets shot dies. Years ago, Garris had taken two bullets while protecting her husband during a pitched battle in Afghanistan. He had lived. Lawrence would, too.

Observing Meredith from down the corridor, Diane paced herself, advancing toward the nurse's station. The timing had to be just right. She needed to bump into Senator Beemer like it was a coincidence. If need be, she would walk past the station, then turn around and walk back like she had forgotten something. She had her cell phone in her hand like she had just used it or was about to make a call. Encountering Lawrence's wife in the hall was gravy.

Like herself, Meredith was fit as a fiddle. From the neck down, they could have been twins. But unlike Diane's natural blonde hair or the short auburn wig she had on as part of her disguise, Meredith's hair was as black as a raven's wing, feathered, long, and flowing. Her skin was smooth, with a flawless olive undertone. Dressed in a gray skirt suit with a white blouse, she looked like a politician's wife or a Wall Street broker. She was ALL business.

Diane was also ALL business. She believed the key to her vocation was all about choosing the right tool for the job. Another of Diane's commandments: don't get sold on just one. Be professional. Bring a minimum of three tools, not counting bare hands. Scenarios change. Sometimes, it is necessary to switch horses in the middle of the stream. It is always best to have options. Though the Beemer operation had been meticulously planned, it was still risky. The hospital, the high-profile target, the extra security outside the building, and outside the target's door had all been factored in. Diane chose the three tools she would be comfortable with going forward. Like any new job, the hard part was getting through the door.

They had stationed two uniformed cops outside Lawrence's door. One cop had made himself comfortable on a plastic chair. Diane thought they probably designed it specifically for cops who love Portland's trendy donuts. He was at least fifteen pounds overweight. His uniform muffin topped over his waistline, and his black boots showed little wear. Diane dismissed him immediately. He would not be a problem. But the other officer—the exact opposite. Thirty or so and built like a linebacker. And though he was indoors, and it was long after midnight, he wore black polarized sunglasses, the type hunters used to pretend they were Navy Seals. She could see he was wearing body armor underneath his shirt. Diane's assessment: He wouldn't be a major problem if she had to go off-script, but he might slow her down a little. Proceed with caution.

Baranski and Meredith were in their own world, conversing near the circular nurse's station positioned like a tollbooth in the middle of the corridor. Two nurses worked in its center, one was on a computer. A skinny guy. The other nurse looked like she was in charge and had worked the night shift since its creation. She was somewhere in her late fifties. She wore fashionably oversized red glasses and had a wrist tattoo of Obama, making her look hip. It was Portland, after all.

No sign of the senator. He might have been inside Lawrence's room. The timing was critical. Diane dragged her feet. She was fine; it was all part of the dance. With her official badge, she belonged.

Lawrence's door opened, and the sitting cop sprang to his feet. The cop with sunglasses rigidly stood at attention, adding another inch to his tall frame. With a flick of a wave, Senator Beemer signaled they could relax. Both cops looked to Sergeant Baranski for permission to stand down. He did not give it.

Someone's cell phone chirped. Five heads bobbed like hill pigeons. Diane's wasn't one of them. She had turned her phone off in the restroom. She was now on her own. No turning back.

"Elizabeth," Beemer said, delighted to see her return.

"I'm sorry that took so long."

"Is everything okay?"

"I'm breaking in a new babysitter. She's still learning the routine."

Interested in why he was speaking with a nurse and not a doctor, Meredith zipped over to greet her father-in-law.

Under a watchful eye, Baranski eased himself closer to Beemer. He had met the nurse minutes earlier. Since the senator had introduced them, he took it for granted she was not a security threat. But something felt off. Vibes. Through his new girlfriend, Baranski was into yoga, meditation, and, recently, a plant-based diet, and was getting in touch with his inner feelings. Being an excellent student, he listened and paid close attention to his vibes, and his vibe was telling him to keep an eye on Nurse Anderson.

"You've met Sergeant Baranski," Beemer said.

"Hello, again," she said.

Baranski responded with a faint smile.

"Meredith, let me introduce you to Elizabeth Anderson," Beemer said. "I'm grateful Elizabeth has kept my coffee cup filled to the brim. I'd be sawing logs right now if she hadn't."

"We haven't met yet. Have you been in to see my husband before now?" Meredith asked.

Baranski leaned in, keen to hear her answer.

"No. I'm halfway through a double shift. Until now, I've been on the lower floors. They've asked for volunteers who could work longer. So, here I am. I'll be here till the morning. Or longer, depending on how it goes. I was at the rally and want to help your husband, Ms. Beemer." She turned to Beemer. "You've got my vote."

"Thank you, Elizabeth," Beemer said.

Diane needed to move this along before an actual nurse showed up. "I'd better go in and check on Lawrence."

"Yes. Of course," Meredith said.

"I'll join you," Beemer said, and Baranski moved to follow.

"It's okay. Why don't you stay with Meredith," Beemer said to Baranski.

The room was as dark and twinkly as Dante Green's. The difference between the two was that Lawrence had amassed a bountiful collection of flower bouquets, get-well cards, and premium candy boxes. Diane flashed back to Dante's threadbare room. A shame.

Double-checking that the door was closed tight, Diane listened. Lawrence's ventilator performed as maestro for an orchestra of machines, playing a mechanical purring score.

Lawrence's eyes were closed. An actual nurse had pulled the top sheet back. His bare chest showed traces of smeared blood. Tubes were inserted into his nostrils, and hoses ran like freeways into his arms. The bullet had entered through the right side of his neck, between the mandible and the clavicle. It had missed the esophagus by a fraction of an inch. Diane had seen worse, much worse.

Though he did not look it, Lawrence's chart confirmed the odds of surviving were in his favor. This was unfortunate for his family. For a nanosecond, Diane thought perhaps in a different life, meeting Frank Beemer and his daughter-in-law would have been a pleasant occasion. But tonight, it was not in the cards. Lawrence Beemer had to die. Because the bigger picture would not work if he survived. In war, they called it collateral damage. Diane knew all about collateral damage. The senator knew about collateral damage, too. This was one reason they had chosen his family. In time, Beemer might understand that his son's death held a higher purpose.

"Care for a chocolate?" Beemer offered.

"No, thank you."

It was time. No need to make a long night even longer, especially if Cherry had something special planned for her the following afternoon. The woman FBI agent.

Three tools. One would do.

Drifting to the right side of the bed, Diane scanned the room. Acting like she was searching for something specific.

"Is there something I can help you with?" Beemer asked. "Something I can get you?"

"Another pillow? I think he'd be more comfortable if I elevated his head."

Beemer looked confused. "I know you know your job, but is that a good idea? To move his head?"

"Yes. It will be better for him."

While Beemer checked the closet, she reached for her cell. Three tools. All hidden inside her modified cellphone.

Some time ago, back in the nineties, the Russians produced Novichok. Scientists claimed the group of fifty or more nerve agents was the deadliest. The poison came in both solid and liquid form. They designed Novichok to be undetectable and to defeat NATO chemical protective gear. The elegant beauty of Novichok was it was safe to handle. It was a winner and quickly became the savvy assassin's go-to. Naturally, the intergovernmental organization, the Organization for the Prohibition of Chemical Weapons, objected to its use. They wrote a clunky, ineffective, piecemeal treaty, knowing what they were in for. Scientists are like chefs. Once the dish is in a cookbook, improving the recipe is easy. During the Balkan War, weapons were expensive for all participants. The timing was ripe for something new in the way of the poison. The difference between the flashy Russians and the Serbians— Serbians could keep a secret.

Diane checked Lawrence's eyes to see if he was experiencing REM. If he was dreaming, so much the better. He was.

Poking the tiny slot at the bottom of her cell phone where the charging cable is usually inserted, she ejected a stainless steel vial. It looked a part of the phone, a mechanism. However, when pulled apart, it exposed a sharp tip at one end. Needing both her hands for the next part, she slipped the phone back into her pocket.

"Here you are," Beemer said, handing her a pillow.

Carefully lifting Lawrence's head with her right hand, Diane slipped the pillow beneath with her left. Without Beemer catching on, she skillfully maneuvered the vial to the back of Lawrence's neck, then kept her left hand still, while reaching over and around Lawrence's face with her right hand and fluffed the pillow.

The door opened. Baranski.

"Excuse me, Nurse Anderson. I'd like a word with you, privately," he said.

"One moment."

"Now, Nurse Anderson."

Giving the pillow one last pat with her right hand, she gazed up at Beemer and forced a smile, slipping the vial into her pocket with her left hand. "Don't leave him alone. You'll want to stay with him for as long as you can."

Beemer nodded.

She had almost made it to the door. Reaching into her right pocket, she pulled out her cell. "I'm sorry," she said to Baranski, "my phone. It buzzed. I'm breaking in a new babysitter. Do you mind?"

Baranski raised his eyebrows and nodded to go ahead.

Offering thirty seconds of parental advice, Diane acted like she had ended her call on the phone that was powered off. Then she followed Baranski out the door.

"How can I help you?" she asked.

"I made a mistake allowing you inside. You gave me the impression you'd been assigned to his room. You are not. Tell me why we're having this conversation?"

From across the hall, Meredith glanced up from her phone, curious.

"I'm sorry. I didn't mean to cause alarm," Diane said to Baranski. "I met the senator in the break room. While we were having coffee, he said I reminded him of his daughter, Elizabeth. He's worried. I'm a nurse and care about the family just as much as the patient. I thought he could use a friendly face."

"You said they assigned you to this floor."

"No, I didn't."

"I think you did," Baranski said, then asked for the clipboard from the officer sitting down.

"I can't find your name on my list."

"I can't help you with that. I've been working at this hospital for three years. This is the first I've heard about being on any special list to do my job. Maybe this is an issue I should bring up with my supervisor or union rep," Diane said, raising her voice. "Sergeant Baranski, I understand you see Lawrence Beemer as someone more important than our other patients. However, I do not. I care about them all equally. As I've said, I've been working several floors tonight. Senator Beemer asked me to swing by if I could, so I did."

"I don't believe you."

"For God's sake! It's okay, Sergeant," Meredith said. "It's just a case of miscommunication. She was only thinking of Frank."

Glancing at her watch, Diane took a step backward. "Please let the senator know my thoughts are with him. And with you, too, Ms. Beemer. I should get back to my other patients."

"Thank you," Meredith said.

Leaving Baranski reviewing his clipboard, Diane eased down the hall to the elevator, down to the lobby, and out the hospital's front door.

Having breathed hospital fumes for hours, the night air was more than welcome. The bus stop was across the street in front of the neighborhood park. She thought about taking the bus, but it felt like forever since she had had any exercise. She needed to move. She walked.

Downtown Portland at night can be threatening to some, but not to Diane. Taking NW 23rd, she took her time and did a little window browsing. A home improvement store had a sign in the window claiming they had only the finest cookware, bakeware, cutlery, and gadgets. Cherry fancied himself as quite an excellent cook. She would like to come back and shop for him, but knew that would not happen.

Restaurants and bars were winding down. Mexican food sounded good. At a hole-in-the-wall, Diane ordered a stuffed chicken tortilla with avocado and black beans off the takeout menu. Cutting left on Burnside, she passed the bookstore and crossed on Tenth. The aroma wafting from her food stirred more than one homeless person nestled in dark doorways. Hungry as she was, she left the bag of food with an older woman housed on a flattened cardboard box, petting her bony puppy and talking to herself. She reminded Diane of her grandmother in Serbia.

Usually, Broadway Avenue was a steady stream of Ubers and Lyfts, loaded with drunken partiers searching for one last call. But not tonight. The Square looked like a ghost town. The yellowish-orange glow from sodium-filled streetlamps spilled onto the glazed bricks adorned with the names of donors etched into them.

Approaching the Expedition, the same hotel they had used during the operation, Diane watched a red Ford pull into the valet parking spot. A squat, muscular guy with bug eyes got out of the front passenger side. Two other men, cut from the same tough cloth, got out of the back. Diane knew the type. They were a crew. It could be the cartel searching for Garris Kelley. Too bad for them. They were wasting their time. Kelley was with Cherry somewhere in cowboy country.

The driver was the last to get out. He did not fit in with the others. Nervous and uptight, he was probably just an innocent driver who was in way over his head.

One of the guys from the backseat tipped the valet, and the crew went inside. She entered right behind and stepped inside the elevator with them. The bug-eyed guy reeked of tequila. Still wearing her red wig and padded plump bodysuit, none gave her a second look. They got out on the sixth floor, and she on the twelfth.

She knocked her costume jewelry wedding ring on the door to suite 1216.

Marty Moore, the celebrity chef, answered and welcomed her inside. "You hungry?" He poured her a glass of red wine, a Coleman library vintage.

"You ever tried hospital food?" she answered.

"Knock on wood, I haven't had to."

"I picked up some Mexican on the way over, but I gave it away."

"I'll order room service."

Removing her wig, Diane placed it into a plastic bag Marty had ready, then handed it back.

Two blankets covered the sofa from one end to the other. One pillow. Marty's bed for the evening. She had taken the suite's bedroom.

Kicking off her shoes, Diane kicked back in the chair near the fireplace and took a sip of wine. Marty brought her a cell phone, then he made himself scarce.

Tapping the speakerphone, she said. "Hey, Cherry on top."

"How did it go?"

"It's in Mother Nature's hands now," Diane said.

CHAPTER 15

THE MITCHELL BROTHERS' TRUCK, PARKED OUTSIDE MCCOY'S hangar, saved Garris the trouble of tracking them down. But it also put him on guard. He nosed the General's Jeep right behind it; boxing them in seemed like the right thing to do.

There were just enough questions floating in the ether for Garris to pull his Beretta, but not enough that he needed to aim it. Keeping it down to his side, he approached the three men inside the hangar. McCoy was not one of the three. He was nowhere in sight.

There was a new player. Not a sibling. Nothing Mitchell about him. He was tiny in comparison. Rat-like, with beady black eyeballs and two coffee-stained buckteeth the size of razor clams. He wore grubby camo dungarees and looked like he had been deer hunting, despite the crowbar in his hand, advancing the slim chance Coleman could be right. Maybe under McCoy's guidance, these boys were forming a boy band—a militia.

As Garris approached, they fanned out. They had been tinkering with something and attempted to hide it behind them.

Four opened beer bottles and a party-size bag of barbecue potato chips littered the cement floor. It was a good sign that McCoy was nearby and oversaw their project.

"Good evening, Mitchells," Garris said. "That wouldn't be the General's new push-mower behind you?"

Faced by a CIA operative with a gun, the brothers and the rat did not speak up, thinking it was best to wait for the General.

Stuffing his Beretta behind his back, Garris plucked a beer for himself, then waved them to separate. When they did, they revealed a wooden crate that was a little smaller than a pine box coffin.

"Where's the General?" Garris asked, directing his question to the brains of the family.

Tommy was about to answer when the thunderclap of a flushing toilet came from the back of the hangar. A moment later, McCoy walked around the tail of his airplane.

"I see you've met William," McCoy said, glancing at the rat.

William flashed Garris a clammy smile.

"I'm late for the party," Garris said. "What's in the box?"

"You're just in time to find out." McCoy waved his hand, and William drove the chiseled edge of his crowbar into the crate and pried off the lid. Four Christmas morning smiles.

Andrew and Tommy reached inside and hefted the body of a military-type drone from the box and set it down on the crate's lid. It looked like the amateur version of the Air Force MQ-9 Reaper—an armed, multi-mission, long-endurance, remote-piloted aircraft.

They left the wings in the box, but based on his experience, Garris guessed the drone would have a seven-foot wingspan when fully assembled.

"Explain," Garris said to McCoy.

William came around holding the crowbar, flanking McCoy's right. He mimicked a kung-fu stance he must have seen in movies. It amused Garris that William would risk getting his clock cleaned to defend the three-star general. McCoy signaled William to relax. They were all friends.

"I'm a hobbyist. Would you like to help?" McCoy said.

"I've got nothing better to do." After a long draw on his bottle, Garris set his beer down and poked around inside the crate. No weapons. Good to know.

Finding the manual, Garris handed it to Andrew. "Here. Read it out loud, and we'll get started."

Andrew stood frozen. Something was wrong. Being the vulnerable Mitchell brother, he looked to Tommy to save him.

"C'mon, Andrew. Try. There's no YouTube video for it," Tommy said. "You can do it."

Garris put his hand out for the manual. Andrew had a problem with his reading skills. No need to embarrass the guy. "It's okay. I've had a little more practice with these things." Frustrated studying the booklet for a few minutes, Garris tossed it aside. "You know what, Andrew? We don't need it." Reaching inside the toolbox, he grabbed a crescent wrench. "Things are always more fun just winging it."

With Tommy and Andrew busy wrestling the rest of the heavy pieces out of the container, William traded the crowbar for a screwdriver and started attaching the brackets to the fuselage.

Garris stepped next to McCoy. "We need to talk, General."

McCoy nodded. "Let's see how far they get on their own. Follow me." McCoy led Garris out of the hangar and into the darkness. "Watch your step."

With no flashlight, Garris followed McCoy behind the hangar, down a path that led deeper into the woods. For five minutes, Garris watched his footing and dodged tree branches. Finally, the forest opened into a clearing, where a cabin sat in the silvery light from the half-moon.

Showing Garris inside, McCoy lit a candle and set it on a rustic table. "Sit."

The cozy cottage had one bedroom with a wood stove and a white porcelain sink. Pretty much standard for a cabin. Not-so-standard, or at least what surprised Garris, was the fine-gauge Belgian lace curtains hanging from every window. And someone had thoughtfully arranged wildflowers in vases and placed delicate teacups and saucers in an orderly fashion on a shelf above the sink. McCoy had not mentioned he lived with someone.

"Why sleep in the hangar, General?"

"The cabin doesn't belong to me. The owner's gone, and I take care of the place. We'll leave it at that. You wanted to talk. What's on your mind?"

They could have talked in the hangar, but McCoy wanted Garris to see the cabin. However, he was not ready to say why. Not yet, but soon.

"That's quite a toy your boys are putting together," Garris said.

"I thought they'd have some fun with it. I don't have to tell you it's not military."

"Small-scale, Reaper, replica. Made in China. Two thousand bucks at Tammie's Hobby Shop. I got that. You planning on modifying it?"

"Meaning, am I weaponizing it? Yeah, I might attach small guns to it. Hunt rabbits and squirrels," McCoy said. "But let's talk about you. You didn't catch your shooter. He's still toying with you."

"If things are moving in the direction I think they are, he'll make his move tomorrow."

"How so?"

"Tonight, I had dinner at Coleman's ranch."

"So, it's true. He owns a spread here."

"Yeah, about the size of Hawaii. This afternoon, I had a close encounter with another drone. This one was not interested in rabbits and squirrels. It was practicing tactical maneuvers. I didn't know it then, but it was on Coleman's property."

"Your compass is pointing toward Coleman?"

"An FBI agent came to town, a guy by the name of Ron Boyle. Coleman claimed he's investigating a group forming a hostile militia or something equally nauseous."

"An FBI agent, and you, an Agency operative, in my neck of the woods. I'll sleep better tonight."

"Not so fast. There's more. Boyle went dark, and another agent got worried and came here to find him."

"Two FBI agents and you. I'm tossing my sleeping pills."

"It turns out Boyle is fine. He left Traughber and is now in Salem to follow up on a lead, but listen up. Coleman brought up Tommy and Andrew."

"Being the guys in the militia? Which would mean I'm involved."

"Can you think of a more qualified commander?"

McCoy sighed. "And here I am, drinking beer in the hangar with three Sons of the Pioneers, putting together a warlike drone. Looks suspect to me."

"You said you had guys. Other men, besides the Mitchells."

"To help maintain the airstrip."

"Right."

"Am I on your radar?"

"No. But I had to consider you. When we go back to the hangar, your boys will have the drone built to float down a river. They aren't capable of doing what I saw today."

"They mean well."

Garris took a moment, opting for a diversion. "Coleman offered me a job."

"Come again, soldier?"

"He's hosting a winemaker's clambake at his estate in the Willamette Valley. He asked me to join his security team. If I say yes, I leave tomorrow."

"Don't you still have a job?"

"Do I?"

The general snorted. "I never could get a straight answer out of you CIA clowns."

"I'm being set up, General."

"You've thought that all along."

"That's right, but I didn't know by who or why."

"Rudyard Coleman."

"He could be the who."

"And the why?"

"Coleman has more money than he knows what to do with. It's possible a team of very expensive contractors executed the hit. I think I met them tonight. All but their team leader. They're planning something else besides the winemaker's soiree. I need to find out what."

"You're going to let them play with you? Go along with their setup?"

"It's the only way."

"Is it just you, or are all CIA agents knuckleheads?"

"That's classified."

The general got up from his chair and went into the other room, returning with a photograph, which he handed to Garris. A picture of a much-younger McCoy, holding hands with a woman with a beautiful smile. They stood on a beach. Obviously in love.

"I didn't drop out of sight because of that peckerwood Cahill. The media manufactured the feud. But I purposely added fuel to the fire. Time was running out, and I needed privacy. The woman. That's Marie. And this is her cabin. It was our hideaway. Marie is gone now."

CHAPTER 16

COFFEE WAS RIGHT ACROSS THE STREET. JIMMY COULD THROW a baseball through the shop's window. It was that close. The dark, rich aroma of beans brewing was too much for him. All he needed to do was order through the app and then run over to pick it up. He needed his morning cup of Joe. It was more important than a bowl of cereal. Tempting as it was, a cup of coffee was a high price to pay for his life. So he stayed with the Ford. Besides, he could not have called, anyway. Dom still had his phone.

Twenty minutes passed. Ozzie came out of the hotel holding a sixteen-ounce cup in his hand. It smelled heavenly.

"Get the door."

Ozzie sitting beside him again was the last thing Jimmy wanted, so he shepherded Ozzie street-side and opened the car's back-right passenger door.

The gunsmith and Dom came down together. The gunsmith, whose name Jimmy finally overheard, was Armin.

Armin also had a coffee. Dom did not.

Fingers crossed, they would be heading to the airport. Jimmy waited behind the wheel for his instructions.

Armin closed Dom's door for him and stayed on the sidewalk. He was not going with them.

"Siri," Dom said into Jimmy's cell phone, "directions to Traughber City."

BREAKFAST HIT THE TABLE at eight-sharp, prepared by the woman who had walked the horse and served dinner the night before.

Crispy bacon, blueberry pancakes made from scratch, and eggs fresh from the chicken coop that Garris had passed by on the way to the main house.

She poured him a cup of coffee. He thanked her.

"You're welcome," she said, disappearing through the kitchen door.

Outfitted in matching black T-shirts and tan tactical pants, Hawkins and Parks dished up their breakfast, then moved into the other room and to sit in the same chairs they had used the night before.

Joining them, Garris moved the comfy chair the Beluga had used to the head of the table—the CEO's spot.

Since they were now possibly teammates and Garris was considered a short-timer, Parks made an effort to play nice. He started by giving Garris a history of Coleman's ranch, noting that in the mid-1800s, the Travis Mining Company owned the property, and gold was their thing.

Parks chronicle was not news to Garris. He was reciting the same text, almost verbatim, that Garris had read on the postcards in the Grand Meeker Hotel's lobby.

Having heard enough, Garris said, "What's your timeline, Parks? Coleman has the illusion you guys are something special. I don't. So why don't we get going? I'd like the chance to see what I'm missing."

"Slow down, compadre. Coffee first. Hawkins and I are going to finish this delicious breakfast. Then we'll take you to the shooting range. We might not impress you, but you will be surprised. That's a promise," Parks said, flashing a playful grin.

"Don't bet on it," Garris said. He turned to Hawkins. "Coleman has a shooting range?"

"It's just a spot far enough away from the main house where we can practice without making a disruption."

"I know you're carrying," Parks said to Garris. "Since we might work together, I'd like to know what you've got?"

Pushing his chair back, Garris picked up his napkin, wiped his mouth clean, then stood, towering over the table. Parks flinched.

With his right hand, Garris raised his polo just above his belt, took out his pistol, and set it on the table.

"I knew it," Parks said. "I told Hawkins you'd have a Beretta M9. I have a Glock 18."

"Duly noted." Garris settled back in his chair. "Who's the woman who's been doing the cooking?"

"Don't have a clue. Not my business."

"I believe you, but don't you find it strange a woman serves your food, day in and day out, and you don't know a thing about her?"

"What? Am I supposed to know everyone in the world who can flip a pancake? She's never given us the time of day. Besides, Coleman said to leave her be. The food's edible. That's good enough for me."

"I think she's Coleman's assistant," Hawkins chimed in. "I've seen them in the office, going over paperwork. Finances, that sort of thing."

Parks glanced at his watch. "After our demonstration, we're flying to Portland. If you're in, Coleman wants you to leave your plane here. We move as one unit. So you'll need to get your things together after we finish."

"I fly when and how on my own terms. If I'm onboard, then I'll meet you there."

"You take Coleman's money, you take our orders, same as everyone," Parks shot back.

Picking up his Beretta, Garris gave it a long, icy gaze. "Let me talk with my union rep, and we'll see what we can work out."

"Fine. Whatever, asshole. Do what you want," Parks said. "Geez, Louise. What a diva."

Garris slipped his pistol back where it belonged.

After the two had polished off their breakfast, Garris followed them outside. Hawkins pulled around their vehicle, ready to go.

"Get in the Gator," Parks said with delight.

Painted green and yellow, the Gator was a utility vehicle manufactured by a tractor company, Parks said. Garris thought it was a golf cart.

Parks took the wheel with Hawkins beside him. Left with no choice, Garris crammed himself into the bed at the back.

Taking the dirt road around the pond, they passed two old bunkhouses. About a mile from the main house, Parks rolled up to the front of a shaky gabled barn. Garris guessed the Travis Mining Company had left it, in ruins. Gray, washed-out, hundred-year-old boards. Rusted hinges and a roof that drooped in the middle.

"Out," Parks commanded.

"You first."

"This is your stop. Not ours."

Garris got out and watched Parks and Hawkins putter off to the north, then out of sight.

The time had come. An old barn. Nobody around. Far enough from the main house that if anyone heard gunfire, they would assume it came from the firing range. Not a bad place for an ambush.

Brushing his wrist against his side, Garris felt his pistol. He had read the setup in Hawkins' and Parks' eyes at breakfast and flipped the Beretta's safety off as he picked his gun up from the kitchen table. There was never going to be a trip to the firing range.

Thirty feet from the barn door, Garris glanced up at the opened hay hood. Perhaps it was a diversion, and he was supposed to think someone was hiding up there, ready and waiting to shoot. Maybe there was. And perhaps while thinking about that, he would get it in the back of the head. But he still had a head on his shoulders, so he stopped thinking and followed his instincts.

There is not much to do when caught in the open, with not even a shrub to crouch behind. Two choices. Walk away, or roost. Figuring acting like a hen would not get him far, Garris walked, but not away. Around. Around the rickety barn.

The left side was in no better shape than the front. More rotting and busted boards. They had left rakes, shovels, and other rusted farm tools around the barn and in the tall grass.

Near the top of the barn, underneath the soffits, he saw two abandoned bird nests and one active hornet hive.

A few yards away, a 1951 flatbed Ford had been dumped in the berry bushes. In its prime, the automobile was a gem. Now forlorn and forgotten, its rusted frame and overgrown interior made it the perfect playground for a game of Hide and Seek.

Gripping his Beretta, Garris surveyed the ground for fresh footprints. None. He circled the truck slowly, eyes scanning every potential hiding place. Each step was measured, and every breath was calculated. He stopped six feet away. Listened. Nothing. He picked up a rock the size of a baseball and stepped another three feet. Listened. Nothing. He chucked the rock inside the cab through the narrow space where the windshield should have been. Driver's side. It made a loud, echoing bang, but no heads popped up. Peeking inside, Garris saw that its formerly royal-blue seat cushion was ripped, exposing corroded, coiled springs. He moved closer to the barn's corner.

Seven minutes had passed since Hawkins kicked him off the Gator. Timing was everything. Somebody was waiting for him on the other side, but it was too soon to find out who. Garris knew that everyone danced to the rhythm of their own innate clock. People can only wait for so long before they get antsy. Garris decided not to do the expected. Instead, he would wait them out. He would wait all day if it meant not getting dead. Eventually, whoever set the trap to snare him would wonder why he had not turned the corner. Then they would get impatient and make the mistake.

Three minutes later, the earthy crunch of footsteps on gritty dirt broke the standoff, and Garris dropped behind the back bumper of the Ford.

"Kelley," a voice echoed. "We're just talking. I know you've got your gun drawn. Put it away."

Betting on instinct, Garris hesitated for just a second before tucking his Beretta into his jeans, keeping his polo shirt slightly above his belt. A silhouette emerged from the barn's deep shade, stepping into the sun. The face was unmistakable. Cherry Mackey.

The notion that Cherry was the mastermind behind the attack on the MAX had gnawed at Garris since he first glimpsed the Gilberts' card adorned with the three cherries. It was more than a mere doodle. It was Cherry's playful John Hancock. Now, as he stood eye to eye with the enigma known in hushed circles as the black eye of the CIA, the weight of their shared gaze confirmed all that Garris had suspected.

Garris stepped out into the open. Cherry had his shooting hand poised an inch from his holstered pistol. The two men squared off halfway between truck and barn. Twenty feet apart. Alone. The next move was anybody's guess.

"Given our history, this might be the time we put our hands in our pockets and take a breath. Both of us," Cherry said, and he did just that.

Garris achieved the same result by flipping the bottom of his polo shirt over his pistol.

"Remember my promise? If our paths ever crossed, I'd shoot you at first sight," Garris said.

"Now you're thinking otherwise?"

"It could go either way. I might have to flip a coin."

"Before you test your luck, we should talk."

"You put a hotel doorman in the hospital. That's hitting below the belt, even by your standards."

"I've put others in the grave. What's your point?"

"You missed your primary objective."

"Did I?"

"Frank Beemer's still alive. Not a scratch."

"There's always next time," Cherry said.

"Not if I make good on my promise. I've got no problem putting you down."

Cherry stood his ground. "Likewise. But consider this, Garris. If we do this now, and you end up dead, I'd be down a man on my team. I can live with that. But I could use an ally," he said, building his case. "As for you, you suspect I had something to do with that Portland debacle. Maybe I did. Kill me, and you'll never know."

Detainment was not an option. A showdown was on the table. Garris believed he was faster to pull. Cherry thought the same. Stalemate.

"But let's toy with the notion and say you're right," Cherry continued. "You know how we work. If I had something to do with targeting the train, that would just be the beginning, the smokescreen, and there's more to the job."

It was true. Garris knew Cherry's playbook inside and out, and he thought there was something much bigger than Portland in the works, leaving him with no choice but to change tact and pursue his suspicions. He would have to dive headlong into the conspiracy. "Are you still in? Or are you out?" Garris asked.

"Of what? The Agency? I'll tell if you tell."

Garris did not. Cherry did not.

"Garris, help me with Coleman's party. Give me three days, and I bet you'll put the MAX behind you."

A split-second impulse surged within Garris to finish Cherry then and there. But that would not kill the root of the problem. Cherry had a crew. Killing him would not stop the others from carrying out whatever else they were planning. Somebody would step in to take Cherry's place. Maybe Parks, with his own dark ambitions.

Keenly aware of the complexities at play, Garris weighed his options, options that would take him further into Cherry's game. "I'll shadow your guys. Once I get a good read on them, then and only then, will I decide."

"All right," Cherry agreed. "At least that's not a no, so I'll take the win. Let's take a walk."

Cherry took the lead, guiding Garris through a field of tall brush and morning sunlight. "Keep your eyes out for snakes and scorpions," he cautioned.

Using the warning as an opening, Garris asked, "What's your deal with Coleman? You're not really his bodyguard?"

"I am. Well, head of his security. The money is more than good, it's phenomenal. But the real jackpot is he'll buy any high-caliber toy I want. No strings attached. The kind of toys the Agency would never let me get near."

"Drones?"

Cherry laughed. "Did you really throw a rock at my drone? Thanks for that. It made my day. Lucky for you, your FBI girlfriend's an excellent shot. Maybe we should ask her to join us, instead of you."

"I'm not buying it. Playing with drones isn't enough for you to quit your day job. Is Coleman under investigation by the Agency? Is that what's going on?"

"You and I, we get paid to lie. Would you believe anything I answered?"

"Try to give me something resembling the truth."

"Okay. Truth. I like the guy. How's that? Coleman comes across as another arrogant, rich idiot with more money than he knows what to do with. He is. But he's also brilliant. He's a big-picture guy. I think you'll appreciate his vision once you talk with him more."

"Are we talking about the same guy? Rudy Coleman, the winemaker?"

"It's Rudyard Coleman, the vintner. Give him a chance, Garris."

"At a hundred bucks a bottle, he can put a cork in it. No thanks. What about the others?"

"Hawkins and Parks? They're on board, too."

"Where'd you find them?"

"Parks was with the Rangers. Hawkins with the Seals. The best of the best. The Beluga, Bruce Gillman, he's not really one of us. He's an ex-cop. Not as disciplined, but he serves a purpose. Just look at the size of him."

"What about Ron Boyle?"

"The FBI agent? I don't know much about him. Only that he was poking around, looking at some of the local stock he suspected was up to something. Last I heard, he's following a lead in Portland, or maybe Salem? Diane knows more about him than I do."

"Diane?"

"She's one of ours. Your partner, Gayle. She's hooking up with Diane later tonight."

Cherry cut away from the main trail to lead them up a hill. As they gained elevation, he stopped, nodding to Garris to take notice. From this heightened angle, they could clearly see the target painted on the barn side.

Pulling out his cell phone, Cherry made a call. "We're set." As he slipped the phone back, he flashed a smile. "Showtime."

On cue, a high-pitched noise echoed across the valley from the north, in the direction Hawkins and Parks had taken. Soon after, the outlines of three drones materialized. Unlike the ones Garris and Gayle had seen the day before, these were war machines primed for action.

Cherry's eyes beamed. "My toys."

In predatory air-strike formation, the drones dropped seven feet above the field, aiming straight for the hill. The engines went silent. With unified precision, the drones shot straight up toward the sun like fireworks, then split off and disappeared. They looped back from the east and regrouped in an arrow-head formation, shooting past Garris and Cherry, skimming inches over the hill. They fired at the barn. Splintered timber exploded.

"Pretty cool, right?" Cherry said. His phone chirped. He listened, then hung up. "We're going back to the winery. Now."

"What's the rush?" Garris asked.

"No rush. That was Coleman. Plans have changed, that's all."

FOR TWO GUYS AS fit as Garris and Cherry, the hike down the hill and up another was easy. Then, with their silent rivalry fueling them, they raced for a mile across the field to the main house. It was a good clip, but not good enough to beat Hawkins and Parks, who had taken the Gator. The guys already had the gear stowed in Coleman's plane and were hanging out on the porch.

Wasting no time, Cherry briefed his team about Coleman's sudden change in plans. They were now on a tight schedule. They would fly to the villa in the Willamette Valley immediately, then have a late dinner. The following day, he would have breakfast with Garris before showing him around the vineyard's premises to bring him up to speed.

Garris had his own dinner plans. He had invited Gayle to his hangar, though he was not sure she would show. It depended on her meeting with Diane, the woman whom Boyle supposedly trusted.

CHAPTER 17

BREAKING THROUGH THE TREE LINE, GARRIS SPOTTED MCCOY'S troopers on the airstrip huddled around the drone. They hardly looked like a militia, as Coleman had implied, more like teenagers at a science fair. Leaving the keys to McCoy's Jeep Commando in the ignition, Garris joined them.

After Garris heard about the drone's successful maiden flight, with Andrew at the controls, McCoy pulled Garris aside. "I reached out to the curator at the culture center. She didn't know Gilbert's history. Now she's curious. I'll let you know if she finds anything."

Garris nodded. "Coleman's making moves. It's thrown his security team off-kilter. They're flying to his tasting room as we speak. I'm going to shadow them, but I've got another favor to ask."

"What do you need?"

"Coleman said Agent Boyle left Traughber City to follow a lead in Salem. I'd like to know who he talked to and where he went while he was here. Coleman's security are ex-Special Forces, led by a loose cannon I know from the Agency. If Boyle got in their way, they wouldn't think twice about getting rid of him, even if he was FBI."

"Then that would go the same for you, wouldn't it?"

"When the time is right, they'll come for me. But for now, they need me."

DOUBTING SHE WOULD RETURN to Traughber City after this, Gayle insisted she and Bruce Gillman drive her rental car to Coleman's vineyard in the valley. She would drop the car off at the airport when she flew back to DC, after she found Boyle. The car was a compact, four-door, American-made, standard rental, black with black interior. Just the way the FBI liked them. She had paid a little extra for the satellite radio, and the car fit her like a glove. The Beluga, not so much. He was at least six-foot-six and weighed more than three Gayles. But he made no complaint. He did not say a word, for eighty miles. Then he said he had to use the bathroom.

Another forty minutes down the road, Gayle pulled into a two-pump gas station in a ten-building town. The gas station also served as the town's Post Office. The General Store was right next door. Its loss leader, scotch-taped to the front window, advertised cheap smokes and cold beer.

The second Gayle switched off the ignition, the Beluga bolted out of the car. For a big guy, he could move like the wind when he needed to.

Two old codgers lounged on a bench outside the market. Over the years, they had seen their share of tourists whiz by. It was ordinary. To see a giant whale making tracks was a treat. The older men worked at the gas station, though their slow call to service belied that fact. It was the nametags stitched to the chest pocket of their baggy overalls that gave them away. Duffy and Elgin.

Duffy, the youngest old guy, set his newspaper down and dragged his feet to the driver's side, in no great hurry. He had the rest of his life in front of him, right there at the filling station. Politely asking Gayle what he could do for her, knowing all along it would be a fill-up.

With a sign prominently posted on top of the pump stating there was no opportunity to get gas for at least a hundred miles, it was always a fill-up.

Seeing how she had nothing better to do until the big fella came back, Gayle stepped out to stretch her legs, allowing Duffy the opportunity to chat about his town's glorious history. It turned out that the town was established by hunters and trappers who had immigrated to the area in 1882 from eastern Washington state by dogsled.

Finished with his business, the Beluga dawdled back to the car with a giant hot dog loaded with mustard and catsup. It looked tiny in his hand. Trading places with Gayle, he stayed with the car with Duffy while she went inside, devouring his dog in four bites.

The Beluga found Duffy intriguing, but he asked him no questions, as the FBI woman might have. During the drive, she had been relentless, asking him questions nonstop. And the questions she had asked, he would have liked to have answered but could not. Not yet.

Relishing Duffy's yarn about the town's first livery stable, the Beluga's attention turned to the red Ford Escape that pulled up to the pump on the opposite side of the island. The car was pointed in the direction of Traughber City.

Duffy bailed on his story. He had his job to do, leaving the Beluga alone to either stay by the car or wander around the parking lot. The Beluga wandered.

Meandering around to the other car's front end, he glanced at their license plate. The car came from a dealership in Portland. Eighty percent of the vehicles he had seen on the road so far had come from there.

If Cherry's crew were around, he would stick with the vindictive ex-cop act and play the giant buffoon. But he was still working undercover, and the police detective part of the Beluga wanted details. Details told the story, like the two advertisement stickers on the back of the red Ford's window. The vehicle was for hire. Not a taxi but a private ride summoned by a phone app. The Beluga was sure the car was a long, expensive way away from Portland, and they must be traveling to Traughber City. But why? What was in Traughber City for these guys?

The back-right door of the Ford opened. A squat guy with biceps more prominent than his head got out. The Beluga thought the guy's giant eyeballs made him look like an insect, like a fly. Raising the Beluga's interest, the bug wore a pair of fancy, dark blue denim jeans and a tight red linen shirt. Too snazzy to be a cowboy country local.

Duffy glanced at the Beluga, then at the bug guy. Two odd-looking creatures at his filling station at one time. Like the circus had come to town. Duffy hoped his brother, Elgin, appreciated this moment.

The Beluga caught the bug inspecting him. It was a given he would. Everywhere he went, people would stare. He was tall enough to clean the gutters without a ladder, and as wide as a combine harvester, he could bulldoze a cornfield with his chest.

But the way this bug was glaring at him was different. As if to say, if I had to hurt this whale, where would I start?

Ozzie, the bug, flashed Beluga his signature toothy smile that he practiced in the gym's mirror. It was all about intimidation. Stupefying Ozzie, the Beluga distained to give him a second look.

That didn't work for Ozzie. Here he was being friendly, and the big ape was disrespecting him. Nobody disses Ozzie. Now, he would have to go over to find out what the big blob's problem was and set him straight.

The filling station door chimed.

Duffy watched the whole thing go down. First, Gayle popped out the door, holding a bottle of water. Ozzie stopped in mid-stride. Another guy, smarter-looking than Ozzie, got out of the Ford's front passenger side.

Dom glanced at the Beluga. He couldn't help himself. Then Dom looked at Ozzie, then at Gayle. He ordered Ozzie to get back into the vehicle. Ozzie didn't move, his eyes now fixed on Gayle.

The Beluga caught the way he was ogling her and disapproved. His job was to keep Gayle safe.

Then Jimmy got out of the car. Duffy didn't think the driver fit in with the other two men. Jimmy didn't seem to notice Ozzie, or the Beluga, or not much of anything. Fumbling through his wallet, he was concerned about how he was going to pay for the gas. Eventually, he smiled, handing his credit card to Duffy.

Ozzie rounded the other side of the gas pump, heading toward Gayle. The Beluga was too far away to stop him. Duffy grabbed a tire iron propped against the pump and stepped in front of Ozzie. Clearly, Duffy had used the tire iron before.

The Beluga slipped his hand inside his coat, right where a pistol would be.

Ozzie put it together. The big guy was not the woman's husband or boyfriend, but her bodyguard. Ozzie knew his gun was out of reach in the car's footwell, and if he touched Duffy, the big guy would shoot him dead. Not worth the headache. Flashing the Beluga another toothy grin, he backed up. "No drama today," Ozzie told Duffy, retreating to the Ford. "But I'll be back, old man. This is the only gas station in a hundred miles."

FOR A CHANGE IN scenery, Garris opted to fly over the mountain range. It was a longer route, adding a half-hour or more travel time. Instead of heading north, then tracking the Columbia River west, he dipped his Piper south for thirty miles, then cut over to Highway 26 to the east. More mountains, fewer farms. It would be worth the extra half hour.

Between Prairie City and Mount Vernon, he contacted Olive, and she gave him the unwelcome news concerning Lawrence Beemer. He and Lawrence were not close friends, but they had shared enough history that he asked for a few minutes after receiving the news before they continued their briefing.

When he called back, he walked her through the scenario with Coleman and Cherry Mackey and then asked if she had seen anything in the system relating to Parks and Hawkins. Cherry had claimed Parks was an Army Ranger and Hawkins a Navy Seal. They looked right. Physically, they were in peak condition. They had professional knowledge of firearms, and they had the edge. But it's easy to walk into a bar and find a guy claiming to be Special Forces to get the girl, a free beer, or both. If their alleged backgrounds were authentic, they had likely gotten into some trouble. They were working with Cherry, so they weren't angels. Maybe their track record would shed some light.

Before signing off, Olive's voice hardened. "If Cherry was involved with the MAX, why not take him down now?" It was a fair question. Maybe he should. But Cherry signaled something far more ominous in the works, something that likely involved the ultra-rich winemakers attending Coleman's party. He admitted it was a risk but said he would wait a little longer. Once he found out what Cherry and his crew were up to, then he'd take care of Cherry. Guaranteed.

With the help of a strong tailwind, Garris arrived at the airport in good time. He made his final approach from the south and landed with plenty of daylight to burn.

Taxiing onto the gravel, Garris passed four aisles of hangars and turned the corner to his row. A black four-door sedan with tinted windows sat parked in front of his hangar. Apart from Liz Beemer, no one should have known about his hideaway.

He reached for his Beretta and laid it on his lap, then angled the Piper onto the tarmac outside the hangar and put on the brakes. Revving its twin engines, the prop wash kicked a cloud of dust in the air, blanketing the sedan.

Releasing the cockpit's door, he waited. If they were the cartel, he was ready.

After the dust settled, Sergeant Carl Baranski appeared. "I'd feel better if you'd put your weapon away," Baranski called.

"Liz Beemer told you where to find me," Garris said, stepping off the wing.

"Her brother died this morning."

"So I heard."

"The family's at the hotel. They want to see you. Pronto."

"Help me get the plane inside."

Twenty minutes later, Garris was set to go. Then, enlightening Baranski that he had a thing about police cars—he never got in one—Garris said he would drive himself and to meet Baranski outside the hotel.

AFTER TWELVE LAPS AROUND the block, Garris surrendered and pulled his green 73 Opel GT into a twenty-dollar-a-day parking lot, then met Baranski waiting in on the hotel steps.

Inside the lobby, Baranski pressed the button to the elevator.

"I'll meet you up there," Garris said.

"What? Where are you going?"

"I'm taking the stairs."

"Do you want me to go with you?"

"Why would you?"

Garris found Baranski waiting outside the same suite he had occupied a few days earlier—room 1217.

Liz answered the door with a faint smile and eyes reddened by tears. She showed them in. Garris was taken by the amount of flowers and fruit baskets. It was remarkable that it was the same suite.

"Dad's been on the phone since this morning. Help yourself to whatever you like."

Garris glanced at the mini-bar.

Beemer paced back and forth near the window, phone to his ear. He motioned Garris to take a seat. Baranski positioned himself near the door.

Meredith was busy on her laptop, handling the necessary details of the newly widowed. By the looks of it, Garris thought she was well composed, saving her grieving for later. Liz handed him a bottle of sparkling water, then pulled up a chair. "At 1:55 this morning, Lawrence's body shut down. Some bizarre infection from the wound the doctor hadn't caught. It was sudden. I'll need to wait for the autopsy report before I can make any sense of it."

Meredith closed her laptop. "I thought he was doing better, so I walked and got a coffee. Thank God, Frank was with him."

After his call, Beemer jotted something on a writing pad and handed it to Baranski. Baranski read it and excused himself to join the two officers in the hall.

"Thought I'd see you at the hospital, at least once," Beemer said to Garris, his voice edged with bitterness.

"I was out of town."

"Out of town? What was so important you couldn't wait until Lawrence was out of the woods?"

"You might say I had a job interview."

"A what?" Beemer's eyes widened with anger.

"A job interview."

"You're with the CIA. You have a job."

"Do I?"

Putting on a stoic front, Beemer's response was a heavy silence laden with mixed emotions. Sensing the need for clarity, Garris added, "Rudyard Coleman has asked me to lend a hand at a wine soiree he's throwing at his villa. If I accept, I'll start tomorrow."

"Rudyard Coleman? I know Rudyard," Beemer said. "He threw a campaign party for me two months ago."

"He said that."

"But, Garris, I don't get it. I practically begged you to help me find the guy who killed Lawrence."

Now would have been the time to tell them he was on the killer's trail, to offer a fragment of solace in their anguish, but Garris knew better. It was too soon to give away any information. "Let the police do their job, Frank."

"Damn it, Garris. They're not you. It's been days. They haven't come up with diddly squat. You can find the guy. It's what you do."

There was no doubt why he'd been invited to Beemer's suite and why Baranski had left the room. Beemer was about to pick up the dance Liz had started at his hangar a couple of days earlier. Garris had to shift the balance of power. "Then what? Will you say it? Spell it out. What would you like me to do once I find him?"

Beemer saw through Garris's move—the challenge to voice the unspeakable. Garris knew there were too many ears in the room to get an honest response. Beemer was okay with Liz being present, but not Meredith. He had no choice but to move on. "Forget it."

Garris softened his voice. "I'm sorry I couldn't help Lawrence. I had a choice. You or him. I went with you."

"In Afghanistan, you took bullets for Lawrence. That must have left an impression. He didn't hesitate when it was his turn. He stepped right between the gunman and me," Beemer said.

"He died a hero."

Beemer poured a drink. "Now I wonder if I had only made different choices. My staff is getting calls and emails saying I should have been tougher on gun control. That Lawrence's blood is on my hands and I got what I deserve. Can you believe that?"

"You're supporting the president's policy, Dad," Liz said.

"Yeah? Well, maybe if I'd listened to my conscience and not Paul Cahill, if I'd stuck to my gut, it would have been harder for the damn murderer to get his hands on a gun."

In a perfect world, perhaps, Garris agreed. But men like Cherry, they would always find a way.

Beemer's cell phone chirped. Not his regular phone, but a different phone he kept in a custom-made, stainless-steel case and carried at all times.

"Excuse me," Beemer whispered. Then mouthed, "It's him," and walked to the bedroom. "Thank you for calling, Mr. President," he said, closing the door.

That was Garris's exit cue.

TWENTY MINUTES LATER, BEEMER came back out, looking even worse than when he had walked in.

"Where's Garris?"

"Dad. Did you think he was going to stick around while Paul ran his mouth?"

"Too bad. He missed his chance to hear my major announcement."

"Announcement?"

"We're going to have a public memorial service for Lawrence."

"What the hell? No, we're not. I don't want a public anything," Meredith protested.

"It's a request from the president. We can hardly refuse."

"Really, Dad? How could you let this happen? This is a private family matter. Not a campaign stunt." Liz paused long enough to regain her composure, her tone softening with genuine concern. "It's too dangerous. The killer hasn't been caught. It would be ridiculous if you allowed yourself to be an easy target. Again."

"I'm not the least concerned about that. Let's be realistic here. It's just an assumption I was his intended target," Beemer said, downplaying the situation. "Besides, I'm not going to let my constituents down. I'm not going to retreat into hiding. As far as I'm concerned, it's business as usual. End of story."

"When?" Liz asked.

"In two days. Wednesday at noon."

"No, Frank. No," Meredith protested again.

"I know. I know, Meredith. I tried to dissuade him. But Paul insisted. Remember, he is Lawrence's godfather. He needs to do this."

"Call him back. Shut it down, Frank," Meredith demanded. "I'm serious."

"I'm sorry. I'm not going to do that. It's already been settled. Paul Cahill, the president of the United States, is giving the eulogy. Like it or not, this is a prestigious gesture. I just got off the phone with Mayor Baas. The venue is at the riverfront park. Afterward, Paul has arranged a private gathering at Rudyard Coleman's winery."

"What the—" Meredith snapped.

"Why there?" Liz asked.

"Paul asked if I'd been in contact with Garris. I impulsively mentioned he was here right now, in my hotel room. I screwed up. Somehow, I let it slip that Garris is working for Rudyard. Paul just took the ball and ran with it."

"Dad!"

"Go to hell, Frank," Meredith said.

CHAPTER 18

ON HIS WAY OUT, GARRIS GIFTED BARANSKI AND THE TWO officers with a box of premium chocolates from Beemer's suite. It seemed like the right thing to do.

Avoiding the elevator, Garris bounded down five flights of stairs and stopped abruptly. Someone else was in the stairwell. They were three or four flights above him. Not once had he seen anyone use the stairs higher than ten. Was he being followed? He would not be surprised if Cherry had him tailed. Or could it be the Trevano cartel?

Stepping into the corridor, Garris eased the door open and pulled his pistol. Closer and closer, boots tapped, echoing through the vestibule. Almost there. Unexpectedly, a woman passed by.

"Gayle."

She looked back over her shoulder. "Garris? What are you doing here?"

"I take the stairs instead of the elevator," he said, tucking his pistol away.

"Wise guy. You know what I mean. What are you doing at the hotel?"

"Beemer wanted to see me. Lawrence is dead."

"Diane told me."

"Why are you here? I thought you'd be at Coleman's."

"Diane wanted a pre-meeting here. I just left her suite."

"What's up?"

Gayle gave a half shrug. "I couldn't pin it down. There didn't seem to be any reason to meet."

"Let's go somewhere we can get a bite," Garris said.

"How about a rain check? I need answers, and Diane hasn't even scratched the surface. She wants to continue our conversation at the winery."

"Gayle. It might not be safe at Coleman's."

"Give me the specifics."

"I didn't tell Beemer, but I made contact with the MAX gunman this morning."

Gayle's eyes widened. "You thought you might. But he's not in custody, or you would have said so by now."

"I don't have anything concrete. No physical evidence, but I know it's him."

"What's his connection to Coleman?"

Garris checked the halls for listening ears. "At dinner, we met Coleman's security team. Parks, Hawkins, and the big guy, Gillman. But we didn't meet their leader. Charles Mackey. He goes by Cherry. I've worked with him in the past."

"At the Agency? Is he still with them? Wait. Hold on. You wouldn't have a clue, would you? In your world, trust is scarce, even among allies. You could say you're still in the Agency, or not, but who'd know for sure? Right?"

"That's a fair assessment."

"Okay, Garris, I know it's a stretch, but hear me out. If Cherry Mackey was working inside, could the Agency have orchestrated the attack on the MAX? That would mean the Agency attempted to assassinate a senator. An order like that could only come from the top. Beemer's pal, Paul Cahill."

"That's a hellish leap. No, Gayle, the president can't order hits. And the Agency doesn't either. At least, not on United States soil."

"Really? Ever hear of JFK?"

"That's a conspiracy theory. We have our limits."

"How can you be so sure?"

"Obviously, I can't."

"Right, you can't. So what do we do?"

He motioned toward a set of chairs near the elevator. "Sit down. Let's piece this together. Let's say Cherry still has a foot in the door in the Agency, or he's freelancing. It doesn't matter. He's still planning something. And let's say Gordon Parks and Bob Hawkins are ex-Special Forces. That means it could be anything from another hit, to robbing a liquor store. Cherry basically copped to the MAX operation and wants me to be part of the next wave. That means he thinks I'd be sympathetic to their cause. I can't stop a train wreck if I don't know what track it's on. So I have to play along. Cherry knows this and is counting on me taking the bait. It's a move right out of the playbook."

"If Senator Beemer was his primary target, then he's still in danger."

"Yes. But it could be something entirely unrelated. I just don't know. Yet."

Gayle ran her fingers through her hair. "So, again, we're back to square one. You need to cooperate with Cherry, and I need to find Ron. Diane claims she's been in touch with him, but she hasn't given me any details. What do we do?"

"She's on Cherry's crew, so she's involved somehow."

"Now you're on Cherry's crew. Does that make you involved?"

"Fair point. Coleman did say she's been in Portland this whole time, isolated from the others. Which means she might not know what Cherry's up to, any more than I do. Or, if she does, she might not have been included in the latest developments. When I was at the ranch, Cherry got an urgent call. His timeline has been moved up. When you go to the villa, keep your eyes open. I'll be there first thing in the morning."

Gayle nodded.

As they entered the lobby, Garris stopped and asked the doorman if there was any news about Dante Green. Negative.

Out of the corner of his eye, Garris spotted someone lurking in a dark corner of the lobby. Thick black hair. Oblong face. Dressed in an expensive eel-skin jacket, black slacks, and Italian dress shoes, he looked like a mortician who would be right at home with the hotel's upper-end clientele. He was waiting for someone. Garris knew he was the guy.

Moving outside, Garris whistled. Gayle had snagged a parking space right in front of the hotel. Lucky her.

She slipped behind the wheel. It was not just McCoy's 'Vette or the Jeep Commando; she even made an economy rental car look good.

"I'm going to take a walk to the hospital. I want to visit Dante," Garris said.

"I'm sorry about dinner."

"I'll see you at Coleman's in the morning."

"First thing."

Under the amber glow from one streetlamp to another, Garris followed Broadway Avenue and crossed Burnside. Allowing the guy in the eel jacket he had seen in the hotel to catch up, Garris stopped at a bookstore and did a little window browsing. The guy clearly was not one of Cherry's. He was physically solid, but not in a Special Forces way. Plus, his clothing was a giveaway. He would never be caught dead in a red trucker's cap. He was cartel.

Moving on, Garris continued down Burnside to Tenth, where he took a right. A Mexican restaurant on Twenty-Third looked and smelled delicious. He had not eaten, hoping to have dinner with Gayle. Maybe the guy following him was hungry, too.

Beef burrito in hand, Garris sat at the restaurant's outside picnic table. The guy stayed back a half a block. His loss. After cleaning his plate, Garris resumed his walk.

The red sign to the hospital's emergency room was brightly lit, and the light spilled over to a neighborhood garden across the street. With few lights of its own, the park was dark and vacant.

Using trees for cover, Garris waited for the patter of Italian shoes to pass.

Allowing the guy to get a few paces ahead, Garris stepped out from behind a tree and sized up the guy. Up close, he looked more substantial. If the police drew a chalk outline around Garris, he would be that size.

"This looks like a good place as any," Garris said.

Caught off guard, his prey jerked around.

"They won't have far to come to get you." Garris gestured to the hospital.

The guy laughed. "True. Better still, they don't come for dead stiffs. You will be doing them a solid."

"Not a pretty picture for either of us, is it?"

The guy shrugged.

"You're with Trevano."

"How can you tell?"

"Have you looked in the mirror?"

Tugging at his jacket lapels, the guy laughed. "I am not typical Portland. I see your point."

"You've lost the element of surprise," Garris said. "But we're here now. Alone. No witnesses. What's your plan?"

The guy dropped the smile. Garris thought he might.

He was big and no doubt lethal. But he had made a series of mistakes, starting with the flashy fashion statement that got him noticed at the hotel. Then there were his sloppy tailing skills. And now that he had voluntarily walked into the garden without backup, Garris saw him realize he was in way over his head and understood the consequences.

"You killed Hector."

"Did I?"

"Your president said so."

"What do you think?"

"It doesn't matter. It's what Edgar thinks. Hector was his big brother."

"It does matter. Edgar isn't here. You are."

"No shit," the guy said. "Do me a favor. When I put a bullet between your eyes, I want you to see Edgar's face, not mine."

Garris smiled. "The power of positive thinking. I like that. What's your name?"

"Why would I tell you?"

"Why not? You know mine. But if you'd rather not say, I can live with it."

"Armin."

"Okay, Armin, we're off to the races. Let me break this down for you. If you believe Edgar, who believes the president, then you have to accept I killed Hector. And that would mean his men, too. President Cahill claimed there were more than a dozen. So you know what I can do. You might be good at your job, but are you good enough to go at me alone? Face it. You screwed up. No doubt, Edgar sent more men to Portland than just you. Why didn't you wait for them? We all could have settled this at one time and place."

"I don't need them."

"Maybe not. You could get lucky. I did just eat a burrito. But I have time. Shall we call them now?"

"They're not here."

"Where are they?"

"You were supposed to be in Traughber City."

"So, they're in Traughber City?"

"Not any longer."

"I see you have a predicament."

"I have a predicament?"

"After you saw me in the lobby, you couldn't wait to call Edgar. Am I right?"

Armin answered with silence.

"And he ordered you to get the job done?"

"Something like that."

"You didn't like that idea."

"Would you?"

"How many are in your crew?"

"Why should I tell you?"

"Why not? I'm giving you time to think through your next move. I already know mine."

"Two. No, three, not counting the driver."

"Get your cell phone."

"What?"

"You heard me. Call Edgar, then hand me the phone."

"No, I'm not going to do that."

"Why not?"

"He'll kill me."

"No, he won't."

"You don't think so?"

"I'll ask him not to."

"That's not enough."

"I'll say, please, if it makes you feel better. Now, call him."

"I have a gun."

"You wouldn't be much of a *sicario* if you didn't."

"It's a trick. You wish me close enough to hand you my phone, then you'll do something."

"Fine. Have it your way. Dial Edgar, then toss me your phone from there."

Armin wasn't sold.

"Come on, Armin. Edgar's expecting a call. He'll want to know if I'm dead yet. Obviously, you're experienced or he wouldn't have sent you. But I'm thinking not in a showdown. Look what you're wearing. Your jacket's going to slow you down. It's going to get in the way when you go for your gun. It looks nice, but style costs. It's not worth losing your life. Now, give me your phone."

Hesitantly, Armin reached into his pocket.

"Go ahead. Dial, then toss it."

"You'll drop it."
"Not if you lob it."
"It's expensive."
"If I drop it, I'll buy you a new one. Scout's honor."

Armin dialed and tossed it. Garris snagged it with his left hand.

"Armin," the voice said over the phone.
"No, Edgar, it's Kelley."
"Garris Kelley. The star of my movie. Is Armin dead?"
"Not yet. Maybe later. We'll see."
"Go ahead, kill him. I don't care. I have others. As long as I'm head of this family, I'll keep sending more."
"Duly noted."

Garris didn't need to be looking over his shoulder. Unfortunately for Armin, he would have to be slowed down. It would be unpleasant but better than the alternative. With nothing else to say to Edgar, Garris tossed Armin the phone way up high.

Armin wasn't a pushover, but phones mean so much to so many. It was instinct. As Armin reached for it, Garris charged and grabbed him by his jacket, then yanked him down to his knee. Armin's head snapped backward, then forward. He teetered sideways to the ground. He was not gravely injured, but his jaw would need medical attention.

Garris slipped his hand inside Armin's jacket to his waist. "I'm letting you go, but I'll have to take your gun."

"Watch your back," Armin warned. "I'll still have to kill you."

"I know. That's our predicament."

"I'M ON MY WAY out the door," Diane said to Cherry over the phone. "Gayle might beat me there. Baranski, the cop, he's been in and out of the Beemer's suite. If I accidentally run into him in the hall, he'll recognize me from the hospital."

"I'm surprised Beemer's holed up there. Garris must have had something to do with it."

"It's not a problem."

"How did it go with Gayle?"

"It's just like you said. She's so driven to find Boyle that she's not focused on what's in front of her nose. I told her I was seeing him tomorrow and invited her to come along. I've set up a wild goose chase to keep her busy. I'll keep her away from you and the boys."

"Thanks."

"That is unless you'd like me to take care of her sooner. I've already got some ideas."

"No. Not yet. We can't risk Garris catching on. We need to lead him slowly, and I'm pushing my luck as it is."

"You're the boss, Cherry on top."

"Stop it."

"Never."

THE PATIENT'S DOOR WAS open. Garris knocked lightly.

"Yes."

"Mr. Green. I'm Garris Kelley."

"I've seen you on TV. Come in."

Small room. Two beds. One occupied.

Dante's grandfather had pulled his chair close to the bed. He had been reading to his grandson. "They say talking helps," he said, gesturing to the other available chair, and Garris sat down. "Thank you for stopping by. I appreciate it." He set the book on the bed, then reached to shake Garris's hand. "I'm Calvin Green."

"How's he doing?" Garris asked.

"Not sure."

"Is there anything I can do for you, either of you?"

"You can take your check back. Five thousand dollars is too generous, Mr. Kelley. And I respect the gesture. But Dante and I can do for ourselves."

"I'd still like you to keep it."

Calvin sighed. "It would help. I'm not sure how we're going to pay for all this."

"Settled," Garris said. "Let's talk about other things."

"Okay, by me."

Calvin wore a blue short-sleeved seersucker shirt. When he leaned into the light, Garris glimpsed the tattoo on his wrist. Two dog tags with Calvin's name on them.

"Marines," Garris said.

"Lance Corporal. 1st Battalion, 8th Marines."

"The Beirut Embassy bombing. October 23, 1983, 6:22 am. You were there."

"I was about the same age as Dante is now. It was the deadliest single-day death toll the Marines had since the battle of Iwo Jima. The equivalent of 21,000 pounds of TNT."

"Two hundred and forty-one Marines died that day."

"They did. Not too many people remember that. Are you a brother?"

Garris put his hand on Calvin's shoulder and looked him in the eyes.

"Oh. You were a Raider," Calvin said knowingly, referring to the Marine's Special Forces. "That would make sense."

"I'm the reason Dante's here," Garris said. "I asked him to help me, and he did. No questions asked."

"That's my Dante. The police said they think he stopped the killer from getting to Senator Beemer."

Garris nodded.

"His son. He was here. Upstairs. In a nice big room with a view," Calvin said without a hint of bitterness.

"He died."

"I heard that. I don't know what I'd do if I lost Dante. I've had him since he was a boy. Or he had me, is more like it. Being just a child, one might think I was taking care of him. But I think it was always the other way around. Always. I don't know how I got so lucky. Dante has a way of making me feel that what's left of me matters."

"I know what you're saying. The bond."

"You do?"

"My grandpa raised me."

"He did?"

"He did. And he made me feel I mattered." Garris paused. "Calvin, I'm going to get the guy who did this to Dante."

"Then what?"

"I suppose it will depend."

"On the weather?" Calvin asked.

"That's right."

"Then I'll pray for rain and hope it thunders."

"Would you like to take a walk or something? Stretch a little. I can stay with Dante."

"Thank you. That might be a good idea."

When Calvin got up and limped out the door, Garris recalled Olive's one-page file that said he had lost his left leg on a Sunday morning in Beirut.

CHAPTER 19

THE FOLLOWING MORNING, GARRIS WOKE UP IN HIS OWN BED. He checked his watch. Half past five. He put on a pot of coffee, then took a cup outside to wait for the sunrise. The stars twinkled, then faded as the sun rose across the runway above the eastern tree line.

The mom-and-pop country airport where Garris kept his plane and collected his mail had been in business for more than forty years, built on land that had once been the family's dairy farm. Some pilots, including Garris, swore they smelled the rich aroma of Holstein cows lingering from a few of the older hangars. It was more likely the odor had drifted in from the nearby dairy farm that was lucky enough to have stayed in business. In recent years, many Oregon farms had been bought out and transformed into profitable vineyards. And Rudyard Coleman had his fingers in all four corners in the state.

Cherry had scheduled breakfast with Garris for seven-thirty at Coleman's signature wine-tasting room, a villa at his Willamette winery—the gala's location.

His phone said driving the back roads would take fifty minutes. Like General McCoy, he had a couple of modes of transportation. And maybe because he had recently driven the general's Jeep, Garris drove his 1990 Cherokee. Perhaps Olive was right. A fondness for old airplanes, old cars, and Dutch beer served in little green bottles; he and the general had a few things in common. But Garris would not go so far as to say they were soulmates.

Not committing to staying overnight but being prepared, Garris packed a bag with a compartment for an extra gun and ammo. He threw in a couple of shirts and a black sports coat, thinking he might be required to spiff up for the party.

He tossed the bag in the back seat, then hit the road, looking forward to the plate of pancakes and bacon that Cherry had promised.

Out of the airport, Garris headed southeast, driving up one hill and down another, among the same brambly hills and acres of sun-kissed wildflowers that Liz Beemer had the pleasure of discovering. He passed the same rusted automobiles, the same llamas and goats. Then, cutting south, he entered a rural valley filled with nothing but grapes as far as he could see.

A glance at his phone showed ten miles to go. He'd be right on time. Then he hit a roadblock.

Up ahead, coming his way, a black-and-white Dodge Charger flashed its blue-and-red bar, then dramatically cranked the wheels to block traffic. It was the law.

Garris pulled over, but before he rolled his window down, he reached into the back and double-checked his bag to make sure it was zipped and that his pistol was not exposed. Why ask for trouble?

"Good morning, Deputy."

"You're expected, Mr. Kelley," the officer said, glancing in the backseat.

"Yes, I know. For breakfast. Am I missing something, Deputy?"

"You don't know?" the officer asked.

"By the looks of it, this has nothing to do with the wine soiree at Rudy's."

"President Cahill will arrive tomorrow to attend Mr. Lawrence

Beemer's memorial. It's possible he will attend a private party at the winery afterward."

"No, kidding?"

"No, sir."

"But he hasn't confirmed?"

"No, sir. It's just a possibility. The Secret Service are on the Coleman premises. They are aware of your presence. As is the president. You are allowed to continue to the property. I'll move my vehicle to let you pass."

"You're not going to search my car for weapons? I know how uptight the Secret Service can be."

"No, sir. That won't be necessary. Word has been passed down. You have top security clearance. Have a nice day." The officer tipped his hat.

"Thank you, Deputy."

"You're welcome, Mr. Kelley. It's been a pleasure to meet you. It was an awesome thing you did to that scumbag, Trevano."

"It's only a rumor I was involved."

"Plausible deniability. Yes, I understand, sir." With a nod, the Deputy pulled his patrol car over to the roadside, signaling Garris to pass by.

He had driven the country road hundreds of times, but now Garris saw the splendid landscape through a specific lens. Coleman owned every hill, rock, tree, and grapevine in sight.

A sign advertising the tasting room said to take a right in one mile. When Garris arrived at the gate, two special agents confronted him. After a quick chat, during which they flaunted their presence to make damn sure he knew they were there, Garris had learned no more than what the deputy had given.

Driving the steep private road, Garris guesstimated that the winery sat on fifty to seventy manicured acres.

Another agent waited at the top of the drive and flagged Garris into a reserved parking space beside a gray Rivian. The agent had orders to escort him inside. But Garris would not be hurried.

Acting like a tourist admiring the architecture, Garris inspected the building. How many windows did the place have, and were they bulletproof? Besides the main entry, how many other potential exit points were there? He glanced up at the red-tile roof. Then he inspected the exterior's yellow clay walls. The entrance faced east, allowing an excellent view of Mt. Hood and Mt. Adams. The alignment meant a shadow would fall on the parking lot and the door by the early afternoon.

It was a given the Secret Service agent was a smart guy. He knew what Garris was up to. "You have another thirty seconds," he said.

Ten seconds later, Garris said he was good to go, and they moved inside. There, Garris started the process all over again.

Coleman called the villa a tasting room. It was much more. It was everything his ranch was not, way over the top and with a theme-park vibe, reminding Garris of a fourteenth-century monastery he had once visited in Taormina, Sicily.

The villa was at least seven thousand square feet. High ceilings. Marble floors. Endless corridors. Landscape paintings mounted in expensive frames. Rudyard Coleman portraits mounted in expensive frames. Statues of people. Garris had not the faintest idea who they were but crossed his fingers he would find one of Ezra Meeker.

Sam Riggins, the agent, introduced himself and told Garris to wait in the reception area. Then Riggins got out his phone and strayed off to make a call.

Having time to look around, Garris started with the wall behind him. It was Coleman's Wall of Fame, a mosaic of photographs showcasing Rudy Coleman rubbing shoulders with celebrities who had visited the winery. Actors, athletes, and politicians were prominently featured, including a recent picture with Senator Frank Beemer.

Garris walked down the corridor into a spacious room with towering ceilings and counted five chandeliers and three fireplaces, along with more paintings, sculptures, mirrors, and expensive flower arrangements. Garris figured it made sense that when Coleman charged a hundred bucks for a mediocre bottle of wine, he would throw in a few bells and whistles to heighten the experience. It would take the attention off the beverage's mediocre caliber.

In light of the impending presidential visit, Garris noticed at least five special agents scouring the perimeter. No stranger to the security process, he thought it peculiar they had allowed him inside without immediately asking for his identification. He respected the Secret Service. They had a tough job. Maybe because the president's trip to Portland was last minute, the visit to the winery was deemed "highly unlikely," and the agents could modify protocol?

Agent Riggins arrived on Garris's left. "You're not allowed to be in here."

Glancing through the window on the far side of the room, Garris spotted a familiar face, the woman from the ranch. She smiled at him, then slipped out of sight.

"Who was that woman?" Garris asked Riggins. "You must know."

"I do."

Before Riggins could elaborate, the door behind the receptionist opened and Coleman stepped in.

"Garris," Coleman said. "Good to see you. I had some doubt you'd show."

He would get to Coleman, but Garris wanted Riggins to answer his question. He eyed Riggins for an answer.

Lowering his voice to a whisper, Riggins said, "I'm not permitted to say."

"As you might have guessed," Coleman said to Garris. "Should you accept my offer, your duties will have elevated into something much more prestigious than the vintner's conference. And I have you to thank for it."

"Me?"

"What? Did Senator Beemer leave you in the dark? I thought he was your friend. Let me enlighten you. Frank let it slip during a call with the president that you'd be moonlighting for me. That tidbit gave him the idea that my winery would be the perfect setting for a private gathering following the memorial. As you can see, this place is not only beautiful but, being strategically built on top of the highest hill in the area, it's extremely secure."

Turning to Riggins, Garris said. "This doesn't seem rushed to you? It's only been one day, and the president is organizing an outdoor event. You guys are supposed to take time to scout and secure your locations. Lawrence's killer hasn't been apprehended. Senator Beemer could still be in danger."

Riggins hesitated. "I'm not allowed to discuss this. Off the record, it's important to the president to show the public he supports Senator Beemer during this time."

"Sounds like he's on the campaign trail."

Coleman interjected. "Garris, why don't we have breakfast on the terrace? Afterward, I'll show you around the property."

"You? Where's Cherry?"

"Busy. Whether the president attends or not, the Beemers will still be here tomorrow. Cherry and his team are preparing. You'll be joining them after we're through."

"And Agent Wilson? We were to meet this morning. Did she spend the night?"

"She did. Gayle left word that she'll call or see you this evening when we all get together for dinner. Diane thought it best they hit the road running." Coleman motioned Garris to follow him. "Now, I'm sure you've brought an overnight bag. I'll have it brought to your room. You'll be in the Sangiovese suite, next to Gayle's."

CHAPTER 20

ONE NIGHT AT THE GRAND MEEKER, A MORNING BREAKFAST at Rosie's, then Jimmy and the crew were on the road, heading back to Portland.

Jimmy was not the kind to wish harm or misfortune on anyone, but when he heard that Armin had paid a visit to the hospital, he wanted it to be the numb-nuts riding shotgun. Ozzie.

Dom volunteered no details, but Jimmy put it together from Ozzie, who had run his mouth for nearly the entire drive. Garris Kelley got the drop on Armin. It got worse. Kelley took Armin's phone and made a call to Edgar. This was a big boo-boo. Dom knew it. Armin, for damn sure, knew it. Once they found Kelley, Armin would take an early retirement. Boasting that he was super-tight with Edgar ever since giving him a cool video game, Ozzie was sure Armin would be dropped in his lap. It was something to look forward to. Just because Armin looked intimidating did not mean he was. Kelley had no problem handling him.

Backtracking the route he had driven the day before, Jimmy pulled into the same two-pump gas station in the same ten-building town.

Just as before, the two older guys sat on the bench outside the store.

Elgin made a move to help the customers, but Duffy recognized the vehicle and stopped his brother. He'd take it.

Jimmy rolled down his window and asked Duffy to fill it up. Then the passenger door opened, and Ozzie stepped out. He looked Duffy in the eye, then told Jimmy to get out of the car. Not inclined to do so, Jimmy got out.

"Jimmy. Give the old man a hand with the gas," Ozzie said.

"I tell you what, mister. You get back in the vehicle, and I'll check the tires and the oil," Duffy said, glancing at the tire iron propped against the pump.

"Jimmy, do it," Ozzie ordered, glaring at Duffy. "And you, my new friend, you're going to show me where the gents' room is."

"It's inside," Jimmy said.

"Not today, it isn't. Come on, old man. And don't forget your walking stick," Ozzie taunted. "Go ahead, pick it up."

Duffy picked up the tire iron.

"Good, now let's go. I bet the gents' is in the back."

The Ford's back window rolled down.

"Get back in the car, Ozzie," Dom said. "We don't have time for this shit."

"I've got to take a leak."

"Then make it quick."

"It won't take any time at all."

Dom nodded.

Duffy led Ozzie toward the store. He gave Elgin a brotherly smile. Elgin was confused, not understanding why his brother was taking a customer to the back of the garage.

The nozzle clicked. Rounding up, it came to fifty-two dollars. Jimmy waited to give his credit card to the older man.

Ozzie came around the right side of the store. Alone. Passing in front of the hood, he told Jimmy to get in the car.

"I haven't paid for the gas yet."

"Don't worry about it. I paid it forward."

Jimmy got behind the wheel, dread freezing his insides.

TWO AGENTS CAME AROUND the corner on their way to the vineyard. So far, Garris counted seven on-site. A modest enough number, giving him the impression that the president's chances of visiting the winery were slim to none. But he had only seen the inside of the tasting room and the terrace.

"When did the Secret Service show up?" Garris asked Coleman.

"They called yesterday afternoon, asking if hosting such an event was doable. I said, of course it was. Before I knew it, they'd flown in from San Francisco and were here before midnight."

"They're staying here, on the premises?"

Coleman nodded. "Open your eyes. I have plenty of rooms."

"And they're okay with Gayle being here?"

"At first, there was some resistance. But since she's with the FBI, they worked it out. You're both staying and are cleared to roam as you please."

"Good to know," Garris said. "I'd like to check out the grounds."

"I was just about to give you the ten-cent tour. Cherry should be ready to see you by the time we finish."

"It's your dime. Let's go."

Standing on the terrace, Garris imagined he was somewhere in Europe, maybe Italy. The late morning sun tapped four hills and washed down into the valley and over Coleman's terrain.

Though it was close to harvest time, the busiest time of the year, the vineyard was quiet. The staff had been ordered to abandon their tractors, forklifts, and other machines until it was decided if the president would visit. They had replaced the laborers with a White House event planner and her team, who were milling about, looking for the best place to set up additional tables.

While the Secret Service gave him the once-over, Garris returned the favor, then focused on Coleman.

A born showman, Coleman was like a walking/talking late-night television commercial. He could not resist, and quickly confessed that his wine was no better than the wine down the road, admitting that it was his marketing and presentation that separated him from the pack. He believed it was essential to his bottom line that his customers get involved with the process of winemaking. Not only did participation lead to immediate bottle sales, but it also paved the way to joining the prestigious and expensive wine club, where the real money was made. He had decided early on to go big or go home, leading him to building the villa-style tasting room. The perfect spot for capturing money.

Tucked behind the villa, off the terrace, they passed a splendid butterfly garden, the perfect place to drink and picnic. Just beyond the garden, they came to the vineyard. At its entrance, a footpath led to the "Signature" winery a short walk away. As part of the marketing strategy, the production facility had been designed to draw the attention of curious customers. It was functional, but built for show. Consumers could leisurely stroll over with their pinot glasses and witness the production of the latest Coleman vintage, imagining themselves involved and part of the process, though, in truth, the main industrious winery was located much further away in the eastern sector of the vineyard.

Leading Garris inside, Coleman shifted gears. His voice dropped, and he transformed into a tour guide, pointing to the rows of oak barrels forested in France. Garris gathered he was supposed to be impressed. Then Coleman spoke about the gnarly wine crusher and destemmer. It was custom-made and might be the largest ever built. Garris said it looked like a steel coffin with a seven-foot spiral drill bit. Coleman joked it would be a pity if anyone accidentally fell inside it.

Moving on, they passed grape containers and wine presses the size of jet engines, twelve-foot-high stainless steel container tanks where they stored a thousand gallons of fermenting grapes. He encouraged Garris to climb the ladder to the steel catwalk to look down inside them. Thick, soupy, blood-red juice, full of grapes, skins, seeds, and stems.

Next on the tour was the storage area. Rows and rows of barrels and bins, with Coleman's name stamped on each one.

The tour might have been impressive on a different day, but joining a wine club was not on Garris's mind. He was looking for a clue as to why Cherry wanted to enlist him. What was the big picture? The answer might be concealed right where he stood, in the villa or the garden. If so, he had missed it.

Coleman launched into his rehearsed bit about the bottling process.

"Rudy, the shows over. I've seen enough."

"You've made a decision? Will you join my team?"

"Call Cherry. Tell him I'm in, with the wine party."

"And what about Lawrence Beemer's memorial? There's still a chance the president will make an appearance. I'm aware he's keen on seeing you."

"I'm thinking about it. But let's be clear. I don't need to be razzle-dazzled. I'm a beer drinker. Cheap beer, the kind that comes in green bottles. Now, why don't you point me in Cherry's direction so I can justify what I'll be charging you."

"Would you like a glass of wine first?"

"Maybe a beer. I just had breakfast."

Coleman laughed. "I keep those in the outbuilding. Don't tell anyone, but I don't mind a cold brewski myself sometimes."

"I didn't need to know that."

Coleman guided them to a nearby inconspicuous shed hidden from the view of the villa, housing hand tools, hoses, buckets, gloves, boots, and a Gator, identical to the utility vehicle he had used at the ranch.

"See the hill about a mile out?" Coleman asked.

"I see four hills."

"To the left. Do you see the communications tower?"

"Got it."

"Cherry's up there with his men. Go ahead, get in the Gator. But pay attention. There are a thousand rows of grapes in this vineyard. It's like a maze. You could easily get lost."

Lost? Garris listened up.

"I have tags and markers on the wood posts. They're color-coded at the top. Red, white, and blue. What you'll want to do is go straight down this row. It's called Main Street. Can remember that?" Coleman smiled.

Garris didn't.

Coleman continued. "Follow Main. About two minutes in, there's a post with a blue band at the top. The tag will have the number 19 on it. Turn left there. Follow it for roughly thirty seconds, then swing right at row 58. Then, just keep going straight. There's a clearing to park at the foot of the hill. You can hoof it from there."

Coleman was grinning. Maybe not. It could have been the Botox.

The distance between rows was eight feet. This gave Garris room to play. He had never been behind the wheel of a Gator. But, being a car guy, he was interested to find out what it could do. He stomped his boot on the electric cart's accelerator. He bounced around a little, almost side-swiping a vine or two. There was no speedometer, but he figured he had it going right around fifteen and could go faster.

Coleman said it would take two minutes to reach Post 19. Checking his watch, Garris smiled. He had made it in one minute and forty-one seconds. After taking the left turn, he stopped and got out his cell.

"Olive."

"Garris, I'm glad you called. Where are you?"

"I'm in a golf cart in the middle of Coleman's vineyard."

"Golf cart? You don't play golf."

"Nope. Too much real estate for this man's diversion. What do you have for me?"

"Beemer is holding a public memorial for Lawrence. Get this. It's tomorrow, in the park downtown, along the river. Cahill made a big announcement, saying that, Lawrence Beemer being his godchild, he would attend."

"So I heard. Cahill set it up. It was his idea."

"Unbelievable."

"Not for him."

"I'm trying to get you Cahill's itinerary. You know the Secret Service are tight-lipped, but I know an agent who knows an agent and so on. Do you know Cahill requested a private gathering at Rudyard Coleman's winery afterward? Have you seen any signs of this?"

"The Secret Service are on the premises as we speak."

"Is Cahill going out of the way to see you?" Olive laughed.

"Don't jinx me, Olive."

"I've been digging into the woman you were interested in at the ranch. So far, no luck. According to his file, Rudyard Coleman never married. So, no divorces. Since his status as a successful vintner has risen, he's been seen with a few minor celebrities but no long-term relationships. I dug into his taxes. There are several staff members taking care of his ranch, including a personal chef. But not the woman who made your dinner. The chef was male, and he moved on four months ago. Coleman had a personal assistant. Female. Caitlin Armstrong. Thirty-two years old. College graduate, University of Oregon, paid ninety-three thousand a year. I'm texting you her photo now."

Garris's cell chimed, and he pulled it up. "Not her."

"I'll keep digging. I'm still working on Gordon Parks, Bruce Gillman, Bob Hawkins, and the FBI agent, Ron Boyle."

"Thanks, Olive. I'll call you later." Garris ended the call. Just as he was about to move on, his phone chirped again. He thought it was Olive calling back.

"Yes?"

"Garris, it's Gayle."

"How did it go? Did you reach Ron?"

"Not yet. He's not making it easy. Diane arranged a meeting in Salem, but he never showed."

"You tried his cell?"

"So many times, I lost track. Straight to voicemail every time. But I got texts. Two of them. One said, if I'm worried about him, don't be. He's fine, but it's too risky to communicate, and he'll get in touch soon. The other said, in case I got any funny ideas to come to Oregon, don't. He said to stay in DC and not get involved." Gayle chuckled. "Too late for that."

"Is there anything in the text to prove it was him? Something only you and he'd get?"

"There was. The text included a five-pointed star emoji. You know, like a badge. It's an FBI thing. Do you CIA guys have an emoji?"

"No, we're not as clever as the FBI. Your emoji thing might be a good sign, but it's still generic. Someone could have taken his phone."

"Right."

"You've been with Diane. What's your take on her?"

"She's smart, complicated, and I don't trust her a lick. Just to be on the safe side, I slipped her a few unpredictable questions about Ron. She answered well enough, so they did spent time together."

Garris sighed, hinting his concerns.

Sensing he was gearing up to give more cautionary advice, Gayle changed the subject. "How's it going on your end?"

"I'm hiking up a mountain about a mile east of the villa. Cherry's running drills up there; I want to see what kind. I'll see you at dinner."

"Sounds good."

"Gayle, do yourself a favor."

"I know. Keep my eye on Diane."

"DID YOU SEND THE text?" Cherry asked Parks.

Parks held up Ron Boyle's cellphone and waved it in the air. "An hour ago."

"Good. That should give the FBI a little hope."

CHAPTER 21

HUNCHED OVER ON A PARK BENCH, ARMIN DELICATELY SIPPED his iced coffee through a paper straw, avoiding the tender spot on his swollen jaw.

"Armin. Get your ass up, and get in the car," hollered Ozzie, with his arm hanging out the window, slapping his palm on the car door. "Hurry up."

Armin stayed put until he had finished his drink, then took his sweet time getting to the car. He had dropped the ball, but he was not going to pay for it by listening to Ozzie drone on and on about it. Armin had one good way to shut him up. Slipping into the backseat behind Ozzie, he reached for his gun. Shit. Garris had taken it.

"You're slow. You know that?" Ozzie said, egging him on. "So slow, Kelley ran circles around you. You know what I'm going to call you? Turtle. Yeah, that's you. Mr. Turtle."

"Enough, Ozzie," Dom said, then slapped the back of the driver's seat. "Jimmy, drive to the hotel. Go."

Jimmy did not go.

"What's happening?" Ozzie asked. "I'm working with two guys who don't understand time is money?"

Never having a panic attack before, Jimmy thought he was having a heart attack. The world seemed to be closing in on him. His chest was tight and he could not breathe. At the gas station when Ozzie had returned to the car and the older man had not, Jimmy's nerves got the best of him.

Dom recognized the problem. Like a big brother, he reached over the seat and put his hand on Jimmy's shoulder. "It's okay, Jimmy. Breathe. You're going to be okay."

"What? Is he sick or something?" Ozzie asked. "There's a hospital right over there. We could drop you off, Jimmy, but then Armin would have to drive. So we'd never get out of the parking lot. I can't win."

"Ozzie, give it a rest," Dom growled. "It's just nerves, Jimmy. Nothing's going to happen to you. I promised your cousin Renn. Start the car and drive."

Taking one helluva deep breath, Jimmy put the Ford into drive and took the first right, crossing Burnside, the street dividing Northwest and Southwest Portland, Jimmy drove one block, then stopped.

Roadblock. Two cops.

An officer approached the car. Jimmy rolled down his window.

"You need to turn around. The downtown blocks are closed."

"We're staying at the Expedition Hotel," Jimmy stammered, struggling to mask the rising fear in his voice.

"Not today or tomorrow, you're not. The president is coming to town. No vehicles allowed."

"President? What president?" Ozzie asked across Jimmy.

The officer crouched down. As he locked eyes with Ozzie and gave him a burrowing stare, Jimmy could feel his fingers unwillingly tightened on the steering wheel. "The United States president, moron. Now do a U-turn, and have a nice day."

Jimmy made the U-turn.

As if nothing happened, Dom said, "Jimmy, you live here. Where's another hotel?"

"With a pool," Ozzie added.

"I don't know. By the airport, I guess?"

"I got a better idea," Ozzie said. "If the president of these United States is coming, this town will be crawling with cops. We'd leave a paper trail if we check into a hotel now."

Dom leaned forward, intrigued. "Go on."

"Why don't we stay at Jimmy's?"

Jimmy thought he might throw up, pass out, or both.

Dom mulled it over, weighing his options. "Jimmy, take us to your place. We'll drop our things off, then see what's going on with this president's business."

"Do you have a big tub, Jimmy?" Ozzie asked. "I'm a soaker."

"No."

"Damn."

Armin held up his cell. "I've got it right here. President Cahill will attend a memorial tomorrow for Beemer's kid. It's going to be at the water park on the river."

"Waterfront Park. Not water park," Jimmy said.

"We just got lucky," Ozzie said, turning with a grin to Dom. "Kelley will be there. One hundred percent."

THE DISTANCE FROM THE winery to the hill was close to a mile. At the bottom sat a red pickup truck. It had to be Cherry's, which meant there was a road leading back to the villa.

Hiking up the switchback, the higher he climbed, the more Garris could see how much property Coleman owned. Besides the villa and the winery, there were three other smaller production facilities similar to the one he had toured earlier. He noted they were strategically located to service a different quadrant of the vineyard.

Reaching the communications tower at the plateau, Garris spotted a dirt road and understood why Coleman had the smirk on his face. Garris had to laugh, acknowledging he could have driven the Gator up, bypassing the climb.

Their backs to Garris, Cherry and Parks continued tinkering with a drone. Two others sat on the ground next to their controllers. They were identical to the one he had encountered at the ranch.

Partially hidden in the knee-high brown grass, Hawkins lay prone, his nose facing north, toward the villa. Though the rifle was out of view, Garris caught a glimpse of its distinctive Leupold scope, a scope Garris knew fit nicely on a McMillan TAC-50 long-range sniper rifle.

"If you ask me, that's a little overkill for pigeons."

"I wasn't expecting you so soon," Cherry said.

Connecting the dots faster than Cherry predicted, Garris asked, "Does the Secret Service know what you're doing?"

"They have their job. We have ours. Plenty of real estate for everyone. Besides, they'll be clearing out tomorrow after the president makes his appearance. But we need to be ready for the next day."

"Protecting rich winemakers."

"That's right," Cherry said. "Now form up everyone." He kicked Hawkins's boot. "You, too. Leave your toy and stand up."

Cherry pulled out his cell and opened a document. "This is mostly for your benefit," he told Garris. "Parks and Hawkins know the basics, but with the president's visit, I might make one or two adjustments. Twenty-five vintners from all over the world will be on the premises the day after tomorrow. The combined worth of these winemakers is way over a billion dollars. A meeting of such magnitude, with so many vintner tycoons, is unprecedented. It's up to us to provide protection. We watch them like hawks. Coleman wants them to feel at home, but doesn't want them walking away with any trade secrets. Here are the assignments. Diane will be inside the winery. We'll post the Beluga outside, in the garden area. Maybe he won't look so threatening in an open space. Parks, you'll operate the drones, providing surveillance from above, and Hawkins knows his assignment." With a grin, Cherry turned to Garris. "You're the pony show, Kelley. Coleman wants to show what his money can buy. You'll mingle with the guests. Tell tall stories and whatever else Coleman tells you to do."

"I can't wait," Parks said. "To see the infamous CIA boy being Coleman's arm candy. Now that's worth getting popped in the nose."

"Why wait?" Garris said, then popped Parks in the schnoz. Backhanded. Not hard, but just enough to get his attention. He was there. It seemed like the right thing to do.

"Damn it!" Parks said, holding his nose and sniffing loudly.

"Enough," Cherry said. "You'll be fine, Gordon." Cherry threw Garris a look. "Just leave him alone, okay?"

Garris shrugged. "You're the boss."

Cherry turned to Hawkins. "A few of our out-of-town guests were supposed to arrive tomorrow and spend the night. That can't happen now. Secret Service won't permit them on the property. So we've asked a few local winemakers if they'd like to open their doors."

"What's your assignment?" Garris interrupted.

"I'll be roaming. Handling things we didn't foresee," Cherry said. "Okay, that's it for now. Garris, you can go back to the villa. Gordon and Bob. Pack it up."

BACK AT THE BOTTOM, Garris took time to peek in the bed of Cherry's truck. Nothing suspicious. Then he checked out the dirt road. As he thought, it led to the villa. But it also forked and curved to the right, in the opposite direction.

In no hurry to go back to chit-chat with Coleman, he climbed into the Gator and followed the road, discovering it wrapped around the hill to another vineyard. Olive had said Coleman owned seven in the area. Each grew a different variety of grapes.

He kept going on the road. It took five minutes to pass the last row, and then opened to a grassy field. On the far side of the barbed wire, he recognized the country road he had driven to get to the villa.

Eventually, he reached a cattle gate made of steel pipe. No one would have suspected the land behind the gate was part of Coleman's empire. Good to know. Garris spun the cart around and headed back. Parking the Gator at the outbuilding in the same spot, he followed the path leading to the villa.

The party planners had added ten tables to the garden's permanent picnic tables to prepare for the two upcoming events. A stocky woman with short, red-rooster hair was waving her phone, directing an assistant to go to the van for the tablecloths. As he approached, Garris waved hello, crossed the lawn, and took the steps up to the terrace. He looked over at the garden layout. It was all coming together nicely. The event planner knew her business.

Stepping into the villa, Garris saw no one: no agents, no employees, and no sign of Coleman. Having the place to himself, he started to roam.

"Would you like a glass of wine?" It was the woman from the ranch—the woman with the horse.

"I'd take a coffee if you have a pot on."

"In the kitchen. Follow me."

The kitchen was modern, Italian-themed to match the rest of the villa, with all sorts of appliances Garris never considered having in his hangar. A heavy-gauge rack hung above a granite island counter, with copper and stainless-steel pots and pans hanging from hooks. Stainless-steel knives filled heavy wooden blocks. Not one, but three stainless steel refrigerators, and wall-to-wall glass cupboards.

"Take a seat," she said, tossing her hat, then went to work on a fancy espresso machine.

Garris pulled up a stool. "That's a nice-looking horse," he said. "The one I saw you with yesterday."

"Do you know horses?"

"Just enough to know yours is a palomino, and palomino is a coat color, not a breed. Many people get that wrong," he said with a smile. "We haven't met. I'm Garris Kelley."

"Yes, I know. I am informed of who comes and goes," she said, setting a hot cup in front of him. "I'm Ella."

"Thank you, Ella. And for the dinner last night and breakfast."

"You are most welcome."

She had piqued his interest from the moment he first saw her at the ranch. "If you don't mind my asking, where do you fit into the Rudy Coleman machine?"

"Rudyard would say I'm his personal assistant."

The first box ticked. Olive had looked into Coleman's employees. No personal assistant matching Ella's description. So who was she?

"Then I'd punch him in the arm," she added with a smile. "Actually, I help him out from time to time. Sometimes at the ranch. Sometimes here. Whenever he needs help with parties and other things he has a hard time with. Rudyard is good at business, obviously. All you have to do is look around to know that's true. But, sometimes, he has so much going on in his head that it's hard for him to track day-to-day tasks. It's a friendship, Garris. We look after each other." She changed the subject. "Would you like something to eat? I'm baking pies, and I have one that just came out of the oven."

Garris inhaled, guessing the aroma. "Smells like boysenberry."

"Raspberry."

"My favorite."

She sliced a large piece and spun him a plate.

"Thank you." He took a large bite. "It seems quiet here except for the agents and the crew setting up for the party."

"Only essential personnel are allowed until it's decided if the president will attend tomorrow."

"So, that means you'll be here?"

Ella poured herself a glass of white wine and settled into a white farmhouse chair. "I'd like to be. Rudyard spoke to the Secret Service. They're thinking it over. Thus, the pies."

"A bribe?"

"Who doesn't like raspberry pie? It's a sad occasion, but it would be special to meet President Cahill."

"You think so?"

"Love him or hate him, he's still the president. What he does or does not do makes a difference in this world. I heard he wanted to meet you, and you turned him down."

"I went to a baseball game instead," Garris said, leaving it at that. "I was looking for Rudy. Is he around?"

"Rudyard will be back for dinner. He has a surprise for you and Gayle Wilson this evening."

"I don't like surprises."

"Then you've come to the wrong winery. He has one or two in store for you."

"I'll have a talk with him about that."

"Please don't. It would ruin everything."

"All right."

"You were friends with Lawrence Beemer," she said.

"We were co-workers for a short time."

"You were in the Marines together. The news reported you were shot, protecting him."

"Twice. Upper body."

"Really?" Fascinated, Ella's eyes widened. "If it's not a trouble, could I see?"

"My scars? Not the first time I've been asked. A bartender down in Austin said she'd buy me a round if she could take a gander. I told her they shot me twice. She popped two bottles and put them on the bar. One per bullet. That being said, it's hardly the thing to show over pie."

"Later, maybe?"

"Maybe. Depends on the beer, I suppose."

Ella took a sip to gather her thoughts. "Lawrence didn't have to be shot. It was so senseless."

"How do you mean? Like the wrong place, wrong time?"

"That too," she said, like she was going somewhere, but she changed her mind. She picked up her glass, set it in the sink, and left without another word.

CHAPTER 22

"THERE'S A COFFEE SHOP ON THE CORNER IF ANYONE'S INTERested," Armin said, closing the door to Jimmy's cramped apartment. He dropped a duffel bag next to the coffee table and took off his jacket.

Ozzie and Jimmy sat on the couch, playing a video game. Given the game was about a rogue assassin, Ozzie had an advantage.

At the kitchen table, Dom tapped away on Jimmy's laptop, searching for news related to Garris. "What did you find out?"

Walking past Dom to the fridge, Armin threw a couple of six-packs inside. "It's true. The president is coming." He picked up the duffle bag and dropped it on the table. "They are setting up a stage at the park's south end. They call it The Bowl. There's a bridge at the opposite end, the Hawthorne Bridge. The park has an esplanade that runs along the river. Across the river, there is a science museum. Very popular. It has a real submarine. You can go on it."

"Cool," Ozzie said.

Armin unzipped the duffel bag and pulled out a sleek new pistol. He set it on the table with the nose pointed away from Dom but toward the jerk on the couch. He continued. "You're allowed to walk around most of downtown. But as we already know, no vehicles. At least to the west.

The north will be the same since that's the direction the stage is facing. I don't know the situation south of the stage. They're expecting people to use the authorized buses and the transit train, an then walk to the park."

Without missing a beat, Ozzie chimed in. "Thank you for that excellent report."

"Did they catch the guy who shot the senator's kid?" Dom asked, belaying Armin's response.

"Not yet," Armin said.

"With all the cops, plus the Secret Service, how are we going to get to Kelley? Do we want to wait a few days and let things cool down?" Ozzie asked.

None of this conversation was going down easily for Jimmy. It was dangerous just knowing their names. Now, they were talking about killing someone. If they went through with it, killing Garris Kelley, he would be an accomplice to murder. Plus, the question of waiting until the president left town meant they would be sticking around for another two or three days. Jimmy set the video game controller down and went to the bathroom to see if he had anything to settle his nerves.

"Waiting's not an option. Edgar wants it handled now," Dom said.

"But we don't know where Kelley is," Armin said.

Jimmy came back and picked up his game controller.

"We don't know where Kelley is now, but we know where he'll be tomorrow," Ozzie said. "Kelley is tight with the senator's family. He'll be at the park."

"You haven't been paying attention," Armin said. "There's going to be a crowd to see the president. There's just the four of us. We can't cover every street."

FOUR of us? The words jolted Jimmy

"Why don't you stop with the games and try to help come up with a solution?" Armin said to Ozzie.

"Armin. You don't think I'm paying attention? It's you that's not listening. Open your ears. Kelley's been trending high this week. He won't be in the crowd. They'll make sure he's on stage with them." Ozzie paused the video game and slapped Jimmy on the thigh. "Whadda you think we should do, Jimmy?"

Dom could see Ozzie was on to something. He closed the lid to the laptop, giving Ozzie his full attention.

"What?" Jimmy asked.

"Simple question, Jimmy. You've been listening. Your three roommates have a problem. We need to take care of a guy. How should we proceed?"

Oh, crap! Jimmy realized what Ozzie was getting at. The answer was right in front of him. Lifting his index finger, Jimmy pointed to the TV screen. Ozzie had paused the video game on an image of the assassin. The assassin was on a bridge, aiming a sniper's rifle.

Dom got out of his chair.

"Armin," Ozzie said, delight in his voice. "You might get a second chance to redeem your royal screw up."

"No, no, no!" Jimmy said, shaking his head. "C'mon, guys. You can't be serious."

"Relax, Jimmy," Ozzie said. "Little known fact: Armin used to be in the military. An All-Star. Sniping's his thing. Isn't that right, Armin?"

"It's too risky," Dom said. "Come up with something else, Ozzie."

Ozzie waved him off. "No, it's not."

"Yes, it is!" Jimmy shouted.

"Shut up, Jimmy," Ozzie said. "You're demoted. Back to driver."

"But the cops will have the entire area surrounded," Jimmy argued. "It would be crazy!"

"Relax, Jimmy. We're not after the president," Ozzie said.

"I feel sick."

"Get away from me. Go to the bathroom," Ozzie ordered, then turned to Dom. "You said Edgar wants it done now. This is the way to go. We might not get another chance before Edgar thinks we can't finish the job. If that happens, then we're all dog food. And that goes for you too, Jimmy."

"I don't have a rifle," Armin said.

"Go get one," Dom's response was immediate. "I'll call Edgar."

"Jimmy," Armin said. "Grab your car keys."

"IT'S IMPORTANT TO MY family you're there," Beemer said over the phone.

Garris watched the agents watch the party planners in the garden while listening to Beemer try his hardest to convince him to be part of Lawrence's memorial.

Beemer tried a softer approach. "He thought of you as a very close friend."

"Bullshit, Frank. I saved his life. That doesn't make us golf buddies. Why are you doing this? This should be a private family matter. Not a campaign rally. Cahill put you up to this, right?"

"He's a good friend."

"Some friend."

"He's also your president."

"I voted for the other guy."

"He wants you there. You've captured America's attention."

"Bullshit again. America thinks I have it out for Cahill. A vendetta."

"Of course they do. Who do you think perpetuated that idea? Cahill, that's who. Now he wants to look magnanimous."

"You guys are pathetic."

"What can I say. It's politics."

Garris's cell buzzed. McCoy was trying to reach him. Before ending the call with Beemer, Garris gave him an answer. "Frank, if it's important to Meredith, I'll do it. But you're going to do something for me."

"Name it."

"The kid you were with in the hotel room, Dante Green. You know he's in the hospital. Same one as Lawrence."

"I heard that."

"But you didn't visit him."

"No. I suppose I should have."

"Yes. You should've. Here's what's going to happen. Dante gets moved, and not to just any room. I want him looking out at the city, breathing in the skyline. As far as medical attention, if Lawrence was getting the gold-standard care, Dante gets platinum. And you pay his bills. All of them. He was there to help you. You owe him."

"Consider it done."

Garris hung up, then answered McCoy's call. "General, sorry to keep you waiting." He turned back toward the winery.

"Nothing on television, but I heard on the radio Beemer's throwing a kumbaya barbecue for his son," McCoy said.

"Trust your radio. Shoot your TV. I just got off the phone with Frank."

"And Cahill? He's going to be there?"

"It was his idea, and I just agreed to be part of his dog-and-pony show."

"Which one are you, the dog or the pony?"

"The jackass."

"Are you being modest?"

"Like never before. It gets better. There's a private party at Coleman's winery afterward."

"And Cahill will be there campaigning."

"He hasn't committed, but it was also his idea."

"He sets the stage, then sits back and watches the dance. The man craves attention."

"I need to figure out Cherry's endgame and shut him down before things get rolling tomorrow."

"Do it, then come on back for a beer call. I've got a cold one in the cooler with your name on it."

"Did you just seriously say that?"

"Yeah, why?"

"Something Olive said just popped into my head. Never mind," Garris said with a trace of amusement in his voice, then shifted gears. "Cherry put on a show for me. He has drones and a guy who knows what he's doing with them. How 'bout you? Find anything?"

"I've got Andrew on his computer. Nothing yet."

"And Tommy?"

"He flew my drone into the trees. He's dealing with that."

"Okay. I'll be in touch."

"Roger that," McCoy said.

The door to the winery was unlocked. Though Coleman showed him around earlier, Garris had the time to take his own private tour. As his hand reached for the door, he heard footsteps; then Gayle came around the corner.

CHAPTER 23

YIN AND YANG. DIANE AND THE BELUGA.

Diane breezed up the hill. The Beluga stopped every ten feet to catch his breath.

With the drones packed for transport, Parks was digging a hole, as Bob Hawkins ate an apple, watching him. Cherry stood at the edge of the plateau, texting. Diane nodded to Frick and Frack, then went over and joined him.

"Give him another five minutes," Diane said, updating Cherry on the Beluga's ETA. "If he stops to smoke, we'll need to get a wheelbarrow."

"Let him take his time," Cherry said, putting his phone away. "Tell me about the Fed."

"At first, she was uptight. But the moment she got the text from Boyle, she loosened up. I think, given a chance, Gayle would have been a wonderful agent. Beneath her tough facade, she's friendly, thoughtful, a good listener, and she's definitely had excellent interrogation training. She's determined to find her partner."

"Did she say anything about Kelley?"

"Every time I brought up his name, she changed the subject. But he's here to help her find Boyle. And she thinks he's cute."

"Seriously?"

"Don't be jealous. She's entitled to her own opinion. I think you're cute, Cherry on top."

"Stop it."

"Make me." She smiled her oft-repeated invitation.

Finished with the hole, Parks tossed the shovel. Hawkins threw his apple core into the good-sized hole.

"Did Kelley see the drones?" Diane asked.

"He did. The rifle, too. He's primed for tomorrow."

"The same with Gayle. Since she's heard from Boyle, she should be interested when I suggest we get together."

"She'll be more than interested," Cherry said. "She'll insist. I just sent her another text from Boyle's phone. It turns out he wants to see both of you."

"Good."

"I'm not going to ask what you have in mind for her."

"Don't. Let it be a surprise."

There was no need for the wheelbarrow. The Beluga had never smoked a day in his life. Though, by the time he reached the top, he was drenched with sweat.

"You all right?" Cherry asked.

The Beluga took off his windbreaker, but he kept his cowboy hat, which he had grown fond of. He rested his hands on his knees.

"Catch your breath. Then come over here," Cherry said.

Showing signs of impatience, Diane left Cherry at the ledge, conveying that Bruce Gillman had enough time.

"Nice view, isn't it?" Cherry said. "The way the sun's hitting all the rows of grapes."

"I like clouds," the Beluga said.

"Who doesn't? Tell me about the drive with Gayle."

"What about it?"

"How did it go?

"What do you mean? It was a drive. We're here. End of story."

"What did you talk about?"

"We didn't talk."

"Three hours in a car, and you didn't have a chinwag?"

"She's not much of a talker."

"She's the FBI. They're always asking questions."

"Not her."

"How about you? You're a detective. You must have been curious about what she knew about her friend Boyle."

"I used to be a detective. The answer is still no. Boyle never came up."

"Okay. Just thought I'd ask. You know, maybe Gayle had little to say to you, but she and Diane talked up a storm."

"I'm so happy for them I could cry."

"Diane got the impression that Gayle thinks we were in Portland and not in Pendleton the day the MAX was hit."

"She's entitled to her own opinion."

"True. The thing is, I trust her judgment."

"If the Fed said something to that effect, she was probably fishing. And if she knows more, she didn't get it from me."

"I want to believe you. Because we went to great lengths not to leave any evidence linking us to the incident."

"I don't know what you're talking about. You told me you were going to Pendleton. If you went somewhere else, I wasn't told. And I don't care. Are we done with this conversation?"

"Yes, I think we are," Cherry said, then gave Diane a wink.

Diane was all business. She believed the key to her profession was choosing the right tool for the job and not getting sold on just one. This was a different scenario than Lawrence Beemer. She had other tools to choose from.

The Beluga had his back to Diane, listening to Cherry, standing close to the edge of the cliff.

She had her pistol, the SIG Sauer. That was not an option with the

Secret Service on the property. They were probably out of hearing distance, but why take a risk? She had asked Parks to bring a shovel. One with a specific size and shape. A thirty-nine-inch, round-point bronze shovel with the edge sharpened. She considered using it, but she reconsidered after sizing up the mountain of a man with a skull as hard as a bowling ball. Ultimately, she chose the Sheffield Fairbairn-Sykes dagger. With its thin six-inch blade and only weighing seven ounces, it was a British Special Air Service favorite and fit perfectly in her palm.

With one fluid motion, Diane made eye contact with Cherry and lunged toward the Beluga, at the same time winding her right arm like a major league baseball pitcher. With a flick of her wrist, she came up, under, and over and launched the dagger, the Beluga's nape being the bullseye.

Cherry's expression tipped him off. Something was coming from behind. The Beluga ducked left, but, being a slow creature, Diane jabbed the dagger into the back of the Beluga's neck, two inches in, four inches still out. All was not lost. He gave her an elbow, sending her flying before she could drive the blade into his brain. He reached for his pistol, but he had left it in the pocket of his windbreaker.

Sometimes, it's necessary to change horses in the middle of the stream. Diane picked up her second tool, the shovel with the razor-thin edge.

Reaching behind his neck, the Beluga yanked free the dagger.

Yin and yang. Shovel and blade.

With Parks, Hawkins, and Cherry rooting for Diane from the cheap seats, the Beluga understood there was no happy ending in his future. The obvious move was to charge Diane. Then, if he were lucky, he would grab the shovel. But even if he did, he would still have to deal with the other three. At the end of the day, he knew he was a goner. So why bother with Diane? This was all Cherry's doing. Cherry had not moved from his position. He stood four feet from the ledge, his hands down. No weapon.

A standoff. Ten feet apart. Diane waited for the Beluga to make his move.

A master of misdirection, the Beluga glared at Hawkins, flames shooting from his eyeballs, then grinned at Parks and tossed him his black Stetson. As expected, all eyes followed the hat. Using that diversion, the Beluga charged Cherry.

Cherry was seconds away from either being stabbed, catapulted off the hilltop, or crushed.

If only the Beluga would have moved as quickly as he had at the gas station when he needed to visit the toilet. But no. Adrenaline pumping like never before, Diane caught up with him. With both hands wrapped around the shovel's handle like a baseball bat, she swung for the bleachers. The shovel's sharp edge penetrated the Beluga's meaty neck. But only an inch. It was bad, but it could have been much worse. He dropped the dagger, reached up, and gave the shovel a tug. The blood gushed out in an arc, and he tipped over like a bull. Dust clouds burst beneath his body.

"Get him in the hole," Cherry ordered.

Bob Hawkins swore he would never, ever, ever mess with Diane.

CHAPTER 24

"HAVE YOU BEEN INSIDE?" GARRIS ASKED GAYLE, POKING HIS nose in the production facility.

"Yesterday," Gayle answered. "But I've only seen the vineyard from a distance. Let's take a walk."

"How about a drive?"

"Another convertible?"

"Close to it."

Guiding her to the equipment shed, she slipped on her sunglasses and hopped in the Gator. It worked for her. She could do no wrong.

They had planted rows of grapes north to south to get the most sun. With all rows looking the same, Garris started in the direction he had taken earlier, leading to the southern hill. With luck, he would bump into Cherry or the crew and surprise them.

"We have some catching up to do. I'll go first," Gayle said. "Last night, Diane insisted we stay up and have a glass of wine by the fireplace. We'd already spent most of the day together, and I got the feeling she was running out of things to say. I had the feeling she was trying to keep me busy and distract me. It was late, and I thought we were the only ones up. But then I spotted Bruce Gillman lurking in the corridor.

Eavesdropping. Two glasses later, I called it a night and went to my room. Have you been to yours yet?"

"No."

"Great bed. The pillow was to die for."

"Good to know. I usually sleep with my gun under the pillow."

"Really?"

"That information is on a need-to-know basis."

"It wouldn't take much to find out."

"Probably not."

"Okay." She paused, filing that information. "So listen. Not a minute passes, and I get a tap on the door. It's Bruce, asking to come in. We'd spent hours driving, and the guy hardly said a word until we stopped for gas. Something happened at the gas station. I can't put my finger on it, but he changed. I got a whole different vibe from him for the rest of the trip. He was still quiet, but he seemed friendlier. Now he shows up at my door, insisting we talk. He starts by saying Ron was a pretty good guy. Remember that Bruce drove him around Traughber City?"

Garris nodded.

"He said the day before the MAX shooting, Cherry, Parks, and Hawkins went to Pendleton. Cherry told Bruce he wasn't needed, so he would stay to keep an eye on Coleman's ranch. They'd be back in a few days. Bruce was suspicious. Pendleton is only a few hours away from Traughber City, a day trip. This happened the same day Ron went off the grid. He didn't say it, but I think Bruce was trying to tell me Cherry and the guys went to Portland, not Pendleton. My instincts tell me maybe Ron didn't go to Salem. Maybe he followed Cherry to Portland. If I'm right, Ron might have evidence connecting Cherry to what happened on the MAX. I hope to find out tomorrow."

"Say again?"

"I sent Ron a text letting him know I was here. He texted back and said we can meet tomorrow."

"That's good. But why hasn't he called you?"

"He's deep undercover, can't risk it. But don't you see the twist? We thought you'd help me find him. And now he might help you nail the MAX shooter. If you still think it's Cherry."

"I know it's Cherry," Garris said. "I want to talk with Bruce."

"So do I. Have you seen him?"

"Cherry, Parks, and Hawkins are up on that hill. Bruce wasn't with them."

"What're they up to?"

"They brought the drones from Traughber City. They made it a point to show them to me. And they've got themselves a sniper rifle."

"You saw a sniper rifle?"

"Only the scope. It's like a hood ornament on a McMillan TAC-50. Cherry's no stranger when it comes to sniper cells. And he knows I know that."

"Garris. The president is coming here tomorrow. We need to shut Cherry down now. We need to inform the Secret Service," Gayle said with urgency.

"Not yet. Whether he's still an op or not, Cherry will have a rock-solid alibi going back for the last two years. And that goes for his men. The drones and the rifle will be legal. He'll have all the licenses, permits, and paperwork to justify his security job for Coleman. As far as the law is concerned, he's clean. There's nothing to shut down, at least for now."

"Yet you're positive he's the shooter."

Garris stopped the cart. "We have three scenarios. One, Cherry didn't do it. He's legitimately working for Coleman and wants me around for the wine party."

Gayle gave him a skeptical look. "You don't believe that."

"Not for a second. But for some reason, it's crucial to him I'm here. He seems to think Coleman is a philanthropist with a vision. Maybe he thinks I might share that dream with him."

"Did he indicate what it was?"

"No."

"Scenario two?"

"Two, Cherry's freelancing and this all has something to do with Frank Beemer. Maybe he's out to finish the job he botched on the MAX."

"Do you believe that?"

"It's possible. But not likely. He's taking too long, risking too much by delaying."

"Agreed."

"Three. He's working for the Agency and it could have something to do with Coleman's wine party. Coleman said vintners from around the world are expected. International winemakers. It's plausible that one of them is the intended target."

"A sanctioned hit. A foreigner on US soil?"

"It sounds bad the way you say it."

"It is bad."

"Right. Maybe it's not a hit. It could be surveillance. We need to see who's on the guest list and go from there."

"There could be a fourth scenario," Gayle said.

"President Cahill," Garris agreed. "I've been thinking about that. But how could they have ever predicted he would come to Portland?"

"We're going in circles."

"He wants me at the memorial."

"Who?"

"He got Frank to try to persuade me to attend. I've agreed."

"Why on earth would you do that?"

"As long as Dante Green's in the hospital, Frank will treat him like his own son. We'll leave it at that."

"Garris, Cahill has to know the cartel is in town searching for you."

"He knows."

"You'll be an easy target."

"That's right."

"He really doesn't like you."

"Never got a Christmas card from the man."

Suddenly, Ella appeared from around a post. "Dinner's in an hour."

"Thank you, Ella."

Expressing no desire to be social, Ella left without saying another word.

"She doesn't say much. I'm trying to figure out her connection to Coleman," Garris said. "Has she talked with you?"

"Very little. She's Coleman's business partner."

"Is that what she told you?"

"Not in so many words."

"She said she was a friend who helps from time to time. But I think it's more than that."

"I'll see if I can get further with her," Gayle said. "By the way, not to change the subject, but you never told me how you nailed Hector Trevano."

"That's yesterday's news."

"It could be tomorrow's if you step one foot on that stage."

CHAPTER 25

SHOWING GARRIS TO HIS ROOM, GAYLE SUGGESTED THEY meet in twenty minutes to have dinner together.

His overnight bag was at the foot of the bed. In addition to his clothes, Garris had stowed an extra gun inside. His Colt 45 revolver. He checked to see if the Secret Service or anyone else had confiscated it. It was still there.

Taking out a clean polo shirt and his sports coat, he tossed them on the chair. Then, because it was there and seemed like the right thing to do, he lay down on the bed. Gayle was correct. It was comfy. If things were going his way, the shower would be as nice as the one in the Clock Tower suite. It was. He was on a roll.

Eighteen minutes later, he knocked on Gayle's door, two minutes to spare.

Wearing a tailored dark-blue suit and burgundy blouse with a string of pearls, she had no need of her Italian shades. She was striking.

She hooked her arm through his as they strolled down the hall, passing through the tasting room to the outside terrace, where two glasses of Pinot Noir awaited them. As did Rudyard Coleman.

"Good evening," Coleman said. "Please take a moment to enjoy the view. The sunsets are nothing short of magical."

The terrace and garden had transformed into a visceral delight. The meticulous party planners had placed exquisite flower arrangements on every table. Dozens and dozens of white candles outlined the terrace's perimeter. Lanterns hung throughout the grounds. Four additional wine bars were strategically placed to ensure that no glass remained empty. To add a touch of refined elegance, strings and strings of twinkling lights ran along the tops of rows in the vineyard, turning the evening magical.

"This is beautiful, Rudyard," Gayle said. "I feel like I'm in Italy."

"Thank you for saying so. It was serendipitous that we were already preparing for the vintner's conference. Lawrence's celebration of life was so last minute. I hope this will be suitable for the family."

Though Garris enjoyed the view, he had more pressing matters he could not ignore. "Earlier, there were six Secret Service agents milling about," he said. "I don't see them now."

"Less than an hour ago, I was informed that the president's schedule has changed. Though hosting the senator's family was President Cahill's idea, it's now unlikely he will attend. He hasn't officially cancelled, but as a courtesy, they forewarned me not to get my hopes up. Consequently, most of his agents have been deployed to Portland, where they are more urgently needed. Two are still here if the president changes his mind at the last minute. Which they tell me, he often does."

"Where's Cherry, Parks, and Bruce Gillman," Garris asked. "They're not joining us?"

"At my ranch, I invited you to dinner, but it evolved into a business meeting. This is my way of making it up to you. No business tonight for anyone. That includes Cherry and his men."

"I have some questions, and I'd like to go over a few details," Garris said.

"Now look who's turning dinner into business?" Coleman chuckled. "Maybe I can fill in the blanks. I'll keep it brief. I spoke with Senator Beemer's liaison. Because you're this week's hero, you've earned the distinction of becoming President Cahill's new best friend. Congratulations. He wants you on the stage and insists you sit beside him. On his left.

The First Lady, Helen, will be on his right. The senator will be seated alongside his daughter, Liz, and Lawrence's wife, Meredith, on the other side of the stage. And, as they are coming to my winery, they have invited me to join them at the event. Not onstage, of course, but backstage. I'll get to meet the president. I'm hoping to—"

"—taking a selfie with him for your wall of fame," Garris interjected with a smile, cutting through the layers of diplomacy.

"True. You got me there. Celebrity photos equal booming sales," Coleman said. "This neatly brings me to my next point. You'll not only be the senator's special guest, but since you are still working for me, you'll also act as my personal bodyguard. I want you near me."

"You don't need a bodyguard tomorrow. Security will be more than sufficient."

"Of course, I don't *need* you, Garris. The sooner you accept your new normal, the better off you'll be. Consider yourself a photo-op. Being seen with you is a treasure trove of free publicity."

"Do you want a selfie too?" Garris asked Gayle.

Gayle chuckled. "You need to smile more."

"I'm a work in progress."

Garris shrugged.

Coleman turned his attention to Gayle. "Diane informed me you've heard from Agent Boyle. You must be relieved."

"A text. I'll feel better when I see him."

"When will that be?"

"Tomorrow afternoon."

Coleman raised an eyebrow. "Oh? But I thought you'd be here. You're on the list, attending with Garris as his special guest."

Gayle smiled at Garris. "Am I your special guest?"

"Affirmative."

She smiled, then turned back to Coleman. "I'll make sure I'm back in time."

Coleman nodded.

"I'd like to see the guest list for the wine party," Garris said, shifting the conversation back to business.

"Vintners party," Coleman corrected him. "Tomorrow, after the Beemers leave, Cherry will go over everything you need to know."

"That's fine, but I'd still like to see the list. Tonight."

"No reason why not. I'll have it sent to your room."

The clack, clack, clacking of rolling wheels came from the kitchen.

"That would be dinner," Coleman said. "Garris, I have a surprise for you."

The terrace doors swung open to reveal a dinner cart pushed by none other than celebrity chef Marty Moore.

"Garris, I believe you've met Marty Moore," Coleman said.

"I have. Hello again, Marty. How're the grandkids?"

"Isn't this a coincidence?" Marty said.

"I love surprises," Coleman said. "Marty flew in from San Francisco to make the vintner conference special. Now he's also preparing his distinct dishes for the senator and possibly the president."

"It will be another feather in my hat," Marty said.

"And a photo for your restaurant's Wall of Fame," Garris added.

"You know it!"

"I think we've covered enough ground for tonight," Coleman said. "Marty and I will leave the two of you to enjoy the rest of your evening."

Dinner featured Gulf shrimp Saltimbocca with preserved lemon vinaigrette, lobster mushrooms, kabocha squash, and caramelized onions from Walla Walla, Washington. The candle-lit dinner on the terrace was everything Coleman promised it would be. For the rest of the evening, they would keep their weapons holstered and put on the back burner their reasons for being there.

After dinner, they strolled through the luminous vineyard to walk off their meal. Then they backtracked through the garden to the terrace, through the tasting room, leading them to the corridor to their respective rooms.

Garris accompanied Gayle to her door. "I was going to look at the guest list," he said, "but would you like to come to my room and join me for a nightcap first?"

"That's a long way to walk," Gayle said. She stuck in her key and opened her door, then peeked inside. "Oh my, would you look at that? There's a bottle in here."

Garris followed Gayle inside, and because it was there and it was the right thing to do, he closed the door.

THE MATTRESS WAS EXCEPTIONAL, and the sheets were made from organic bamboo. It was, without a doubt, the best night's sleep Garris had had in months.

Following a long, almost-hypnotic shower, he slipped his sports coat over his dress shirt. After checking his Beretta holstered to his side, he headed to the kitchen, hoping to find a pot of coffee. Ella had expected his need and had a cup waiting for him.

"How would you like your eggs?" she inquired, putting a skillet on the stovetop.

"Any way is fine with me." Garris pulled up a stool to the counter. "Thanks."

"You're going to have a busy day," Ella said. "Best to start on a full stomach."

"Agreed."

"Have you seen Gayle this morning?" Garris asked.

"In passing. She and Diane left an hour ago. Diane said they'll be back before the party."

"I haven't met her yet."

"Who?"

"Diane."

"That surprises me."

"Why?"

"I don't know. She works with Mr. Mackey. I assumed you would have met her by now."

"I'm making it a point to see her when they return."

"Would you mind if I ask you a question?"

"Please don't say you'd like a selfie with me."

"A selfie?" Ella smiled and shook her head. "No, thank you."

"Then, ask away."

"You'll be seeing President Cahill this afternoon."

"Maybe. Last I heard, he canceled."

"I'm planning on him showing up."

"Okay. What's your question, Ella?"

"He's been throwing you under the bus on social media. He says by not accepting his invitation to the White House, you've disrespected the office of the presidency."

"Let me guess. You want to know why I stood him up?"

"Was it really because you went to a baseball game?"

"The Hillsboro Hops were on a winning streak."

"Did they win?"

"It wasn't even close."

Ella offered an apologetic smile. "Sorry."

"Don't be. It's baseball."

"Some people will be there today hoping to see you and him go at each other," Ella said.

"It's a free country."

"Aren't you upset he revealed your identity and what you did to Hector Trevano? Now you'll always be looking over your shoulder."

Garris adopted a philosophical tone. "When it's your time to go, it's your time to go. I'm not sweating the details."

"Sometimes, I wish more than anything that the president would go," Ella said.

"I was referring to getting shot in the head, Ella."

"So was I."

"If that's a joke, be careful, Ella," Garris warned. "Two special agents are still on the property."

"They're outside on the terrace," Ella said. "But, you're right. I apologize. That was an awful thing to say. Sometimes, I have a hard time keeping my emotions in check and my mouth shut. Besides, I'm a bit of a hypocrite. Regardless of what I just said, I'm like the others. I'd like the chance to see him. Like him or not, he's still a president."

Garris appreciated her honesty. "Promise you won't shoot him if he shows?"

Ella chuckled. "Him? No. I take back what I said. That was me being stupid."

Checking his watch, Garris changed the subject. "I'd like to take a walk before I leave. Would you care to join me? We could talk horses."

"I have a few things to do. Thank you."

"For what?" Garris asked, puzzled.

"For helping Rudyard. You're going to make today even more special."

CHAPTER 26

"I HAVE CONDUCTED A THOROUGH ANALYSIS OF THE HAWthorne Bridge," Armin reported.

Jimmy closed the door behind them and then handed Dom a coffee, setting Ozzie's on the kitchen table.

"Jimmy, what are you doing? Bring me my coffee," Ozzie demanded, doing push-ups in front of the flat screen.

"The bridge seems like the ideal location to take the shot," Armin said. "However, the cops will probably anticipate that and close it off. But do not worry. All is not lost. The park is the size of a couple of football fields. There could be thousands who show up. The police have blocked off the downtown streets. Only foot traffic is allowed."

"Is that good for us?" Dom asked.

"For maximum impact, I would wait until Kelley is standing next to the president. But if it doesn't look like he will, I'll pop him when he's close to the senator. The key is to get him while he's on his feet so the crowd will see him drop. They'll be terrified and scatter, causing confusion and chaos. The Secret Service and the cops will have their hands full, thinking someone shot the president."

"Making our getaway easier," Dom said.

"Correct. An Armageddon scenario," Armin agreed.

"But if the bridge is out of the question, where's your alternate firing position?" Dom asked again.

"Jimmy found the perfect place," Armin said, giving credit to Jimmy.

"No, I didn't! No, I didn't," Jimmy said. "Guys, please, I don't want to be involved. I'm only a driver. But honestly, it won't matter if you shoot Garris or not. The police will think President Cahill was your target."

"You got it, Jimmy. Which means we won't be suspects," Ozzie said. "Armin knows how to stage these things."

"Thank you, Ozzie."

"No prob, Armin. I call it as I see it."

"I don't follow your reasoning," Jimmy said.

"You're the driver, Jimmy. You don't get a reason," Ozzie said.

"Where are you taking the shot from, Armin?" Dom asked, refocusing the conversation.

"The buildings, hotels, and the bridge sandwich the park on three sides, and it is on the river. The cops have patrol boats in the water. But the cops have left themselves wide open. Across the river on the east side is the freeway. About a mile up, north of the park, under the freeway, is a warehouse district. Most of the buildings are abandoned, no one around but the zombie druggies. There is one building high enough that I can get a clear shot at the stage. That is, of course, if Kelley shows up. We are assuming he will. But we could be wrong, and then we are wasting time."

"I'll call Edgar back," Dom said. "He might not like this idea. Start working on a Plan B."

"I'll come up with something," Ozzie said. "Turn on the TV, Jimmy, and let's play a game so I can think."

"WHAT ARE THE CHANCES? Garris asked.

Special Agent Riggins was on the terrace, sipping his coffee. "That he'll show? Honestly, Kelley, it's anybody's guess. Words out this morning, the president wants to make Portland a quick trip, then we'll move on to San Francisco. There's some fancy Italian restaurant in North Beach. He can't shut up about it. But we never know. He keeps us on our toes. That's why I'm here."

"Just the two of you on the premises. You guys used to travel with an army."

"We still do most of the time. It's not something we advertise, but these days, like other agencies and departments, we've had to cut corners. But we keep the myth alive."

"So if the president makes a cameo, the world stays in the dark, convinced he's up in the stratosphere on Air Force One?"

"You like to put jigsaw puzzles together?"

"He isn't coming, is he?"

"Do you want me to lie to you?"

"If it's a good one."

Changing the tempo, Riggins took the offensive. "And what about you? What's your story? With all your recent escapades, a winery in Oregon is the last place I'd imagine bumping into you. And that goes for the FBI agent, Ms. Wilson. Why is she here? Is there something going on I should know about?"

"Riggins, do yourself a favor. Tell your agents to be sharp today."

Without missing a beat, Riggins said. "We're always sharp, Kelley."

"Then be razor-sharp."

Leaving Riggins to enjoy his coffee, Garris double-timed it to Cherry's truck, hoping to search the truck and find a clue. But he was too late.

Cherry sat behind the steering wheel. Knee-deep in the truck's bed, Gordon Parks had a drone case flipped open. Bob Hawkins sat on the tailgate, wiping down a rifle.

"Good morning," Garris said.

Caught off guard, Cherry got out of the truck. Sensing the change in atmosphere, Parks closed the drone case. Hawkins continued wiping the rifle.

"I thought we'd go over the details for tomorrow," Garris said.

"Plans are changing. We're repositioning to the tower. The teams have been asked to lie low. They'll be there until after Cahill is off the property."

"What about you?" Garris asked Cherry.

"I'm the exception. Being head of security, I'll be at the villa, once I get these guys going."

"I don't see the big fella? Bruce Gillman."

"The Beluga. He's already planted himself up there," Hawkins chuckled.

"I have some questions I'd like to ask him."

"Like what?" Parks asked.

"You're welcome to join us," Cherry interrupted.

"It can wait."

"We'll talk about the vintner's party later tonight. Coleman gave you the guest list. That should get you started."

"I looked it over last night."

"Did anyone interest you?"

"Nope."

CHAPTER 27

AIR FORCE ONE, PRESIDENT CAHILL'S OFFICE IN THE SKY, landed on time at the Portland Air Base. After cutting the engines outside the hangar, the Secret Service ushered the governor, the mayor, and a handful of other dignitaries to greet the leader of the free world.

First, Cahill's staff filed out of the aircraft's rear exit. Then the left front exit door opened and sixty-eight-year-old President Paul Cahill and his wife, First Lady Helen Cahill, appeared. Hand in hand, they descended the airstair.

Abandoning her husband at the limousine with his politicos, Helen immediately walked over to say hello to the crowd who had waited hours behind the security barricade to see her.

Helen Cahill was a beloved figure among the public, admired for her stark contrast to her husband's controversial and eccentric personality. No one loved her more than Paul Cahill himself. He had fallen for her on their first date in college, the night he famously nicknamed her Lightning Bug. Busy visiting veteran and children's hospitals, low-income neighborhoods, and food shelters, Helen was constantly on the go, helping those most in need. Her energy was relentless, and her compassion was profound. Admirably, she never held back from saying what was on her mind. Her word was truth.

The Secret Service made her aware that she had run out of time to shake hands, take selfies, and sign autographs, so she promised the crowd she would return to Portland soon. Almost to the limousine, she stopped and went back, seeking out a young girl who had caught her eye. The girl held a handful of tulips to give the First Lady.

Politely asking the crowd to give the girl space, Hellen motioned her to come forward. "Are those for me?" Helen asked.

"Uh-huh."

"They're so beautiful. Did you know tulips are my favorite?"

"Yes."

"Will you tell me your name?"

"Violet Rivera."

"It's nice to meet you, Violet. Have you been waiting a long time?"

"Forever."

"I'm sorry I took so long."

"Oh, it's okay. I wanted to see you, really bad. Mom says you help kids like me."

Helen scanned the crowd. "Is your mother here?"

"She wanted to come, but she had to work. She has two jobs. My brother, Aaron, brought me."

"That was so nice of him," Helen said, smiling at Violet's older brother.

"I think your scarf is pretty."

"You do?"

Bashfully, Violet nodded.

"Thank you for the pretty tulips, Violet." Helen took off the scarf and wrapped it around Violet's shoulders.

Violet's eyes lit with delight.

The limousine door opened, and the crowd cheered and called for Cahill to pop his head out and say a few words. He did not appear.

Smelling the tulips, Helen gave one last wave, then slid into the limo.

"They love you," Cahill said. "If I get reelected, it will be because of you."

"You bet your sweet ass it will."

With the freeways closed, the motorcade crossed over the river and into downtown Portland in less than half the time it would have taken Jimmy Jimenez.

BEEMER OFFERED BARANSKI SOMETHING to eat, anything off the room service menu. Baranski declined.

Beemer had taken a liking to the dedicated sergeant. They had survived danger together. Promising he would keep Beemer safe, Baranski had not left the senator's side since.

Lawrence's widow and Beemer's daughter, both dressed in black, sat on the sofa nursing glasses of wine, grumbling about Cahill turning Lawrence's death into a circus sideshow.

Baranski's cell chimed. The President was on his way up.

Seeing how the Cahill Show was about to begin, Liz topped off their glasses.

Two agents entered the suite first. The agent in charge asked everyone, including Baranski, to remain seated while they conducted a routine security sweep. The room was clear.

Ten minutes later, the same agent announced the president and First Lady were in the corridor. Then, he asked the senator if he would like to open the door to greet them.

"It's wonderful to see you, Helen. Thank you for coming," Beemer said.

Helen kissed his cheek and said, "I'm so sorry, Frank. If there's anything I can do, you let me know."

"Thank you, Helen. Just seeing you is enough."

"Frank." Cahill palmed Beemer's right shoulder. "Lawrence was a great guy. Truly one of a kind. A winner in every way. That's why I'm here. To salute your son. An American hero cut down in the prime of his life. It's a dirty, rotten shame."

Glancing sideways at Meredith, Liz rolled her eyes and took a drink.

"We'll track him down, Frank," Cahill vowed. "I've instructed the FBI to add more agents. We're going to find the guy who's responsible. And he's going to pay."

"Come and say hello," Beemer said.

"Is the mini-bar open?" Cahill asked.

"Paul, mind your manners," Helen laughed. "Say hello to the ladies."

"Of course. Good afternoon, ladies."

While Cahill offered his condolences to Meredith, Helen started chatting with Liz.

When it was Liz's turn to speak with Cahill, she hesitated, not knowing where to start. The Paul Cahill she had known since childhood would have never capitalized on her brother's death. Or maybe he would have, and she was simply naive.

"You want to say something to me, Liz? Now's your chance," Cahill said, "Best not to keep emotions bottled inside. It will tear you up if you do. It will give you ulcers."

Liz kept her mouth shut.

"Let me get you started," Cahill continued. "You're upset because I asked. No, I demanded your father hold a public ceremony. This was all me. So, don't blame your father. He's a good man. Let me explain. This is an election year. Your father, he's in like Flynn. Oregon loves Frank. Me, not so much. Some do, most don't. I don't understand this state. What with the unemployment rate, the environment, and my unpopular stance on guns, I have to take every opportunity to be seen favorably, or I could lose the election."

"You're using my dead brother."

"Politics is messy. I'm a career politician. Frank is a career politician. And your brother Lawrence was about to join the club."

"What do you mean?" Liz asked.

"You look surprised. Your brother and father had a plan for his future. When Frank stepped down, Lawrence would have stepped into his shoes. I thought it was a terrific idea. He would have approved today's actions, I guarantee it."

"It's true, Liz," Meredith said. "Lawrence told me about it. It was his idea to take the MAX so the public could see him and Frank doing something regular people would do."

"Unbelievable. This is my brother we're talking about. I'm not going. I won't have any part of this."

"Do I have to make a presidential order?" Cahill chuckled.

"This isn't a joke, Paul," Beemer said.

"It's an hour, Liz. Not the end of the world," Helen said. "You'll get through it. Then we'll all go to the winery for a drink."

"Uh, no, Lightning Bug," Cahill said. "Something urgent came up. We're flying to San Francisco right afterward."

"Paul, the party was your idea," Beemer said. "Rudyard Coleman is a great fundraiser of mine. The man practically moved mountains to set up the event on short notice."

"Things change, I'm afraid. You know it's all part of being the president. The big boss. Coleman will understand. I'll send him a gift from the Oval Office. Maybe a signed photo?"

"Sure, he'll understand. But you'll be missing out. He's hired Chef Marty Moore."

Cahill blinked. "Marty Moore? The same Marty Moore from Maison de Prawn in San Francisco?"

"Do you know another?"

"He makes the best *faux filet au poivre*, flambeed in cognac. He's a winning chef. My favorite."

Waving a Secret Service agent over, Cahill whispered into his ear. The agent nodded, then stepped out of the room.

Cahill smiled, a glimmer of excitement in his eyes. "Celebrating

Lawrence's life at Rudyard Coleman's winery is a splendid idea. I'm told Garris Kelley is working for Coleman, so he'll be there too."

"Yes, and at the memorial," Beemer said.

"Well, he better show up this time. I want him on the stage with me, Frank. And I want him to introduce me," Cahill said. "People will love it."

Watching Cahill's shenanigans, Liz just shook her head, disgust visible in every line of her body. "Are the Hops playing today?" she asked no one in particular.

CHAPTER 28

POLICE SHUT DOWN SEVERAL MAJOR STREETS. THEY ENCOURaged those attending to take MAX, the bus, or bike. For those who could not do so, limited parking was restricted to five designated lots.

Four blocks south of the park, Garris backed his Jeep into a space beside a red Ford Escape.

Sitting behind the wheel, alone, the driver had his window rolled down. He stared at Garris.

"How's it going?" Garris greeted him.

"You're him, right? Kelley? I can't believe it. You're standing like, right in front of me."

"What's your name?"

"Jimmy."

"Would you like to walk with me to the park?"

"Me? No. Thanks. But, no. I can't. I have to stay with the car."

"Why?"

"I'm a hired driver. I'm working. I've got to wait with the car in case they come back."

"So you're just going to stay in the car? Could be a long wait. The president's not known for his Haiku poetry."

"Yes, sir. But it's a job, and somebody has to do it."

"Okay. You have a nice day, Jimmy." Garris nodded before weaving around the other cars to the park.

For a second, Jimmy thought he would call Dom and tell him who he had just bumped into. But there was not a chance in hell he would do it. He had nothing against Garris Kelley. Besides, Dom still had his cellphone.

THEY HAD CONSTRUCTED A stage at the south end of the park, the same stage used for outdoor music concerts, with space enough for an entire symphony.

Cutting his way through the growing crowd, Garris attracted the attention of a few fans, who asked to pose for selfies. Largely, they were die-hard supporters of both President Cahill and the senator, there to offer sympathy and support to the Beemer family.

But it was not just sympathizers who occupied the scene. With the recent controversy that President Cahill had intentionally compromised Garris Kelley's identity, some hoped to see sparks fly when the two met that day. There was also the inevitable presence of protesters, who carried anti-Cahill signs and dressed in anti-Cahill shirts and hats. Among the issues they rejected were soaring taxes, skyrocketing unemployment, government spending, and gun control. With mass shootings on the rise, more Oregonians supported stricter gun reform. This would never happen if Cahill had a say, and that cast a dark cloud over Beemer's sunny legacy, being Cahill's golfing buddy.

A special agent swiftly moved in on Garris, gesturing for him to follow her backstage.

Three courtesy tents were available where special guests, including news crews, could mingle under the watchful eye of the Secret Service.

Beemer at the grazing table with Liz. A discreet distance away, on Beemer's left, a vigilant Baranski surveyed the scene.

"Garris," Beemer said, welcoming him with a firm handshake, "thank you for coming. Knowing you'd prefer the shadows to being in the spotlight, this means a lot to me, and the whole family. I know you'd probably rather be anywhere but here."

"Like at a baseball game," Liz said, then kissed Garris on the cheek.

"Lawrence chose honor over privilege. Being a senator's son, he didn't have to wear the uniform but volunteered to do so. I'm happy to be here."

"You might change your mind about that after you hear what I'm about to tell you," Beemer said.

"Go on."

"We both know the game being played today."

"The game you've allowed Cahill to use Lawrence's death as a campaign chip. Yeah, I'm aware."

"I'm not crazy about this either, Garris, but this is where we're at."

"Wrong. I'm not here for Cahill or you. I'm here for Lawrence. But since we're being frank, let's not forget Dante Green. You agreed to pay his medical bills and whatever else he requires."

"Yeah, yeah. Done and done."

"Give me the bad news."

Knowing what was coming, Liz chuckled, an evil undertone evident in the laughter.

"Apparently, because your identity has been compromised and your involvement regarding Trevano has made you a nightly news sweetheart, not to mention coming to my rescue, you've been tracking high. You know Cahill is all about social media. Can't keep him away from it. He believes the war between you two has been a stroke of luck, and it's time to bury the hatchet."

"I have no war with Cahill."

"I know that, but the way he's been framing it, his supporters think you do. And given your reputation, some think you'd kill him if you had the chance."

"Where's this heading, Frank?"

"Cahill wants you beside him on stage."

"What else?"

"When it comes time for the president to give the eulogy, he wants you to introduce him."

"Is that all?"

"That's all."

"Fine by me."

Beemer looked skeptical. "Really? I'm surprised you're taking it so well."

"I can stand in front of a few thousand people with a microphone and say anything I want about Cahill? Count me in."

"Damn it, Garris. Just play ball."

"Dad," Liz said, "give us a minute."

"Don't make this harder than it has to be, Garris," Beemer said before marching off.

Liz leaned in and whispered in Garris's ear. "How long did you think you could hide it? I saw the look in your eyes at the hotel. You're tracking Lawrence's killer. Don't deny it."

Garris reluctantly nodded, confirming her suspicions. "I might be on to something."

Liz exhaled a mixture of anger and hope. "I knew it. Tell me."

"This isn't the time or the place."

"Enough of the bullshit, Garris. Talk to me."

"I'm convinced the man behind Lawrence's death wasn't a homeless veteran. That's why the police haven't found him. It has the marks of a professional job."

"Wait a minute. You sound like you have someone in mind."

"Maybe."

"Then why haven't you done anything? What's the holdup?"

"It's not that simple. I could deal with the assassin now, but I'm sure he's planning something bigger than the MAX. And he has a crew. An elite group of contractors. This means if I move on him now, I might get him, but not the others before it's too late. It's a risk, but I need to wait until I find out more."

"What could be bigger than killing my brother? A senator's son."

"Drop the ego, Liz. You need to trust me. If I'm on the right track, I'll get your guy soon enough. I promise."

"Ah! There you are," Rudyard Coleman said, speeding over in a huff. "We were supposed to arrive together."

"Rudy. Mind your manners," Garris said. "Say hello to Liz Beemer."

Coleman quickly regained his composure. "Excuse me, Ms. Beemer. We met a few months ago at a fundraiser."

"Yes, at your winery."

"I was just about to tell Liz about your party tomorrow," Garris said.

Liz homed in on the conversation.

"Rudy is hosting the world's most notable winemakers."

"Vintners," Coleman corrected.

"Sounds like my kind of party," Liz said.

"It would be my pleasure for you to attend," Coleman said, seizing the opportunity.

"I don't think that's a good idea," Garris said.

"Don't be ridiculous, Garris," Liz said, smiling at Coleman. "Thank you, Rudyard. It would be a welcomed diversion. I would be delighted to attend. In fact, would you mind if I brought a date? I'm sure Lawrence's widow, Meredith, would welcome the distraction."

"Splendid," Coleman said. "I will invite her right now."

As Coleman strutted off with an extra spring in his step, Liz turned to Garris. "Jesus. What's his story?"

"Later. This campaign rally is about to start. I'd like to look around."

"I'll see you out there. I can't wait to hear your introduction." She winked.

The stage had a strategic design: Two staircases, one on each side. One exclusively for the president and First Lady, the other for everyone else.

As Garris moved to ascend the stage, two Secret Service agents asked to see his credentials. He had nothing to show but his smile. One agent talked into his coat sleeve. The other listened to his earpiece, then he gave Garris the okay.

Hidden behind the curtain, Garris widened a slit in the curtain to check the stage arrangement. To his left, stage left, seats were marked for Meredith Beemer, Liz Beemer, the Governor, the Mayor, and three notable dignitaries. Stage right had seats for President Cahill, Helen Cahill, Senator Beemer, and Garris Kelley.

Looking out, Garris noted that the crowd had doubled, blending Cahill and Beemer supporters with vocal protesters chanting and making noise.

A blinding flash of light hit Garris in the eyes. Instinctively, he hit the floor. Though probably nothing, it put him on high alert. He knew Trevano's men were dangerous and had nothing to lose, and with the president and First Lady in attendance, the stakes were unusually high.

As he scanned the area, the Hawthorne Bridge immediately caught his attention. A sniper's dream. There should have been a slew of police up there. But he saw only three. Why not more? It made no sense. The threat upon his life from Trevano was one thing, but the danger to Cahill, the president of the United States, was on another level. At an outdoor venue, it was impossible to cover all the bases. Garris trained his eyes for other glaring holes in security. Plenty of blue uniforms marked the perimeter. Good. A commercial security company checked handbags and patted down spectators before they entered the park. Also good. But across the street from the park, to his left, nearby hotel rooftops posed a significant risk, as they, too, had a clear line of sight to the stage.

His eyes darted to the potential threats on his right. The river, dotted with patrol boats, seemed secure. But parallel across the river he saw the multiple lanes I-5, the interstate freeway always crowded and frequently stalled with traffic. It would take work, but an experienced sniper could jump out of his car, take the easy shot, and be on his way in seconds, barring traffic. Best option would be a motorcycle, but any vehicle would work.

Further north, underneath the interstate overpass, stood a cluster of warehouses and office buildings, their rooftops offering a vantage point too tempting for a sniper to ignore. Garris shook his head in frustration. Waterfront Park was a terrific location for an evening listening to the symphony play Beethoven, but it was the worst possible place for the president's safety. He needed to relay his concerns to the Secret Service to make sure they understood the gravity of the situation. Suddenly, like a New Year's parade, a convoy headed for the park, led by eight police motorcycles, followed by ten black SUVs and two limousines. They turned onto the grass: the president had arrived.

In a choreographed maneuver, four motorcycles broke off and streamed ahead. Skirting around the crowd, the vehicles took a hard right at the river. Six SUVs fanned out. And threading the needle, the president's limo shot forward and disappeared behind the stage.

On the fly, Garris devised a plan to discreetly communicate his observations and concerns to the Secret Service without causing panic.

The plan changed on a dime.

In a sea of faces, a flash of red, slightly left of center, caught Garris's predatory eye—the unmistakable shade of Gordon Park's trucker cap. Why? Parks was supposed to be on the hilltop, watching the villa. Did this mean Cherry was in the crowd? He scanned the mass of bodies pressing toward the stage.

There!

Sporting sunglasses and a Cahill for President T-shirt, Cherry Mackey stood just in front of the stage, and intentionally made eye contact with Garris. He gave a thumbs up. Cherry and Parks meant that the others were there, too. Where was Hawkins? The last time Garris had seen him, Hawkins was on his belly peering through a high-powered scope. A sniper scope.

Cold realization hit Garris. Coleman's vintner party was simply misdirection. The real game was now unfolding.

Garris pushed aside consideration of Parks. The spectacle of Parks operating the drone back at the ranch had been a red herring. It was Hawkins who was the real threat. If he were Hawkins, where would he set up for the shot? Garris looked at the Hawthorne Bridge, relieved to see beefed up security.

Garris replayed the scene from the hill: Hawkins flat on his stomach, practicing with a sniper rifle. Hawkins planned to take the shot in prone position, not standing. On a rooftop. Looking left, Garris scrutinized the two office buildings and a hotel. Lowering his gaze back to the crowd, Garris searched for Parks and Cherry. They were gone.

The ceremony was about to begin. No time left. Garris had to inform the Secret Service.

Almost cinematically, as Garris flew down the steps stage left, President Cahill and the First Lady were ascending stage right—on a parallel path.

Taking center stage to a roar of applause and cheers, Helen Cahill gave an appreciative wave. Then, taking Meredith Beemer's hand, she raised both hands in a sign of united support.

Amid the cheering, President Cahill leaned into Beemer's ear. "Where'd Kelley vanish to? Where is he, Frank?"

Liz piped up. "Has anyone checked the baseball schedule?"

"Not the time, Liz," Beemer said.

"You gave your word he'd introduce me," Cahill said. "He's playing games, trying to undermine me."

"Don't lose focus, Paul. Wave to your voters. This is what you wanted," Beemer said. "Enjoy your moment."

"OKAY. WE'LL SEE YOU there." Diane slipped her cellphone into her pocket. "After this, we'll go pick up the Beluga."

Sitting behind the wheel of her rental car, parked behind a grocery store, Gayle gazed at her phone. Once again, Ron Boyle had not met them as arranged.

"It's been an hour. How much more time do you want to give him?" Diane asked.

"Let me text him and let him know we're leaving."

"I wouldn't worry. He's working undercover and probably has a good reason."

Gayle sent another text, then turned on the ignition. "Where to?"

"Back to the villa."

Running different scenarios regarding Ron, Gayle took a breath and told herself to focus on the present.

On the country road, a couple of miles before Coleman's winery, Diane instructed Gayle to pull over at the cattle gate on the left.

Diane got out and opened it, then told Gayle to follow the dirt road. It would lead to the top of a hill where the Beluga would meet them.

Gayle parked in front of the equipment shed. "It looks like we beat him," she said.

"He'll be here soon. You should see the view from here, Gayle. You'll love it."

Gayle hesitated. Something was off. Diane's enthusiasm felt forced, too intense to be genuine. It was probably nothing, but before getting out of the car, Gayle followed her instincts. She slid her hand inside her jacket, put her hand on her pistol, and swept the safety to Off.

"Come see for yourself," Diane said, waving Gayle to join her at the hill's ledge.

From up high, the view of Coleman's endless vineyard was a sight. Each row of vines had been meticulously aligned, painting a stunning image that blended nature and design.

Believing that the key to her profession was choosing the right tool for the job, Diana followed one commandments: Don't get sold on just one. Be professional. Bring a minimum of three tools, not counting her bare hands.

"Come look, Gayle."

CHAPTER 29

THE SECRET SERVICE TOOK GARRIS SERIOUSLY. HIS REPUTATION preceded him. But moving the president to safety required undeniable proof. They thanked him, then told him they knew their jobs and were confident they had things under control. Garris disagreed but had no time to quibble. He would take matters into his own hands.

As Governor Felita Baas stepped behind the podium, Garris calculated a timeline. He estimated she would speak for five minutes. Liz would do the same. Meredith, being Lawrence's widow, might go a little longer. Beemer, always the politician, would definitely take at least ten.

After the assault on the MAX, many believed Beemer was taking a risk, but Garris was all in: It was Cahill who was in danger. There was no time to second-guess himself. Channeling Hawkins's mindset, Garris concluded that the most opportune time to strike would coincide with the president's opening remarks. That would cause chaos, giving him an advantage. Garris's objective was clear: He had to find Cherry. He was the boss and had the ultimate veto.

Joining the audience, Garris saw things at ground level and began to flesh-out the scenario. Cherry had strategically positioned himself, and with Parks wearing his signature cap, they had planted themselves in the crowd to grab Garris's attention. That accomplished, they had slipped away, leaving Hawkins alone. The pieces were falling into place, but Garris sensed he was being set up.

The governor wrapped up her speech and introduced Liz. Garris had little time left to find Hawkins. If Hawkins had positioned himself on the east side of the river, there was nothing Garris could do about it. That narrowed the possibilities for action to the Hawthorne Bridge or the cluster of buildings across the street. He took another look at the bridge and saw even more blue uniforms, a good sign that the Secret Service might have come around to his way of thinking.

Following the "what would I do" strategy, he narrowed his focus to the two office buildings and the hotel. He factored their proximity, height, and line of sight to the stage to determine which structure Hawkins would most likely choose to take the kill shot and give him the best scenario to make his getaway. Not an easy choice, Garris went with his gut. Hawkins had to be on the hotel's rooftop.

Darting through the crowd, Garris listened to Liz talk about her family spending time on their sailboat harbored at the dock in Portland when she and Lawrence were young. Then, drawing to an end, she told the story about Lawrence's time as a soldier in Afghanistan and how Garris Kelley had saved her brother during an ambush. She called out to Garris, asking him to wave and be recognized. He did not.

As Garris neared the hotel's lobby, he heard Frank Beemer's voice echo from the loudspeakers. It seemed that Meredith had declined to speak, throwing off Garris's timeline.

Garris assessed the hotel had close to twenty floors. Reaching the rooftop would eat up precious time. And he needed a key card to access it. Leveraging his newfound celebrity status, he approached the woman working the front desk.

"Take a good look at my face and tell me you know who I am," he said, almost willing the recognition into existence.

"Are you with the baseball team staying with us?"

"I wish, but no," Garris said. "I'm with the president's security. I need to get to the roof."

Eyes wide, she stammered, "I-I'd better call my supervisor. The door to the roof is locked." She grabbed the phone.

Garris checked his watch.

The manager recognized him. Immediately handing over a master key, she pointed him to the service elevator.

Elevator. Luckily, the hotel only had seventeen floors. As the doors closed, he checked his Beretta. He got out on the fourteenth floor, then bounded up the stairs, stopping at the door leading the roof. He swiped the key card. The door buzzed loudly, undoubtedly alarming Hawkins.

To his left, air-conditioning units, a couple of plastic chairs, and an ashtray. If his intuition were correct, Hawkins would be positioned at the far north end of the building, with his rifle resting on the ledge, or maybe on a tripod, pointing southeast, aimed at Cahill.

Garris formulated his plan: He'd confront Hawkins, with only a split-second to reason with him or fatally neutralize him before he could unleash the kill shot. The dynamic would change entirely if Cherry, Parks, and the Beluga had joined Hawkins.

Garris raised his Beretta and whipped around the corner.

Nobody.

Without hesitation, he hurried to the ledge to check the other rooftops. Nobody on them, either.

Garris called Liz to warn her. She sneaked a peek at her phone and let it go to voicemail.

Backed into a corner, he knew there was nothing he could do but try to pinpoint where Hawkins's shot would come from.

Five minutes passed. Cahill was now speaking about the long friendship he had with the Beemer family.

Ten minutes. Cahill asked Lawrence's wife, Meredith, to say a few words. Again, she declined. Fifteen minutes. Cahill still spoke, still breathed. What was Hawkins waiting for?

Helen Cahill joined her husband at the podium, and the crowd ate it up.

The president waved his last goodbye and left the stage. In less than a minute, the motorcade left the park and merged onto the interstate, heading southbound toward Coleman's winery.

He had gotten it all wrong. Whatever Cherry was up to, the president was not involved, and Garris was back to square one.

As he reached for his cell to call Gayle, he heard a chirp. Not his phone. One at the north corner of the building. His mind raced. Was he right, after all? Could it be that Hawkins had been on the rooftop and called off his mission at the last minute, leaving the phone behind in haste?

He answered the call.

"Garris, how's the view?" Parks.

"Where's Hawkins? Why are you here and not at the winery?"

"Let's just say there was a last-minute change of plan."

"Why wasn't I informed?"

"Below your pay grade, pal. But I'm sure Hawkins will be glad you found his phone." As though nothing out of the ordinary was happening, Parks added, "Oh, and a little heads up. Cahill is pissed."

"Not interested," Garris said, his patience growing thin.

"I'm telling you, anyway," Parks persisted, intent on delivering the bad news. "Your job was to act like his best buddy in the whole world. Now, Colemans' popped his cork. You've embarrassed him. Again."

"What doesn't kill you only makes you stronger."

"Yeah, well, you tell him that. He wants you back at the winery. Pronto."

"Let me talk to Cherry."

"Not possible. The president is on his way. Cherry's orders are to drive to the gas station, the one by Coleman's. We'll meet you there. You'll follow us back to the villa."

"I know my way. I don't need to follow."

"They want us to use another gate. One you don't know about."

It had to be the old gate on the backside of the hill, which Garris did know about. "I'll meet you at Colemans."

"No, dumbass. Meet us at the gas station, like I said. And don't forget Hawkins's phone. He'll want it back." The connection went dead.

Back at ground level, Garris fell in line with a steady stream of people leaving the park. A couple of guys recognized him but resisted asking for anything more than a handshake. Once he entered the parking lot, Garris spotted the red Ford was still occupying the same space.

"Hey, Jimmy."

"I'm glad to see you again," Jimmy said, stepping out of the car. The kid was rattled.

"Yeah, why's that?" Garris asked.

"I need to tell you something. I should have told you before."

"I'm listening."

"You're the guy. The Hector Trevano thing."

"Some say I am."

Nervously, Jimmy looked around, all over the place, except at Garris. "Well, the guys that hired me. The ones I'm waiting for. They're here looking for you."

"I'm guessing it's not because they want a selfie."

"What? No. That's not it."

"Yeah, I figured, Jimmy."

"Edgar Trevano sent them."

"Go on."

"What else can I say? They can be here any second now."

"How many?"

"Three. You should get out of here before they come back."

"It's okay, Jimmy. I have a little time."

"How come you're not scared?"

"Single digits, Jimmy. Nothing to be worried about. What do they look like?"

"Oh, man, oh, man, oh, man!"

"Breathe, Jimmy. Calm down. They're after me, not you. What do they look like?"

"The boss, his name is Dom. He's a regular-looking guy. Dark hair. My size. He looks like a manager for a software company, or something, and he has an accent. Then there's Ozzie, the freakshow. He's a gym rat but he doesn't look like a rat. He looks like a bug. Huge eyeballs that look ready to pop out. He talks all the time. Won't shut up."

"And the last one?"

"Armin. He's a big guy, just like you. He's easy to spot because his jaw is messed up. Like someone beat him up."

"I did. I met him at the hospital."

"That's right. He said that," Jimmy said. "I think he said he was in the army or something. They made it sound like he could shoot you from a mile away."

"From under the freeway. North."

"Yeah. That's right. How did you know that?"

"That's where I would have done it. So why didn't he go through with it?"

"At the last minute, Edgar Trevano said he didn't want the headache it would cause if they were caught. The cops would think they were trying to kill the president and all hell would collapse on them at the first shot. That's what I told them yesterday, but they didn't listen to me. But instead of doing nothing, they figured they'd take a chance they'd find you walking around, like you're doing. You need to get out of here."

"Where do you fit in, Jimmy?"

"Me? I'm just a driver. I don't do nothing but drive. I'm a delivery service. I don't want to be part of it no more. I want out. But they won't let me. Not as long as Edgar Trevano is alive—if you get what I'm saying."

Garris took a moment to think. "How about you help me out, Jimmy?"

"No, please. They'll kill me."

"Nothing ventured, nothing gained," Garris said.

"No, please. No."

"Let me finish, Jimmy."

"What!"

"I only want you to text me if I need a heads up. That's it."

"I don't have a cell phone. Dom took it."

Taking out Hawkins's phone, Garris punched in his number and handed it over. "Don't answer the phone. Don't make any calls. Only texts. Only to me. Got it?"

Jimmy nodded.

"Okay. I need to get going."

"Good."

Garris got into the Jeep, drove to the parking lot's exit, and waited for traffic to clear before pulling onto the street.

"Get your ass in the car, now!" Ozzie called out.

Jimmy cocked his head and saw Dom, Ozzie, and Armin rushing to the Ford.

"I said, get in the car!" Ozzie jumped into the front seat.

"Follow the Jeep," Dom said. "You lose him, you die."

"Do you know who you were talking to?" Ozzie asked.

Jimmy shook his head.

"What were you talking about?" Dom asked.

"Nothing."

"Nothing?" Ozzie repeated. "Nothing?"

"He just asked how to get to the bridge. That's all."

"Garris Kelly," Armin said. "That's who you were talking to."

"Really? No way!"

"You should have called me," Dom said.

"I don't have a phone. You took it."

GARRIS TOOK A SHARP left turn, another left, then merged onto the interstate, southbound.

Jimmy's Ford followed right behind him.

CHAPTER 30

FIVE MILES TO GO. GARRIS'S PHONE CHIRPED. "OLIVE."

"The president has just arrived at Coleman's."

"I'm almost there."

"The MAX transit train forensics report just landed on my desk. You'd better sit down."

"I'm driving."

"Pull over."

"No can do."

"Have it your way. The FBI agent, Gayle Wilson. She was looking for her partner, Ron Boyle."

"Right."

"She can stop."

"Go on."

"The male victim standing next to Beemer was Ron Boyle."

"Wait. You sure? Gayle's been getting texts from him. She went to meet him today."

"DNA doesn't lie, Garris. Somebody has his phone."

"She's in trouble."

"There's more. Bruce Gillman."

"The Beluga. Go on."

"He's a detective."

"I was told he was a former cop."

"Not former. He's still on the payroll. He must have brought his investigation to Ron Boyle."

"How do you figure?"

"Gillman and Boyle were roommates in college."

TEN CARS BEHIND GARRIS, Jimmy put on a show for his passengers, driving like he was keeping on Garris's tail discreetly, but in reality, switching lanes constantly, trying to warn Garris he was being followed. Ozzie had his head down, toying with his pistol, not paying attention to the road.

All was going smoothly until the cell phone in Jimmy's pocket chirped, shattering the ruse.

Dom glared at Jimmy in the rearview mirror. Armin leaned forward.

"Answer the phone you don't have," Ozzie said.

Garris had told him not to.

"Do it," Dom ordered.

Jimmy pulled out the phone, praying Garris wouldn't say anything that would give him away. "Hello."

"Who the hell is this?" Parks, the caller on the other end snapped.

"I don't know?" Jimmy said.

"What do you mean, you don't know? Who am I talking to?"

"Jimmy."

"I want to hear," Ozzie said. "Put it on speaker."

Jimmy did so.

"Where did you get this phone?" Parks asked.

Jimmy lost his ability to speak.

Ozzie jabbed the nose of his pistol into Jimmy's ribcage. "Answer him."

"I found it. It was on the ground. By the car," Jimmy said, trying to sound casual. "Finder's keepers, right?"

"Bullshit. Put Garris on."

"Garris Kelley?" Armin said from the backseat.

Ozzie snatched at the phone. "Whadda you know about Kelley?"

"Who's this?"

"Shut up and answer my question."

"Moron," Parks shot back, "I can't do both."

Ozzie rolled down his window and chucked the phone.

"Did Garris give you the phone?" Dom asked. "Tell me the truth, Jimmy."

"No. Like I said, I found it in the parking lot, by the front tire."

"If you're lying, you're dying," Ozzie threatened.

The likelihood of his death loomed once more. Jimmy realized he knew too much, and his ass would be trash once they had finished with Garris. He needed a way out. But for now, Jimmy thought he was lucky they had not tried calling the number Garris had added to the phone.

GLANCING IN THE REARVIEW mirror, Garris got it. The cell phone was too dangerous, so Jimmy was improvising, changing lanes every so often to grab his attention. Clever.

The Trevano crew was closing in. He would have to deal with them eventually, but first, he had Cherry on his plate while, at the same time, finding Gayle. The two were linked. Gayle was with Diane. Diane worked with Cherry. Playing along with Cherry was his best chance to find Gayle.

Cherry's truck was waiting at the propane refill station, engine running, Parks in the driver's seat. Cherry had the window down with his arm hanging out. He waved Garris over.

Jumping into the Jeep, Cherry signaled Parks to go.

"Tail him," Cherry told Garris.

Dom had Jimmy pull over across the street from the gas station. They watched one guy get into Garris's vehicle. Armin pointed out the guy looked like a bald version of Garris and had the swagger of an operative or ex-military.

Dom shrugged him off; they had Garris in their sights, and if anyone got in their way, there was an easy solution.

Dom had Jimmy follow Garris, maintaining a safe distance.

The same sprawling farmland and vineyards. The same tranquil country road. Garris was right: They were heading to the backside of the hill on Coleman's property.

"The Secret Service has the main entrance blocked. We'll use another route," Cherry said.

Garris had an inkling of where that might be.

"You didn't seem too surprised to see us downtown," Cherry said, probing Garris's frame of mind.

"Why would I? It was open to the public," Garris said indifferently.

"Just thought you would be surprised, or at least curious."

Pushing to unravel Cherry's game, Garris asked. "Why was Hawkins on the roof?"

"You can ask him yourself," Cherry teased. "Before we go back to the villa, we need to swing by the tower. He's up there waiting for us."

As they neared the old sign, Cherry directed Garris to pull over, then got out and opened the cattle gate to allow Garris to drive through. Stopping just past the gate, Garris glanced in the rearview mirror. Cherry closed the gate but deliberately left it unlocked.

While navigating the hill's steep incline, Garris discovered there was more than just the one road, with several routes cutting through the vineyard to the villa. Reaching the ridge, Parks waved Garris to pull in beside a black sedan by the equipment shed. Garris recognized Gayle's rental.

Hawkins stood with a woman near the cliff's edge, her back to Garris.

Sensing Garris's presence, Hawkins paused and nodded, then continued his conversation.

"Come on," Cherry said, "I'll introduce you to Diane."

When she turned, Garris recognized her instantly. The blonde woman on the MAX—who had seemingly played a role in saving Lawrence Beemer.

After kissing Cherry's cheek, Diane gave Garris a coy half-wave.

"Where's Gayle?" Garris asked.

"She didn't call you? She's on her way to meet Ron."

She better not be.

Hawkins and Diane stepped away from the ledge, revealing a yoga mat spread on the ground. Not for a second did he think Hawkins was attending a yoga retreat.

Gazing past the vineyard, Garris saw Coleman's villa, where Beemer's party was in full swing. It was too far to make out the details but close enough to see what was happening. All at once, seeing the president and First Lady strolling through the garden, the puzzle pieces fell into place. He knew what Cherry had been planning all along. His aim was to assassinate the president, not at the waterfront park but at Coleman's villa. Far less security, and instant getaway.

Ron Boyle popped into Garris's mind. The FBI agent had also been deceived, and it had cost him. Teamed up with undercover cop Bruce Gillman, Boyle believed they had infiltrated a militia, ignorant of the fact that Cherry, Hawkins, Parks, and Diane were a seasoned assassination crew. Discovering that Boyle was a Fed, they had devised a lethal trap to ensnare him on the MAX. He never saw it coming.

"Congratulations, Garris, I see you figured it out," Cherry said, his voice dripping smug satisfaction. "You couldn't have shown up at a better time. We've been planning this operation for months, and just when we were about to call it off, you showed up, rescuing the senator, giving us the best-case scenario. Thanks for that."

"Senator Beemer and Boyle were decoys. It was Lawrence all along."

"I won't say yes. I won't say no. But tell me, could you devise a better way to lure the president to Portland?"

"If you murdered the son of Cahill's best friend, then he would come to pay his respects," Garris said. "Good plan. What made you so sure it would work?"

"It's an election year. How could Cahill resist the publicity?"

Garris nodded, acknowledging the logic. "So what happened? Why didn't Hawkins take the shot from the rooftop?"

"That would have worked, too. We planned for alternative scenarios because we didn't know which location Cahill would choose. But it had to be one of five in the metro area, with Waterfront Park being the best, but still not great. Hawkins spent months preparing to take the shot from the hotel, not knowing you'd enter the picture. When President Cahill heard you signed on, he organized the party at Rudyard's winery. We thought we hit a gold mine because that's a much better location for what we have in mind. But yesterday, he changed his mind, so it was back to Plan A. Then, minutes before he took the stage, Cahill changed his mind again. Coleman said it had something to do with Chef Marty Moore. And … here we are."

"So Coleman's involved."

"Who do you think is funding us? We support his cause to some extent, but we damn sure don't work for free." Cherry's voice trailed off when Parks burst out laughing. "Parks. Stop what you're doing and come over. Everyone, gather around."

Concealing his Glock 18 behind his back, Parks positioned himself behind Garris.

"Okay. We're all here," Cherry said. "You know your assignments. Now it's time to execute them, pun intended. What we do today will shake this country to the core, but it will also save future lives. You are not mercenaries. You are patriots. This country will never know your names. You will never get the credit you deserve. But you will know the truth whenever you hear Garris Kelley's name. You can be proud, knowing that it was you. Any questions?"

Parks, Hawkins, and Diane shook their heads.

"I might have one or two," Garris said.

"I'm sure you do." Cherry grinned, as though they were sharing a joke. "But though your role is significant, it needs no preparation. No explanation is needed. Just be you. We'll do the rest. You're gonna to be famous, Garris."

"Haven't you been keeping up? I'm already famous."

Parks whipped his pistol around and aimed it at Garris. "Sit down and enjoy the show, dumbass."

"Thanks, but I'll stand."

"Suit yourself. You'll be lying dead soon enough."

"Sorry you won't be around to see it."

"Enough," Cherry said, turning away and heading toward the shed where a dirt bike sat ready. He mounted the bike and continued, "It's time to warm up the audience." Glancing at his watch, he said, "Hawkins, you have fifteen minutes."

On the yoga mat, tinkering with his rifle and scope, Hawkins gave him a thumbs-up.

Diane glided over to Cherry and kissed him. "See you soon, Cherry on top."

"IF WE'RE VOTING. I vote we do this," Ozzie said.

Jimmy had pulled over to the side of the road, reasonably sure they were out of sight. They had watched Garris stop at the gate. The bald guy got out and opened it and they drove up the hill. A few minutes later, the bald guy had come back, alone, riding a dirt bike. Out of the gate, he took a left. But if he had come their way, Ozzie said he might have stopped him to find out what was what.

After waiting another five minutes, Ozzie grumbled. "Time's ticking. What are we waiting for? Let's go up there and get Kelley."

"This is not a democracy," Armin cautioned. "Dom's the boss. We go when he says we go."

"Edgar is my boss," Ozzie said.

"Look around, Ozzie," Dom said. "What do you see?"

"Nothing. I don't see jack out here."

"Exactly. You're not in the city, Ozzie. Different rules than what you are used to. This could be an ambush. We don't know what's beyond that fence or who or how many."

"If we are voting, I vote no," Jimmy cut in.

"It's not a democracy, Jimmy," Ozzie said, brushing off Jimmy's concerns. "So shut your face."

They fell into a prolonged silence. Then, with deliberate calmness, Dom said, "Get your guns."

Armin, well-prepared as always, reached over the backseat and made his selection. Then, taking Garris's advice, he took off his eel-skin jacket, because style costs.

"Drive, Jimmy," Dom said.

"Crap!" Jimmy said, anxiety creeping into his voice.

They had nearly reached the gate when a shiny Black SUV with black-tinted windows raced toward them, head-on, forcing Jimmy to slam on his brakes.

A standoff. Neither vehicle made a move. The vehicles squared off, engines idling.

"What do I do?" Jimmy asked.

"Armin?" Dom said. "Care to weigh in?"

Armin said, "It's an SUV. Not a tank."

"What the hell is that supposed to mean?" Jimmy's voice shook with fear.

The SUV's doors flew open. Two solid, impeccably dressed men in dark suits, sunglasses, and earpieces jumped out, tactically using their doors as cover.

"Feds," Ozzie said. "What's the Secret Service doing out here?"

"Armin?" Dom said. "Care to weigh in?"

"Doesn't change a thing. It's an SUV. Not a tank."

"Really, guys?" Jimmy pleaded. "C'mon. Can't we just turn around and get the heck outta here?"

"They'd come after us, Jimmy," Armin said.

"Yeah. Listen to Armin, Jimmy," Ozzie chimed in. "Retreating's not an option. Everything's going to be fine. They follow the rules. All that college training, shooting stereotypical cartoon targets, messes with their heads. In the real world, it slows them down. We're from the streets. We're like lightning in a bottle. Right, Armin?"

"The president of the United States's automobile is a million-and-a-half dollar Cadillac," Armin said. "It's nicknamed the Beast and is rumored to have eight-inch-thick armor, five-inch-thick bulletproof glass, and equipped with shotguns and rocket launchers. The president is well protected. The Secret Service uses Chevy Suburbans. They, too, are rumored to be reinforced. But not with the kind of protection a million dollars can provide."

"I've got your back, Armin. It's your play," Dom said.

"In three," Armin said.

Three seconds passed.

Dom flung open his door in a synchronized maneuver designed to draw attention to the Ford's left side. A beat later, Ozzie mirrored the move on the right side, leaping out of the car. Shielded by the door, Ozzie stuck his pistol around and fired at the Secret Service agent on the driver's side. Jimmy unbuckled his seatbelt and buried his head in the passenger's seat. Two heartbeats later, Armin sprang out, arms fully extended, a pistol in each hand. Pop-Pop, Pop,-Pop. Double-tap. Done. Both agents dropped, each taking two to the head. Quick and easy. It was an SUV. Not a tank.

Armin and Dom got back into the Ford. Ozzie patiently waited for Jimmy to buckle up, then he got in. They drove through the gate and followed the gravel road up the hill.

PARKS WAITED UNTIL CHERRY was out of sight. "Cherry's gone. That puts me in charge."

"Scary thought," Garris said.

"Diane, go get our hero," Parks said.

"Garris, come over here. I want you to show you something," Hawkins said, scooting over to make room on the mat. "Take a look through the scope."

"Try anything, I'll shoot you," Parks warned as Garris sprawled out flat on the mat and put his eye to the scope.

The rifle was aimed at Beemer and Baranski, conversing in the vineyard. Garris adjusted the rifle slightly higher. Meredith and Liz sat on the terrace, a glass of wine in their hands. Below them, Coleman and his friend Ella guided President Cahill and the First Lady through the garden. Cherry was in sight, approaching and moments away from joining them. Calculating Cherry's location, Garris estimated they had five minutes before Hawkins took a shot.

"That was straightforward enough," Hawkins remarked. "You've just planted your DNA on the murder weapon."

"What a dumbass," Parks scoffed.

Hawkins signaled Garris to get up so he could resume his sniper position.

"Like I've said all along," Parks said to Hawkins, "there's nothing special about these CIA dumbshits."

As Diane led Gayle over to Parks, Garris shifted his concern. He could see the sorrow reflected in her eyes. "You okay?" he asked.

"Ron's dead."

Garris knew the game Parks and Hawkins were playing. They expected him to make a move to console Gayle, but wouldn't let him get too close.

Recalling Cherry's words, "You can't take one without the other,"

Garris took two steps then stopped, shrewdly positioning himself equidistant between Parks and Hawkins. He knew that for Gayle and him to have any chance, Gayle would have to handle Diane. With Diane being a professional, Gayle would have to rise to the occasion. He was betting she would.

"He's been dead for days, Gayle. So get over it and appreciate the moment, the here and now." Parks laughed. "I'm the boss now. And lucky for you, I'm going to give you a rundown of how the rest of this day is going to go so you're not left in the dark."

"Keep it short," Garris said.

"Shut up, dumbass," Parks said. "Because of the rage that's been building inside you ever since President Cahill blew your cover, thus ruining your career, you've been a ticking time bomb. Blinded by your ego, you had the delusion that with your stellar covert experience, like taking out Trevano, you could execute the president and walk away like it's just another day's work. Given all your exposure, everyone assumes things like this are in your wheelhouse and it won't come as a surprise." Parks glanced down at Hawkins. "Of course, taking the real kill shot would be asking too much from you. More to the point, we don't trust you. So Hawkins will do the heavy lifting and will pull the trigger." Parks turned toward Gayle. "Enter Agent Wilson. She followed you to this hilltop and tried convincing you to surrender. But you're stubborn. Backed into a corner, she had no choice but to shoot you. Sadly, the untested rookie had never shot anyone before. She's shaky. The bullet hits the mark, but it's no kill shot. You get the chance to return fire; with your experience, she's a goner. But that deceptive wound of yours turned out to be worse than you realized. And gradually, you bled out. As for us," Parks grinned, "we were never here."

The sound of tires grinding over gravel shattered Park's diatribe. Caught off guard, a sliver of disappointment clouded his face as he assumed Cherry was returning to abort the operation. It was not Cherry.

"Who's this?" Parks muttered to know one in particular.

"Who cares? I'll get rid of them," Hawkins said, reaching down to his side for his handgun.

Parks signaled him to stay put. "No. I'll go. You have a job to do. Stay focused. I'll see what they want. Maybe Cherry sent them."

Jimmy pulled the Ford beside Garris's Jeep, a car length from the shed.

With his pistol in hand, Ozzie got out and paraded to the front of the Ford. He glanced at the two women near the cliff's edge, then locked eyes with Garris.

"Who the hell are you?" Parks demanded.

"We've come for him," Ozzie said, pointing to Garris.

"Sorry, he's ours. You can't have him."

Holding his two warm pistols, Armin got out of the back and stood by the door. Dom joined him.

"He comes with us," Dom called out. "Hand him over and we'll be on our way. Whatever you've got going on here is no concern of ours. We only want him."

"You the boss?" Parks asked.

"That's right," Dom said.

"Wrong answer—I'm the boss." Parks fired, tearing a hole through Dom's chest, slapping him backward against the Ford.

Shifting left, Ozzie aimed at Garris. Simultaneously, Jimmy stomped on the gas, ramming Ozzie. He swayed like a tree. Jimmy backed up and rammed him again but kept his foot on the gas, pinning Ozzie against the shed from the waist down. Ozzie wiped the blood from his eyes with his sleeve, then waved his pistol toward Jimmy. Seizing the opportunity, Jimmy reached down, grabbed the gun that had fallen on the floor and fired it through the windshield. Ozzie belly-flopped nose down on the car, turning himself into a hood ornament.

If Hawkins was sticking with their timeline, he had a couple of minutes left. But with all the excitement, Garris was afraid he would get spooked and shoot Cahill ahead of schedule.

Hawkins had tried to outwit Garris, tricking him to leave his DNA all over the rifle. But Garris knew what was going on and had used a little sleight-of-hand of his own. Before he had stood up from the yoga mat, he had moved the pistol in his left boot into position. Cherry and the rest of his bunch assumed someone else had checked Garris for weapons. They had not. And because Hawkins was there, and it seemed like the best thing to do, Garris put a bullet into the middle of Hawkins's forehead.

Parks pivoted toward Hawkins' lifeless body, then caught the business end of Garris's pistol pointing at him. Park's eyes widened with shock as the grim reality of his near future set in.

"You should have frisked me," Garris said. "Dumbass." Suddenly, terminally, Gordon Parks was no longer of this earth.

Gayle knew there would be no better time. She spun toward Diane, and channeling the technique she had seen Garris use on Parks on the country road, flattened her hand into a scissor-rock-paper, and chopped Diane's windpipe. But not hard enough. Diane was unfazed.

Evaluating her situation, Diane, being the last of her team standing, saw her chances did not look promising. But, as was her way, quickly chose her tool for the job. A hostage can be a useful instrument under the right circumstances, and it was a given that Garris would not risk Gayle getting killed. She grabbed Gayle by the hair and dragged her to the edge. "You came for Garris," Diane hollered to Armin. "There he is. What are you waiting for? Kill him. Kill him and we both get what we want."

A triangular standoff. Armin, Diane, and Garris. All were armed with loaded pistols on a sunny afternoon.

Armin glanced down at Dom, then back to Diane. "I don't think so," he said.

"What's that supposed to mean?" Diane missed his point.

Armin looked at Garris. "We good?"

Garris answered with a smile, clearly amused by Armin's unexpected decision.

"Are you shitting me?" Diane yelled, turning her pistol away from Garris toward Armin.

Gayle answered with an elbow to Diane's ribs, followed by an Age Zuki, a karate move she had learned at the academy, commonly known as an uppercut punch. Then, because Diane was there and it seemed like the right thing to do, she evoked a memory of Ron Boyle and his penchant for slapstick comedy and followed through with the two-finger eye-poke—in homage to the Three Stooges. Diane screamed, grabbing her eyes, and staggered backward, then toppled over the edge.

"That was for Ron, asshole."

Garris expected she would need a breather, but turning back around, her eyes, calm and composed, shot past him, landing on the mess the Ford had made, signaling they had better check on him.

Jimmy put the Ford in reverse, and Ozzie dropped to the ground. It turned out he was a good buffer. There was no serious damage to the vehicle. Nothing running it through the car wash wouldn't fix.

Armin walked over to join the group. As the imminent threat had subsided, Garris addressed the team. "You two okay driving together?" he asked Armin and Jimmy, "or do I need to split you up?"

Armin and Jimmy exchanged looks, then Armin glanced down at Ozzie. "If you ask me, he did the world a favor."

"What about Trevano?" Jimmy asked. "He'll be coming for all of us when he doesn't hear from Dom or Ozzie."

"Don't lose sleep. He's got a bigger problem than you," Garris said.

"Yeah? Such as?"

"Me," Garris said. With his next move yet to be played, he sent Armin and Jimmy on their way.

Gayle had already demonstrated she was a fierce and cunning fighter, but Garris had to ask even more from her. "How're you feeling?"

"Never better. Exhilarated, maybe? Is that strange? I've never done anything like that before."

"If that floats your boat, I've got something else in mind you might like."

GARRIS LEFT GAYLE BY the yoga mat with instructions for the new plan while he headed to the villa. He had a good idea he would find Coleman puzzled at finding Cahill still upright, sipping pinot noir.

Garris's cellphone chirped. "General, I'm driving to Coleman's."

"How's it going?" McCoy asked.

"There's been some bumps in the road, but I've got no complaints."

"I've got something for you," McCoy said.

"I'm listening."

"I sent Andrew to the center to see if he could dig up anything about the Gilberts: Stephen, Hannah, and Isabella. There was nothing in the archives, but he got the idea to see their exhibit. He spent hours staring at the thing. Then, out of the blue, a man approached him, curious about what he was up to. Andrew told him, and it turns out the guy was the sculptor, the artist who'd created the wax figures. Listen up, Garris. The Gilberts weren't pioneers at all. They were this artist's family. He'd slipped their names on the exhibit as a private remembrance to honor them. His mother, Hannah, had died in a mass shooting. His father, Stephen, was swallowed up by depression and never pulled out. Once the artist and his younger sister, Isabella, were grown up and out of the house, he went behind the barn and pulled the trigger."

"What happened to the sister?"

"Don't know. Andrew didn't think to ask."

"Nice work, anyway. Tell the Mitchell brothers I owe them a couple of crates of beer. Thank you, General," Garris said, ending the call as he arrived at Coleman's.

Garris met Agent Riggins with a handshake and a dilemma. He could tell Riggins to shut the party down and extract the president. The trouble was, Cherry was a master puppeteer and there was not a shred of proof linking Coleman to the mess. Cherry was a wild card, too. Once he figured out that Hawkins was out of circulation, there was no telling what he would do. Garris had dealt with Cherry enough to know he would have a Plan B and C. And Cherry's Plan D had always been to abort and run for the hills.

Predicting the potential fallout with the president if he jumped the gun and it turned out to be a false alarm, Garris chose to fly under the radar until he either spoke with Coleman or found Cherry, even better.

Showing Garris to the terrace, ever observant, Riggins sensed Garris was holding back. "What's with the cloak and dagger? Tell me or I'll have to follow you around like a lost puppy."

Garris nodded. "Any word on Cherry Mackey? Coleman's right hand?"

"Coleman saw how well we secured the perimeter and told Mackey and his team to take the day off. They'll be back tomorrow for his wine thing."

"No, they won't."

"What's that supposed to mean?"

"Look, Riggins, I need you to be with the president. Right now. I'll join you in a minute. Stay sharp. Stay close."

"Give me something. What's the story?" Riggins persisted.

"You need to trust me. Will you?"

Riggins hesitated for a moment, then agreed. Garris reciprocated with an appreciative nod and left Riggins to join Liz and Meredith on the terrace.

"You've got some brass showing up after ditching the bride at the altar," Liz said, greeting Garris with a peck on the cheek.

"Paul's obsessed," Meredith said, fueling the fire. "You're all he can talk about."

"I'll go find him and take my medicine," Garris said, scanning the vineyard, lawn, and garden, searching for Cherry.

"They're in the garden." Liz gave a little wave to her father. Cahill and Helen were chatting with Coleman and Ella, with Beemer angling to get a word in. Nearby, Baranski maintained his vigilance.

When Beemer exchanged a smile with his daughter, Coleman caught the moment and subtly redirected Ella's attention toward Liz, conversing with Garris and Meredith. Ella gracefully excused herself to visit the ladies' room.

As Garris approached the group, President Cahill spotted him. "Helen, look who finally decided to show up," he said. "A little late, don't you think, Kelley?"

"It's a pleasure to make your acquaintance, Madam President," Garris said, greeting Helen.

"The honor is mine, Garris," Helen said, taking his hand. "It's not often I come across someone with the audacity to decline the president's requests once, let alone twice. But do it again, and I'll have you skinned alive and use your hide as a doormat in the Oval Office." She winked. "Only I can tell Teddy Bear to fuck off. Do I make myself clear?"

"As tempting as a personal tour of the Oval Office sounds, I catch your drift, ma'am," Garris said, then turned to Cahill. "Mr. President, I apologize for missing the opportunity to introduce you this afternoon. I was looking forward to it, but something came up at the last minute that required my immediate attention."

"You didn't go to a ballgame, like the last time?"

"No, Mr. President, the Hops are on the road this week."

"So, what was it?" Cahill asked.

Garris glanced at Coleman, hoping to get a telltale sign, but Coleman's demeanor revealed nothing.

"Look," Helen intervened. "Garris, whatever it was, I'm sure you had your reasons. I think you've felt my husband's wrath enough for this week. Besides, today's about Lawrence. Why don't we relax with a glass of wine and enjoy our time together?"

Cahill seemed to agree. "You know what we need, Garris? We need to take a selfie. Let the people know we're on the same page."

THE TAC-50 IS A manually operated rotary bolt-action rifle. It has a 29-inch barrel, weighs 26 pounds, and is 57 inches in length. That made it eight inches shorter than Gayle.

By no means was she an expert, but she had received enough rifle training at the academy to feel confident. She agreed with Garris that, having a bird's-eye view, she should stay behind and be his guardian angel, protecting him from a distance.

Nestled next to Hawkins, who had the yoga mat pretty much covered, Gayle peered through the long-range scope and scanned the scene at the villa.

In the garden, the president and his wife were having a glass of wine with the host, Rudyard Coleman, and his friend, Ella.

Gayle counted eight Secret Service agents. Moving the scope toward the vineyard, she spotted Cherry lurking in a row of grapes, his attention glued to his watch. Probably wondering why Hawkins had not pulled the trigger.

Something caught his attention. His eyes shifted upward and to the left. Gayle followed his line of sight, adjusting the scope to see what had distracted him. On the terrace, Garris chatted with Liz Beemer and Meredith Beemer. Liz kissed him on the cheek. Garris was playing it cool, careful not to draw attention, but Gayle knew he was hunting for Cherry.

As Garris approached the president's group, Gayle refocused her scope. She noticed that Coleman's friend, Ella, had been fixated on Garris, a look of concern etched on her face as she watched him on the terrace. Once she realized that Garris was on his way over to see Cahill, she excused herself and hurried inside the villa.

"BEFORE WE TAKE THE photo, I need to speak privately with Rudy for a moment," Garris told Cahill.

"No, it'll just take a sec. Riggins, get your phone," Cahill ordered. "We're taking a photo together, now. We'll make it a group photo." Cahill motioned Beemer to move closer. "You, too, Rudyard. Get in here."

With phone in hand, Riggins positioned himself, framing the shot. Just as he was about to snap, Cahill raised his hand. "Hold up. Hold up. What am I thinking? Let's wait for Ella. She's done a fantastic job organizing this soiree on short notice."

Ella beamed, not believing her luck. Garris, Beemer, Cahill, and the First Lady were lined up, literally ducks in a row.

It was a small detail, but in addition to her elation, Garris noticed a new accessory swinging by her side as Ella breezed back to the garden. A leather handbag. She clutched it guardedly, as if protecting its contents.

"Ella," Cahill said, "come on. Join us. Next to Rudyard."

She did not join them. Instead, she plunged her hand into her handbag and pulled out cold steel, Garris's Colt single-action Army revolver. The extra gun he had brought and stored in his luggage. She had gone to his room to get it.

"Ella!" Coleman cried out. "Don't do it!"

The desperate timbre of Coleman's plea triggered a connection in Garris's brain. A reference McCoy had relayed during their last call now surged back with newfound significance. Then Garris got it.

ELLA

At the zenith of her mission, exhilarated yet trembling, Ella pointed the pistol at President Paul Cahill's forehead.

A bottle of pinot noir exploded on the table next to Ella. Gayle had missed her shot.

As Ella redirected her aim, Garris knew he couldn't disarm her. With a determined leap, extending his entire frame, he went airborne, soaring past Cahill and diving toward Helen.

Ella squeezed the trigger. The sound of gunfire echoed through the vineyard.

It was a rough landing, but Garris rode Helen to the ground, narrowly dodging the bullet.

Baranski lunged forward, hurling himself over Beemer to serve as a human shield. Riggins mirrored the act, covering Cahill.

Ella aimed the revolver down at Helen to finish the job. Before she could squeeze the trigger, she was violently thrown backward. Gayle's second shot had hit Ella dead center.

In shock, Coleman stared at the unfolding chaos as three agents tackled him to the ground to ensure he presented no further threat.

"I'm sorry I hurt you, ma'am," Garris said.

"I believe I've spilled my wine," Helen replied, her levity a sign she would be fine.

"I'll get you another."

"Please don't. It's not worth—"

"—a hundred bucks? Yeah, I know." Garris looked at the hilltop and gave Gayle a thumbs-up. She responded by firing five rapid rounds into the vineyard, signaling Cherry's location.

Leaving Helen with the agents, Garris sprinted to the vineyard. He recalled Coleman's words about the vineyard being like a maze, easy to get disoriented or lost in.

Garris figured Cherry would execute his Plan D and leave town. Fast. But Cherry needed transportation, and he had left his dirt bike in the parking lot, which would now be secured by the Secret Service. That meant he would probably head to an auxiliary production facility to steal a vehicle. Garris recalled seeing the building; it wasn't too far, maybe fifty or more rows away from where he stood. But he could not afford to be reckless. Cherry knew the property well and might have set a trap or ambush in advance. He could be lying in wait around any corner. Or attack from a row of grapes. Or could be crouching behind one of the tractors or sprayers. Garris had to move cautiously.

Before rounding each end post, he stopped, pulled the three sets of catch wires apart, then peeked into the next row. Satisfied a row was clear, he moved on. He repeated this process for ten rows, but the minutes were racing past, and Cherry had an enormous head start. Garris quickened his pace.

The production facility was quiet.

A shiny cherry-red pickup truck sat idling outside the building, its driver door open. Garris knew bait when he saw it. Cherry was hoping he would be careless and investigate the vehicle, giving Cherry the opportunity to shoot. But Garris, having learned the same playbook, did not bite. He knew Cherry wanted him to think he was hiding behind the forklift parked outside the building. Or behind the giant closed-tank membrane press. Garris knew Cherry was smarter than that. He would be in the building, taking advantage of the confined space.

Beretta in hand, Garris stepped inside. The abrupt shift from natural sunlight to the building's warm fluorescent lights momentarily fazed him, leaving him vulnerable in the open. He quickly sought cover behind the ten-foot grape destemmer and waited for his vision to return to normal. In the meantime, he listened attentively for any sound of Cherry revealing his location.

His patience paid off when Cherry stepped on a hose, causing the metal nozzle to scrape against the cement floor. With his vision fully restored, Garris dropped to the floor and hunted Cherry from beneath the stainless-steel destemmer. While the vantage point was not optimal for surveying the building layout, it provided some protection. From his concealed position, he counted ten enormous dimpled stainless-steel fermenting tanks to his left. The central section of the building was wide, housing dozens of plastic fruit bins, various containers, and a forklift. On the right side of the building, another ten fermenting tanks lined the walls.

Feeling relatively secure, Garris peeked around the right corner of the destemmer. Hundreds of wine barrels, shipping crates, and boxes provided Cherry plenty of hiding places.

Above the fermentation tanks, a steel catwalk served as an elevated platform for winemakers to inspect the contents of the tanks. Garris recalled Coleman's remarks during his tour, when he stressed the importance of punching down the MUST, a mixture of grape skins, stems, and juice in the tank crucial to producing wine. Coleman also underscored the potential hazards of winemaking. Aside from the risks of getting hit by a forklift or a falling barrel, workers needed to be vigilant because of the carbon dioxide (CO_2) produced during fermentation. The combination of yeast and sugar produced a blanket over the grape MUST in the tanks, depriving the area of oxygen. If the workers were not careful, they could easily get light-headed and fall into the tank. If that happened, suffocation could occur within two or three minutes—a nasty way to go.

According to the playbook that Cherry and Garris knew by heart, securing the high ground was a proven tactic to gain the upper hand in battle. In this scenario, the high ground was the steel catwalk.

Using the fruit bins, wine crates, and barrels for cover, Garris snaked his way to the steel ladder. Climbing the ladder would be risky. He would be exposed. But, there being nothing he could do about it, he got on with it.

The narrow steel-grated catwalk allowed Garris only a three-foot-wide path. He leaned over the rail and scanned the ten tanks on the other side of the building. No sign of Cherry.

Taking three steps, he stopped and looked down inside a tank. It was filled halfway with a thick liquid that looked as bad as it smelled. Moving to the next tank, he found the same.

He took another three steps, then stopped. At the far end of the catwalk, Cherry was waiting.

"It's hot up here. Don't you think?" Cherry said.

"I could throw you over the rail. It's cooler down there."

"I tried reaching Parks and Hawkins. Would I be wrong, thinking they're no longer on the payroll?"

"I'd say you're saving a bundle."

"And Diane?"

"You can find her in the vineyard at the end of row nineteen. Look on top of the John Deere."

"That was fine work, Garris. Figuring out, Helen was our target and not the President. How did you do it?"

"You were sloppy at the hotel."

"How so?"

"You scribbled cherries on the card."

"What was wrong with that? I wanted to get your attention."

"It wasn't your penmanship. It was the gift card that went with a bottle of champagne. To the newlyweds."

"Newlyweds? Coleman booked the room," Cherry said. "Help me out, Garris. Am I supposed to know who they are?"

"Stephen and Hannah Gilbert. And their daughter, Isabella."

Garris allowed Cherry a moment to think. "Oh, yeah. Got it," Cherry said. "Ella. Short for Isabella."

"Ella's brother is an artist. He made an exhibit for the museum."

"And you found out that her mother was a victim in a mass shooting."

"I have my team. Their main office is in Traughber City. They dug it up." Garris cocked his head, then said, "Your turn. Why don't you tell me how Rudy fits in?"

"You got the time to hear it?"

"I do, if you do."

Cherry studied Garris, deciding if answering the question would give him an advantage. "In a word. Ella. The way Rudyard told it to me is their bond is beyond ordinary. They were only children, eleven years old, when together, they witnessed Ella's mother brutally gunned down in a grocery store parking lot. Watched her die. Ella might mask it well, but she's a wounded bird. Damaged goods. And Rudyard, he saw it to himself, he'd forever be her knight in shiny armor. He's protected her, shielded her, mostly from herself. But, wouldn't you know, Rudyard's devotion paid off, though he never sought a penny for his loyalty. When Ella's father died, he left her a bundle. She funneled some of the money to kick-start his wine business. You know how that turned out. He's got more money than God. But money is just money. It didn't scrub away the scars from their childhood trauma. No, it didn't. It seems like every single day, there's another headline, another mass shooting. And each time, Ella relives her worst nightmare. It finally got to where she couldn't stomach it any longer and had to make a stand. She didn't want anyone to experience the grief that follows the senseless loss of life. With Rudyard's unwavering support, they hatched a plan."

"Killing politician's loved ones, like Lawrence and Helen, and having Cahill and Frank experience the loss firsthand would lead to changing gun regulation. Is that what you're thinking?"

"Politicians have the power to change the gun laws and save lives. But they sit on their ass. They don't act because it's never their flesh and blood. Never THEIR children, or wife, or husband. We're not calling to take away guns. But they need to do something besides issue statements about how heartbroken they are after a shooting happens. They've got to hold the firearms industry accountable. Guys like Cahill and Beemer can change the world if they want to. They could institute the assault ban. They could ban high-capacity magazines and bump stocks. Insist on better background checks and restrictions. They can support gun violence research and mental health issues. There's so much more they can do, Garris. But they need a wake-up call. They needed to be hit where it hurts. That's what Coleman's plan is all about. And that's where I come in."

"So let me get this straight. You're not going to shoot me. Are you planning on choking me to death on words? Get off your soapbox, Cherry. You were the triggerman on the MAX."

"Ironic, right?" Cherry answered. "Consider that a small sacrifice to prevent others."

"Killing isn't the way to get things done."

"Glad to hear you're still the idealist," Cherry said. "Two old friends up here, face to face. For a moment, I thought one of us might have to hit the 'unfriend' button for good."

"And you'd be right. You're the exception to the rule."

Cherry's eyes narrowed. "You sure you want to do this? You could go down your ladder. I go down mine. Maybe we'll see each other down the road another day. Maybe even work together again?"

"Not this time. I made a promise."

"To who?"

"Dante Green."

"Never heard of him?"

"The doorman at the hotel."

"Why do you care about him?" Cherry asked.

"Think about it."

"I don't have time to think about a doorman. He was collateral damage. He's nothing to me."

While Cherry continued to steer the conversation, his mind working on his next move. Meanwhile, Garris had slowly inched closer. It didn't go unnoticed. Having read the same playbook, Cherry figured Garris was attempting to distract him. But instead, Garris was moving in range.

Garris believed he was faster to pull. Cherry thought the same, and the time had come to prove it. Cherry was a southpaw. A lefty. His fingers reached for his Glock. He was quick to the draw. But Garris was faster, shooting Cherry in the arm above the left elbow. Cherry's pistol flew out of his hand and bounced off the catwalk. Garris charged. Then, snatching Cherry by his left leg and wounded arm, he hoisted him in the air and launched him over the rail and into Tank Number Nine—a pinot noir.

They'd filled the tank to the seven-foot mark. Cherry quickly sank into the thick, seedy purple juice. Suddenly, his head popped up, his arms windmilling and helicoptering everywhere. He tried grasping the side of the tank, but it was too smooth. There was no way out, and he knew it. Caught under a two-foot blanket of carbon dioxide, Cherry struggled to breathe. He was suffocating and gagging on stems. With fear burning in his eyes, Cherry gazed up at Garris. Choking, he managed to say, "For a doorman?"

"Now you have the rest of your life to think about him," Garris answered.

Three minutes later, Cherry disappeared.

Garris stepped outside.

Gayle was waiting in the Gator. "Need a lift? It will cost you."

"How much?"

"Tell me a story. The one about Hector Trevano."

Garris climbed in beside her.

SITTING IN THE DARK, in his favorite movie chair, Edgar watched the news from Portland on his big screen. The day before, there was an incident involving President Cahill at Rudyard Coleman's vineyard.

He thought he heard something behind him and muted the sound. It was okay. It was nothing. He was alone.

Picking up his cell phone, Edgar stared at it. Garris Kelley would surely still be in Portland. He'd need a new crew to go after him right away. A crew who was better than Dom and Ozzie. He still hadn't heard from Armin. What was that all about? Garris must have got him, too.

Tossing the phone onto the seat beside him, Edgar decided it could wait. He wanted to play the video game for a while. The one Ozzie had given him. The one featuring the lone assassin. He turned on the game and shot a couple of DEA agents. It was fun. But not like the real thing.

Then, he felt a presence behind him. He turned his head around to look.

"Hello, Edgar."

ACKNOWLEDGMENTS

Thank you to my wife, Cynthia, who is a constant source of strength, patience, and unwavering support. She weathered the storm of my daily progress reports, becoming a confidant who most likely knows the twists and turns better than I do. Without her love and faith in my ability, I could not have turned my idea into a book. Many times, I have heard that I married above my pay grade. Ain't that the truth.

A debt of gratitude to my good friend Bill Dubey, who dedicated countless hours to scrutinizing and refining early drafts. I am truly thankful.

I couldn't have had a better mentor than Jeffery Deaver. He is beyond supportive. For years, he has been inspiring and encouraging and has generously given his time whenever I was in a pickle.

I have been fortunate to have had the best people show up at the right time. Not only did editor Ann Aubrey Hanson masterfully elevate my story to the next level, but she believed in me and cheered me. Her commitment has been invaluable. Thank you, Ann!

What does the best rock drummer in the whole world have to do with my suspense novel? Kenny Aronoff's unparalleled work ethic was a guiding light when the writing process felt overwhelming. I aimed to channel just a fraction of his energy on days when anything else seemed more appealing than putting pen to paper.

To Ember, Merritt, and Chuck. Through their eyes, I have been able to turn back time and play like a child again.

I thank my agent, Liza Fleissig, cofounder of the Liza Royce Agency. Liza welcomed me to the agency and offered professional advice throughout the writing process.

I would like to acknowledge former Chief of Staff of the Air Force four-star General Merrill McPeak. General McPeak is like Luke Skywalker, Steve McQueen, and Elmore Leonard all rolled into one. He is the real deal. My unlikely friendship with the General has given me invaluable insight and, with his sharp wit, many laughs.

Thanks to Pattie and Mark Bjornson and all the staff at the Bjornson Winery for their professional insight, making the research for this book an enjoyable task.

And a BIG thank you to my entire family, with a special nod to my son Skylar, who shares my interest in movies and novels. When writing *Another Try*, I was writing for Skylar, wanting to tell a story he would be excited to read.

Hey, Don. We've finished.